A POSSIBILITY OF VIOLENCE

By D. A. Mishani

The Missing File
A Possibility of Violence

A POSSIBILITY OF VIOLENCE

D. A. MISHANI

Translated by Todd Hasak-Lowy

Quercus

First published in Hebrew in Israel in 2013 by Keter Books as אפשרות של אלימות

This edition published in Great Britain in 2014 by

Quercus Editions Ltd
55 Baker Street
7th Floor, South Block
London
W1U 8EW

Published by arrangement with Harper, an imprint of
HarperCollins Publishers, New York, New York, USA

A CIP catalogue record for this book is available
from the British Library

HB ISBN 978 1 78087 652 8
TPB ISBN 978 1 78087 653 5
EBOOK ISBN 978 1 78087 654 2

10 9 8 7 6 5 4 3 2 1

Typeset by Hewer Text UK Ltd, Edinburgh
Printed and bound in Great Britain by Clays Ltd, St Ives plc

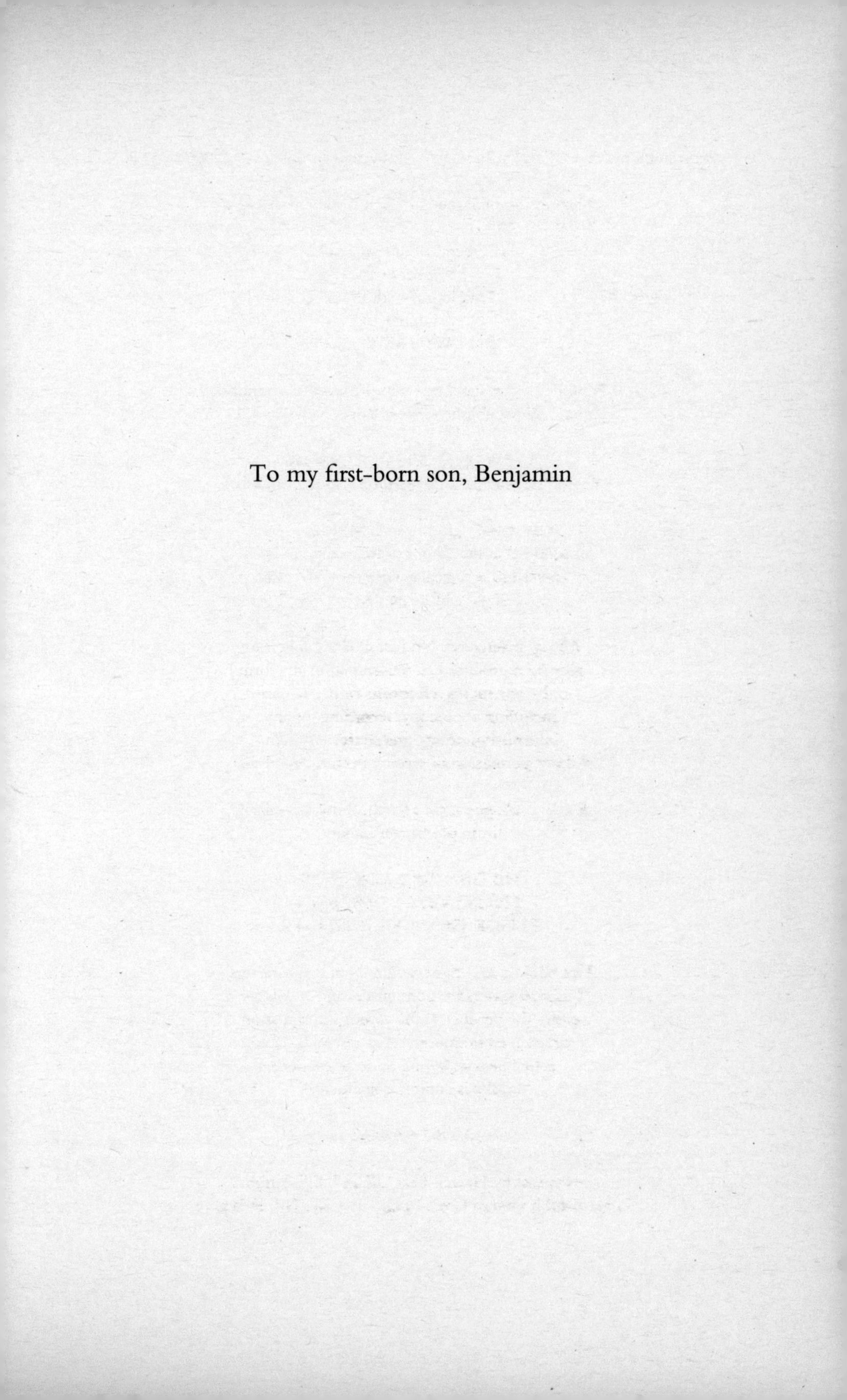

To my first-born son, Benjamin

There are some secrets which do not permit themselves to be told.

EDGAR ALLAN POE, *The Man of the Crowd*

PROLOGUE

During the rush of the long summer they spent together in Brussels, there was a moment when the feeling of happiness and calm that surrounded them cracked, and through this crack another possibility seeped towards him – towards the two of them, actually.

They were sitting on a shady bench on Parc de Bruxelles's wide boulevard, near the Museum of Modern Art. Avraham was sitting and Marianka was lying with her head in his lap. It was six in the evening and the sky was blue and cloudless. She read and he stroked her short hair. He couldn't read any more, since he had spent most of the day reading a detective novel by Boris Akunin in their apartment and at two cafés while waiting for her shift to end. As always, at the end of his reading he managed to prove to himself that the detective in the novel was mistaken.

Suddenly they heard a shriek behind them.

Avraham did not understand why the black woman had screamed, but he saw her advancing towards them. She was pounding her head with her left hand and scratching at her face, and he did nothing. Marianka rose and walked towards the woman, who was tall and wore a tattered dress, similar to a shroud. On her feet she had several pairs of thick wool socks and sandals. Marianka stopped in front of her and spoke. She held the woman's elbow in order to stop her cutting her face.

She said to Avraham in English, 'Someone kidnapped her daughter. She's looking for her and can't find her in the park. I'll take her to the police station.'

Avraham asked, 'Do you want me to come?'

He remained on the bench with the backpack and Marianka's open book lying face down. Watched them walking away. Marianka wrapped her arm around the woman's waist and still held her arm with her other hand. They left the woman's plastic bag next to him, in which he saw only other plastic bags. Countless plastic bags from Toys R Us.

When she returned, Marianka sat down on the bench a small distance from him and asked for a cigarette. He saw that she had been crying.

He asked, 'Did they find her?' Marianka didn't answer. 'Marianka, did they find her? Did someone kidnap her?'

'She doesn't have a daughter,' Marianka told him. 'The police officers know her. She's been wandering through the park for three weeks already. The first few times they searched for her daughter, but then they found out she doesn't have a daughter. At least, not in Brussels. She came from the Congo a few years ago. She scratches herself until she passes out.'

At home they ate a summer dinner that Avraham had put together before they'd gone out. Talked a little bit.

The next morning they were fine, but that evening it seemed to both of them that anything that could go wrong would.

And that's exactly what happened.

PART ONE

I

Chills passed through Avraham's body when he entered the interrogation room for the first time in three months. The air-conditioner had been running since morning and the room was cold. He remembered well the last time he had sat there, and the woman who had sat across from him then.

In the months that had passed, he imagined more than once the next interrogation he'd conduct in this room. He pictured his initial entrance into the room, steady and sure of himself, thought about the first questions he'd ask, in a stern voice. It wasn't supposed to take place on his first day back, but maybe it was just as well that this was how it had happened. Like leaping off a cliff into a stormy sea, with no preparation.

The first details he saw when he sat down across from the suspect were the dark, narrow face, the small black eyes, and, afterwards, the thin arms, from which thick veins protruded. His palms were dirty, as were the nails. Average height, thin, unshaven. Maybe in his thirties. The suspect sat on the other side of the long table. He asked, 'Who are you?' but Avraham ignored his question. He organized the papers in front of him as if he were alone in the room. He hadn't managed to delve into the material, only glanced at it briefly during the short conversation he'd had with the beat policeman who arrested the suspect during the early-morning hours.

According to the report the beat policeman had written, the message about the suitcase was received at the call centre at 6.44. Even though it was likely to be a false alarm, and despite the lack of manpower, a unit was immediately sent to Lavon Street. The police officers on patrol weren't able to locate the scene, so at their request the call centre contacted the woman who made the call, and she came down to the street in a robe and directed the police officers. Less than ten minutes later the bomb squad arrived, ordered the road closed to traffic and pedestrians, and began making preparations to neutralize the suspicious object. The initial inspection of the suitcase revealed a Supratec alarm clock, connected by electric wires to a bottle of 7Up, in which there was an unidentified liquid, and what looked like a detonation device. According to the bomb squad's notes, the suitcase was blown up at 7.50.

A moment before he opened the door to the interrogation room Avraham sent a text message to Marianka: Going into an unplanned interrogation. I'll call when I get out. She answered him straight away: The vacation's over? Good luck!

Everything was ready.

The recording device was working.

He asked the suspect his name and the suspect said, 'Amos Uzan. You a copper? You realize I've been waiting here five hours already?'

He didn't bother responding. 'Date of birth.'

'Mine? July the tenth, 1980.'

'Address?'

'Twenty-six Hatzionut.'

'In Holon?'

'In Las Vegas.'

'Profession?'

'Conductor of the Philharmonic.' Amos Uzan smiled. 'No profession. Write I'm not presently working.'

According to the beat officer's report, Uzan was not a musician. He had been a chef at Café Riviera, afterwards owned a small business fixing motorcycles, and in the end a little kiosk in downtown Holon. In addition to the income from those businesses, it appeared he made some money from modest illegal activities – mainly as a drug mule and hash dealer. He was born in Bat Yam and raised without a father, with two older sisters, in a family social services knew well. Dropped out of high school. Mother was a hairdresser. His first criminal charge came at the age of fifteen. He was stopped with a friend in a stolen vehicle. Avraham looked at him, then returned his gaze to the papers. He said, 'You're suspected of placing, near a nursery on Lavon Street, in the early hours today, a—' but Uzan cut him off: 'What are you talking about? A guy leaves his house to take a morning walk and they arrest him. What do I have to do with a nursery?'

'That will soon be clear.'

'So why did you arrest me, then? Do you even have any evidence?'

From the hurried glance at the file, and from the short briefing with the beat officer, it appeared that they didn't have any evidence. Uzan had been arrested thanks to the resourcefulness of the policewoman, who before the fake bomb was blown up gathered detailed testimony from the woman who had left the message. She was sixty-four years old, retired. Woke up early that morning in order to begin cleaning for Rosh Hashanah. Opened the shutters in the living room and hung the rugs on the windowsill to air them. She planned to beat them only after eight. Her husband was still asleep. When she was spreading out the rugs she'd seen a man enter the courtyard of the building at 6 Lavon. Actually she didn't see him entering but rather crouching among the bushes in the courtyard, as if he were searching for something. At first she thought he was a tenant who had dropped something from above. Afterwards, she'd seen him hide the suitcase behind the bushes, next to the path leading to the nursery. Why did the thing look peculiar to her? Because the dustbins stood just a few metres away, and if he were a tenant in the building, he would have thrown away the suitcase there. And why hide it carefully like that behind the bushes and not place it on the pavement? The building where the witness resided was located at the end of the street, but the sight line from her window was pretty decent. In her field of view there were some treetops and an electricity pole, but they didn't obstruct it. She estimated that she watched the suspect for more than a minute, and said that he didn't leave immediately but instead remained, looking around. Despite the distance, the witness feared that he would see her and she retreated back into the living room. When she stuck her head out again, the suspect had already fled in the other direction, towards Aharonovitch Street. Walking slowly, not running. It seemed to her that he limped. Her description was sketchy, as expected. The suspect was short, with a thin build and, as far as she could remember, wore sweatpants and a hooded sweatshirt that was brown, or some other dark colour. She couldn't see the features of his face.

A few minutes after collecting the testimony, the beat police officer identified the suspect in a crowd that had gathered at the end of the cordoned-off street, his build and clothing matching the description provided by the witness. The suspect had observed the blowing up of the bomb and looked nervous.

When the beat officer asked for his identification, he took off at a fast run. He managed to get about thirty metres before one of the police officers in the area grabbed him. Uzan wasn't carrying identification and denied that he was trying to flee. He denied all ties to the suitcase and claimed that he was there because he had gone down to buy bread and milk. He refused at first to provide his identification number but was persuaded to do so. A check at the Criminal Record Database made it clear that he had a few previous convictions, most of them drug offences.

Avraham said to him, 'We'll reveal the evidence when we decide to. In the meantime, tell me what you did this morning on Lavon Street,' and Uzan replied, 'What anybody does. I went out to get some fresh air.'

'You told the police officer that you went to buy milk and bread. I see that you've changed your story.'

'What'd I say? I didn't change my story. I went out to get some fresh air and to buy milk, too.'

'You went to Lavon to shop at a convenience store? That's quite a way from where you live.'

'Yeah, so?'

'Why?'

'Why do I have to answer you? I can buy stuff wherever I want, no?'

'You don't have to answer. I'm writing that you're not willing to explain what you did on Lavon Street.'

Unlike in the previous interrogation, a suspect sat before him who knew police interrogation rooms well. When he was asked questions whose answers were liable to trip him up he didn't respond immediately but instead paused until he found the right answer. He said, 'I went there because I owe money at the shop in my neighbourhood. Does that explain it?'

'And why did you stop to watch the bomb squad?'

'Do you know how many people were standing there? There was a suspicious object. I stopped to see what it was.'

'And you fled when the officer asked you to identify yourself.'

'I didn't flee – I've already explained that to her. I decided to go then and I didn't hear her call me. Suddenly two police officers jump on me and tell me I'm fleeing.'

'So you didn't flee?'

'Does it look like I fled? Believe me, if I had fled, no cop would have caught me.'

Something in Uzan's answer puzzled Avraham. He opened the arrest report and immediately understood what it was. He looked up and observed the room, as if measuring its size. Two fluorescent lights were lit on the ceiling. In the picture in the police database, Uzan's face was smooth, but since the photograph had been taken he had grown a tiny moustache, Charlie Chaplin-ish, which, in contrast to his nails, looked quite well groomed. 'And where are the milk and the bread?' asked Avraham, and Uzan said, 'What?'

'Where are the milk and the bread you bought?'

'I didn't manage to buy anything. The road was closed off.'

Avraham smiled. 'I see. So you must be quite hungry. And what exactly is your connection with the nursery?' he asked, and Uzan groaned. 'I don't have nothing to do with no nursery. Thank God I don't have kids.'

'So why did you place a suitcase bomb there?'

'You're totally crazy. I'm telling you, I didn't place any suitcase bomb. You all got sunstroke?'

The excitement was gone. As well as the fear that had accompanied Avraham into the room. He was in the right place. He was back to himself, to his role, to the thing he did better than anything else. If Uzan knew that there was a fake bomb in the suitcase, he hadn't fallen into a trap. Avraham suggested he get himself a cup of water from the watercooler at the other end of the room, next to the door, and Uzan said, 'I'm not thirsty.'

'You'd better drink. We're going to spend a few more hours here and it's important that you drink, otherwise you'll get dehydrated. Go and get a drink.'

He waited.

Uzan got up from his chair and went to the watercooler. On his way he passed Avraham, and after pouring cold water into a clear plastic cup for himself, he passed him again on his way back. His steps were light and springy. According to the testimony of the neighbour, the suspect who had placed the suitcase next to the nursery had left the place walking slowly, and with a limp, she thought. The police officer who had made the arrest reported that Uzan took off at a fast run when she'd asked him to identify himself. And he wasn't limping now, either.

Avraham had no more than a few hours before he would have to decide whether or not to bring Uzan before the court to extend his detention, and it was already clear to him this wouldn't happen.

The time was 2.30. Uzan had nothing more to say, and by evening, or tomorrow morning at the latest, he would be free to go home. And Avraham still didn't know if he'd be releasing an innocent man who had gone out early in the morning to breathe some fresh air and buy a litre of milk and a loaf of bread, and been arrested due to a beat officer's incorrect gut feeling, or if he'd be releasing the man who that morning had placed on the path leading to a nursery an old suitcase in which there was a demolition charge that clearly wasn't intended to go off. He said, 'We have testimony that whoever placed the suitcase wore a hood, and you're wearing a sweatshirt with a hood. It's strange that a man would wear a sweatshirt with a hood in this heat, don't you think?'

And Uzan erupted, shouting, 'Tell me, who are you, anyway? What do you care what I'm wearing? I was chilly this morning. And what about *you*? What kind of policeman dresses like that?'

Instead of a uniform Avraham wore white trousers that ended above his ankles and a new peach-coloured shirt. But that was because, officially, he was still a policeman on leave.

He'd returned to Israel a few days before this, at the beginning of September.

He had a few more days' holiday remaining, until after Rosh Hashanah, and he devoted them to preparing the apartment for Marianka's arrival. In the early-morning hours, a bit after sunrise, he went to the beach in Tel Aviv, dipped his feet into the water and smoked his first cigarette, facing the soft waves. The water was warm. When he was in Brussels the sea had aroused in him an incomprehensible longing. Outside, a late-summer heat wave prevailed, unbearable, but inside him was a lightness he didn't recognize. He wore thin, airy shirts in colours he hadn't imagined he'd ever wear. Marianka said that he looked terrific in them. They planned to organize the apartment together after her arrival, to purchase appliances that were lacking, to repaint the walls and add livelier colours, maybe even renovate the bathroom and kitchen, but he wanted to make an early start on a few changes. Mainly he threw away old items. Blackened pots and cracked plates from the kitchen, faded linen, worn-out towels. He stuffed clothes he'd never wear again into plastic bags and cleared shelves in the wardrobe.

When he entered the police station that morning David Ezra rose from his spot behind the duty officer's desk and hugged him. 'That's it? You're finally back?' he asked, and Avraham said, 'Not yet. I just came for a meeting with the new commander. Have you met him yet? What's he like?'

Ezra winked for a reason Avraham didn't understand and said, 'Decide for yourself.'

He went from room to room, knocked on half-open doors, answered predictable questions about his holiday and Marianka. He was happy to see most people, and they were happy to see him. When he turned on the light in his office he was surprised to see again just how small the room was. But its compactness was pleasant and reassuring, and the fact that it had no window gave him a sense of security. The walls were empty and close to him. Three years now he'd wanted to hang a picture on one of them but didn't know which, and now he had a reproduction of a colourful painting loaded with details that had made an impression on him when he'd taken refuge with Marianka in the Museum of Modern Art on one rainy summer day.

The computer was off and he switched it on.

There was dust on everything. A grey layer on the desk and on the shelves and on the black desk lamp. How does dust get into a room without a window? In the bin were bits of a brown envelope and a few crumpled pieces of paper he didn't remember throwing away.

At exactly twelve o'clock Avraham reported to the entrance of the office on the third floor and was asked to wait until the commander, Benny Saban, finished a telephone call. In the meantime, he sent a text to Marianka: About to meet with the new commander. I'll tell you how it goes. Xo. The secretary also spoke on the telephone, not about work.

Saban came out of his office at twelve fifteen and invited Avraham to come inside. He shook his hand and said, 'I can't make head or tail of the mess they left me with here.' He signalled for Avraham to sit and offered him coffee. 'Half the area is sick, like we're in the middle of winter, and the other half is on holiday. I'm working with zero manpower, and since this morning I've had an armed robbery at the Union Bank, a bomb next to a nursery, and someone who tried to set himself on fire on the roof of the National Insurance building. I have citizens who have waited since five to lodge complaints, and detainees I have no idea what to do with. I have no investigating officers, and if I don't get someone in front of them by this evening, the suspects go home.'

Avraham said he'd already had coffee.

Saban interested him. The man had a child's round, soft face, and smooth brown hair that fell across his forehead in a childish fringe. His desk was in order, free of files and papers, except for a thin pile of pages upon which were printed large letters in short lines, ready to be read. He hadn't managed to bring any personal items into the office, and nothing had changed in it. On the walls hung ribbons and certificates of excellence that had been awarded to the area. Avraham asked, 'Can I help?' and Saban laughed. 'Can you fill five positions for me by this evening?' The secretary entered the room without knocking and set a glass plate in front of him upon which were a large mug of hot water and two pretzels, and he sat down and asked Avraham again if he wanted coffee. 'Maybe she will interrogate them,' he said, after she'd left.

Avraham had heard about Saban's appointment to district commander while he was in Brussels, in a phone conversation with Eliyahu Ma'alul. He hadn't met him before and didn't know a thing about him, only that over the last three years he had been a district commander up north, and before that deputy chief of the Planning Division. He wasn't an investigator or a field agent, and had made his way up the organization mainly through a series of administrative positions. The palms of his hands were small and smooth, and the sleeves of his shirt were neatly ironed. From time to time he leaned back in his chair, bent forward again with a sudden movement, and placed his hands on the desk. Picked up a pen and drew sharp lines on the pages in front of him. There was an involuntary twitch in his eyes. For a moment he fixed them on Avraham, and then he began blinking as if something was blinding him, lowered his gaze to the desk, and covered his eyes with an incidental movement of his small palm. He said, 'At any rate, to the matter in hand. I know that your holiday isn't over, but it was important to me to invite you to an early introductory meeting and to hear that you're coming back and that everything's okay. There were rumours you might not be returning.'

Avraham responded that he'd had no plan not to return, and Saban said, 'Good, good to hear. That makes me happy. I heard positive things about you and we need quality manpower. I read about your previous case, and the report that Ilana Lis wrote as well, and I don't think there was any problem with the way in which the investigation was conducted. You have full support from me. The guilty parties were caught and we're moving on. Clean slate.'

Saban blinked again. And tried to smile.

Avraham didn't know a thing about the report that Ilana Lis had written about his last investigation. At whose request had she written it? And who had seen it? And why hadn't she told him?

They had spoken a few times on the phone while he was on vacation and Ilana hadn't mentioned the report. He said to Saban, 'Thank you. I don't know what you read, or where, but the investigation you're talking about is behind me.'

'Excellent, excellent. Good to hear. And, by the way, since you're already here, I would be happy if you stayed for the welcoming toast in my honour this afternoon. Can you? I'm going to talk about what I see as the objectives of the district's policework.'

Avraham promised that he would try his best to stay, and Saban said to him, 'You know what? Take the pages with you – if the worst comes to the worst you can read them at home. I'll print another copy. This is my vision for our shared work in the coming years.' From Saban's damp, combed hair it looked to Avraham as if he had had his hair cut that morning, before coming to the station. Were these signs of nervousness also caused by the speech he was going to give this afternoon? He thanked him, folded the pages of the speech, and stuck them into his shirt pocket.

Saban asked, 'So when are we meeting officially? When are you actually returning?' And Avraham said, 'After Rosh Hashanah. But I could interrogate one of the prisoners today, if you have no one else. I have no problem staying here a few more hours.'

Saban hesitated, and this hurt him. He said, 'But . . . you're still on holiday. And I thought it would be good if you returned to matters, you know, slowly. Maybe you'll join a team that's already started work. It's a shame to waste your holiday.'

Avraham was struck by the desire to enter the interrogation room now, at this moment, precisely because of Saban's hesitation. He said again, 'I can stay. Tell me which is most pressing,' and Saban answered, 'I'm not sure. Maybe the suspect in the fake-bomb case. He's been waiting almost five hours, and we have nothing other than his previous.'

'Fine. Give me a few minutes to study the material and I'll go in. Do you know anything about the file?'

Saban still wasn't sure that this was the right thing to do. He said, 'Not much. It's probably a dispute between criminals, or neighbours. The question is, why a fake bomb, and why next to a nursery? A fake bomb is a warning, no? So another question is, who did they want to warn and what's the meaning of the warning, and, in particular, how do we prevent the next crime before it's carried out? But most important – is this connected to the nursery? This suspect, or someone else, places a fake bomb, in the light of day, when parents are bringing their children to the nursery – this disturbs me. And I'm disturbed by the thought that next time it might be a real bomb.'

He was supposed to call Marianka and tell her about the meeting with Saban, and afterwards he told himself that he'd call when he left the interrogation room, but in the hours to come he was in such a race against time that he forgot, and even when he remembered he simply put off calling.

The first hour of interrogation with Uzan didn't get him any further, maybe the opposite. There was a contradiction between the neighbour's testimony about the limping and Uzan's limber gait, and there were his denials, which became more and more emphatic. It wasn't possible to locate fingerprints on the suitcase, and the forensics team didn't find anything at the scene that could tie Uzan to it. Or in the apartment where Uzan lived with his mother. The beat policeman brought in the neighbour so she could view the suspect, and suddenly she was less certain of her testimony. 'Yes, it could be him, but how can I say with certainty? Do you know from what kind of distance I saw him?' Avraham enquired about the matter of the limping, which, of all things, she had no doubt about. The man who had placed the suitcase had fled towards Aharonovitch Street with a slow limp. At three thirty he moved Uzan to the holding cell and shut himself up in his office to think, as he always did at the start of an investigation.

He still hadn't visited the scene, and he knew it was vital to do this soon. And he couldn't remember whether or not there were traffic lights on Lavon Street. If there were lights and drivers stopped at them, perhaps he'd find additional witnesses who had seen the suspect when he placed the suitcase, or when he had fled afterwards. He checked if someone had questioned the owner of the nursery and the residents of the neighbouring buildings about their ties to Uzan, and it turned out that no one had. In fact, he understood, the investigation hadn't yet begun. It was necessary to search additional places to which Uzan was tied, to try to find evidence of the improvised bomb's design, to interrogate Uzan's mother, who was in hospital, but it was not possible to do all this by evening, and not by himself. And he also shouldn't get stuck on the suspect. It was necessary to consider all the possibilities, not only because of the doubt raised by the limp. He recalled Ilana Lis and her routine warning: 'We shouldn't come to any conclusions in advance, because then we won't examine certain details, while looking too closely at others.' It was possible that the man who placed the suitcase next to the nursery wasn't now sitting in the holding cell at the police station but was somewhere else instead. And perhaps he was planning his next attack, just as Saban feared.

Suddenly Avraham knew that he wouldn't be sorry he had taken on this case.

He looked for something in the drawers and on the shelves. On the floor of the equipment room he found a ream of printer paper, and on the way to his office had already ripped open the packaging and removed a sheet. He wrote a few lines on it:

Nursery.

Precise distance from the nursery. When does it open?

Owner of the nursery – acquaintance of Amos Uzan?

List of parents. Previous crimes.

A threat – maybe for one of the kids' parents?

Scene.

6.30 a.m. (exactly?) More people were passing on the street.

More neighbours who saw?

Traffic lights. Camera?

The suitcase – maybe something unique? that's possible to trace?

Did he get out of a car?

If there was a car, was someone waiting in the car to pick him up?

Neighbours' dispute?

List of tenants.

Criminals in the area.

If we're talking about a warning – what's the message? And to whom? What's the meaning?

What will the next crime be?

Is there a convenience store on the street?

At 4.30 p.m. Uzan was brought back to the interrogation room, but for no purpose really. Avraham had nothing more to ask, and Uzan stroked his moustache and smiled at him with his small eyes and said, 'I ate, I drank, I napped. We had an interesting chat. But hasn't the time come for you to admit you arrested a man for nothing and to let him go?'

Avraham asked, 'What's your hurry? You don't want to have dinner here, too?'

But at five thirty, running late, he went out to the courtyard for the toast in honor of Saban's appointment – and Rosh Hashanah – and when he returned he signed the release forms. 'I promise you that we'll see each other again,' he said to Uzan, and Uzan replied, 'You're just wasting your time, but gladly.'

In the evening, at home, after a quick cold shower, Avraham made coffee for himself and drank it, black, on the balcony in his vest and underwear. The investigation file was open and he again read the beat officer's report from the scene that morning. Afterwards he recalled Saban's speech, which was folded up in the pocket of his shirt that he'd taken off and hung in the bathroom. Most of the police officers thought the speech was ridiculous, but in Avraham's eyes there was something in it that inspired hope.

He longed to tell Marianka about his day, but now, of all times, her phone was off. He couldn't remember if she was on a shift, one of her last with the Brussels Police Department before leaving and joining him.

There was something mysterious, inexplicable, in the difference between Benny Saban's determination and focus when he addressed his new subordinates for the first time and his nervousness and lack of confidence in their meeting in his office earlier in the day.

Saban had stood in the courtyard on the improvised platform and read from a sheet of paper. Despite the heat, he didn't sweat.

At the start of his speech he spoke about the summer.

'We had a long and difficult and violent summer,' he said. 'In June, Tel Aviv's southern neighbourhoods ignited. Refugee infiltrators without work or shelter . . . residents' increasing complaints and cases of sexual assault and burglary . . . organized acts of revenge . . . Molotov cocktails . . . arson of homes and refugee centres. At staff meetings there was a sense that at any moment the fire could start burning up here as well, but we knew how to contain it and prevent it spreading.'

Avraham had been so removed from all of this, on a holiday that seemed like it would never end. He kept himself updated over the Internet, and from time to time with phone calls from Brussels to Eliyahu Ma'alul and Ilana.

His summer had been joyful.

'Afterwards came the protests. Every Saturday evening hundreds of policemen were sent into the streets of Tel Aviv to maintain order and prevent violence during the legal and illegal protest marches. In one of the marches the barriers were breached and windows were smashed at downtown bank branches. At another demonstration one of the protesters set himself on fire and went up in flames. Every officer who could work additional hours did so.'

Later in the speech Saban reviewed the crime rates in the area. 'The data shows that you had an excellent year,' he said. 'You met the objectives that were placed before you, and even exceeded them. You lowered by five per cent the number of house burglaries and property crimes. You recorded a decline of more than ten per cent in vehicular burglary and theft. Thanks to your dedication there was a decline of seven per cent in violent crimes in the area and a decline of eight per cent in car accidents.' Someone in the audience applauded, and Saban said, 'Yes, you definitely deserve applause.' Some joined in the clapping.

The applause died down when Saban lowered his voice and said, 'But there were also objectives that the area did not meet. This year there was a rise in youth crime. An increase in fraud and vice offences. When I analyse the statistics of your area – excuse me, I'm still getting used to this, of *our* area – I see an area where law-abiding citizens are able to sleep more soundly in their homes, but when they leave home there is a greater chance that they will encounter prostitution or drug dealing.' Saban passed his eyes over the faces of the police officers, who listened to him in silence despite the burning heat. He raised his voice: 'My vision, and I know that for some of you this will sound unrealistic, is that the law-abiding citizens in our area will not encounter violence. I want a law-abiding citizen from Bat Yam or Holon or Rishon LeZion to leave his house in the morning, get into his car, drop his children off at nursery or school, stop to get himself a cup of coffee for the road or fill up with fuel, continue driving to his workplace, and on this daily route not experience any type of violence or anxiety. My goal is to create as many areas free of violence as possible in the area. Areas of tranquillity and personal security. Whoever chooses to live a life of crime in criminal areas will continue doing so, and there, too, we will intervene when required. But in my opinion our client is the honest man, the law-abiding, the non-violent man and woman who want to live their lives without encountering violence and without experiencing the fear of violence, or the possibility of violence. Our duty is to serve them.'

At the end of his speech there was applause, but more than a few mocking smiles as well. Saban descended from the platform, and when he met Avraham next to the refreshment table he placed a hand on his shoulder and whispered to him, 'Great that you came, Avraham. How was I?' Afterwards Avraham finally saw Eliyahu Ma'alul, who said to him, 'What's this, Avi, did you lose weight? I barely recognized you.'

Avraham tried not to fall asleep before speaking with Marianka, but his eyes closed. He called her a few times, but her phone was off and he gave up.

Inside him, sleep scrambled fragments of sentences from Saban's speech and caused them to come out of Amos Uzan's mouth in the interrogation room. Uzan looked at him with his black eyes and said, in English, 'My goal is to create in Las Vegas as many areas free of violence as possible.' He woke up in the chair on the balcony, frightened and sticky with sweat. It was after three o'clock. He took off the vest and went to the bathroom to rub himself down. It seemed to him that were he to look outside, he'd be able to see the man with the suitcase, limping in the darkness, but there was no one on the street.

2

Only in the evening, when he put them to bed, did Chaim Sara realize that what happened in the morning had frightened the children more than they let on. Ezer lay on his back in the top bunk and didn't move, eyes open, looking at the ceiling and waiting for sleep to come. In recent nights it had become clear to Chaim that this was how his older son fell asleep, and the position disturbed him. Shalom, the smaller one, was more fidgety than on previous nights; he turned over in the bottom bunk, struggled with the blanket, the pillow; his short legs bumped into the wooden board of the bed frame. Chaim thought that the heat was bothering him.

He had put them to bed for a few days now, and they hadn't asked a thing about Jenny until tonight. They had been satisfied with the few words he had said on the first night. And didn't cry. He sat next to them on a low, blue plastic chair, and waited silently for their sleep to come. The room wasn't entirely dark. The shutters were open because of the heat and humidity, and lights from other apartments in the adjacent building reflected off the walls and the floor. There was no air-conditioning in the room.

But then Shalom turned over on his side, turned his back to him, and asked, 'Why isn't Mummy putting us to bed?'

Chaim saw no sign of longing in the question, and didn't connect it to what had happened in the morning. He said, 'In a few more days she'll put you to bed,' and the boy didn't turn over again. A few minutes later he fell asleep. Chaim was certain that Ezer was asleep as well, but when he stood up Ezer opened his eyes. 'Why aren't you asleep yet?' he asked him, but Ezer didn't answer. He hadn't said a word that afternoon, either. Sat for hours in front of the television with a cautious, wary look in his eyes.

Chaim sat down on the blue chair and continued to wait. Suddenly, from above, Ezer's voice drifted down. 'I know who lost the suitcase next to Shalom's nursery,' Chaim heard him say; and because he wasn't sure that he understood, he asked his son, 'What suitcase?' and Ezer said, 'The suitcase someone lost. The one they closed Shalom's nursery for.'

This is what he told them that morning.

He had to say something when they got to Lavon Street and saw that it was closed to traffic. At the corner of Lavon and Aharonovitch streets people had gathered, and Chaim saw some parents of children from the nursery, among them the young father with the glasses who carried a toddler in his arms. A patrol had closed off the street, and police prevented pedestrians crossing from both sides. But some time passed until he found an explanation. He froze and didn't know where to turn. He was so panic-stricken at the sight of the police that he forgot the boys were with him. The first thing that came to his mind was that he had to go back to the apartment. For a moment it seemed to him that he had forgotten his keys, but when he touched the sides of his trousers he felt them in his pocket. He held the boys' hands tightly and said, 'Let's go back,' but a young woman standing next to them said, 'No point in going back, they'll open it soon,' giving them no alternative but to stay.

Across the street he saw the teacher speaking with two policemen.

And suddenly there was a commotion.

They pounced on a young man, and one of them pinned him down on the pavement, sticking a knee in his back and bending his arms behind him. Someone in the crowd said, afterwards, 'That could be him,' but this didn't reassure Chaim. He held the children's hands and said to them, 'We'll go to Ezer's school first.' So they wouldn't run into the teacher, they crossed to the other side of Aharonovitch Street and walked down it, turned right onto Ha-Aliyah Ha-Shniyah Street, and continued on to Arlozorov Street. Chaim walked quickly and the boys straggled along behind him. He didn't think his racing ahead would upset them. Shalom asked, over and over, 'I'm not going to nursery today?' Only when they stopped in front of the gate to the school did he explain to them that someone had lost a suitcase near the nursery and the police were searching for its owner in order to return it. They'll find it soon and the nursery will open again. The fear dissipated, and he didn't think about it during the day, and in the afternoon they didn't talk about it at all; but if Ezer was still thinking about it, then the children were more frightened than he had sensed.

When Chaim rose from the blue chair his face was at the height of Ezer's bed. He asked him, 'Who lost the suitcase?' and Ezer said, 'I can't tell.' He continued lying on his back, without moving, and staring at the ceiling when he answered.

'How do you know who lost it?' Chaim asked, and Ezer hesitated before saying quietly, 'My first dad told me.'

Chaim shook. In recent weeks Ezer spoke more than a little

about the first dad, and each time he mentioned him Chaim got the chills.

'What did he tell you?'

'That it's a secret.'

He debated whether to continue the conversation or let it go. Shalom moved in his bed and he didn't want him to wake up. He whispered, 'How does he know?' But Ezer didn't answer. His eyes were closed.

Chaim thought about the conversation in the boys' room while he washed the dishes he had left in the sink after dinner and prepared the kitchen for his catering work. What disturbed him was that Ezer needed the first dad because Chaim wasn't enough for him, as Jenny had said a few times. Because he didn't speak enough. Perhaps because he's too old. Because something in him isn't strong enough. He knew he didn't talk to the children enough, particularly Ezer, and that this was one of the things he'd need to change. And he'd need to be stronger. Not show fear or weakness. Give them the feeling that he was protecting them. This was exactly what he had tried to do at Shalom's nursery a week earlier, without much success.

The window in the kitchen was open and voices from the street came his way.

Cars passed and an ambulance's siren could be heard in the room. The fear came and went, unexpected.

It will continue like this for a long time, he thought.

The matter of the suitcase next to the nursery was unfortunate, but if a suspect is arrested, perhaps the investigation will end.

And he knew that they'd manage fine without Jenny,

though there were problems for which a solution still hadn't been found. The nights in particular. He gathered up the dirty clothes in the bathroom and wiped the wet floor with a rag. The socks didn't stink, and he folded them and put them on the small shoes by the door.

Songs played on the radio until ten, and after the news the phone-in programme began.

Jenny usually slept at this time, or sat in the living room and watched movies on television and ignored his existence. Now he was all alone but nevertheless didn't turn up the volume on the radio, so as not to wake the kids. He finely diced onions and red peppers and dumped them into a bowl, and to this he added ten cans of tuna and mixed in a few tablespoons of mayonnaise and a bit of mustard. Afterwards he squeezed a whole lemon over the bowl and sprinkled salt and pepper. On the radio a woman from Beersheba told how she had overcome cancer. After the doctors had given up she turned to a rabbi who blessed her, and only the rabbi had helped. The host said, 'So you actually don't need help, I don't understand why you called,' and the woman said, 'I called to help others and to wish the people of Israel a happy new year.' The host refused to permit her to give the rabbi's telephone number on air and went to the next caller, who had lost his son in a car accident. Chaim cut tomatoes into thin slices and cucumbers into strips and put them on two plates. In the meantime he boiled eggs in the pot on the stove and mashed five into the bowl of tuna, and after this he prepared egg salad in a second bowl. The next caller was a man who refused to reveal his name or where he was phoning from. His wife had left him when he had been diagnosed with diabetes, cheated on him with a friend from work. Chaim couldn't listen to his terrible story and turned off the radio. He worked for a few minutes in silence.

The first dad wouldn't let go of him.

What exactly had Ezer meant when he said that he spoke with him?

If he didn't shy away from conversations he could have called the radio show and asked for advice, but that was out of the question. He knew that children can't thrive in silence, and yet he managed to provide more than a little for his children even without using many words. Shalom had been attached to him since he was born; and Ezer too, until a few months ago, had loved to be in his company and sought it out. Only recently had he grown distant from him and closed up, because of her.

Chaim recalled his father as he followed the quick movements of his own fingers. His father wasn't very verbal either. He was a tailor by profession, but he didn't always manage to make a living from his work and traded fabric or did some sewing in a factory. He remembered him smoking all the time. Always with a cigarette. The swift movement of his fingers when he sewed. What else did he remember? That on Friday evenings he went to synagogue, and also on Shabbat morning and on holidays. That he was tall and thin, very impressive in his clothes. He wore suits for the holidays. When the children woke up he was always awake and dressed and shaved. That he chewed his food slowly. Always finished dinner after his wife and kids. On pleasant nights he sat in the courtyard, smoking and listening to the radio. He died when Chaim was at school, in the Jewish calendar month of Nisan. For some reason they didn't send anyone to inform Chaim and take him out of class. They told him at home, when he got back. He was eight years old, and it was a few nights later that they found him for the first time in the courtyard, walking and talking in his sleep.

When Ezer was born it was clear that he'd be named after him.

He finished his work in the kitchen at eleven and called his mother from the phone in his bedroom. He asked her how she was feeling and she said that her legs were swollen. 'Did you stand today?' he asked, and she said, 'No, I sat.'

He asked her to rest more. Not to stand at all if she didn't need to. She asked him how his leg was and he said much better. Afterwards he asked, 'Did someone come to visit you?' and she said, 'Yes, Adina came.'

'What did she want?'

'To see how I'm doing.'

They were quiet for a moment, but there was no awkwardness in their silence. His conversations with her didn't demand any effort from him. Usually she spoke and he listened. She waited in bed for a call from him and only afterwards turned off the television and the light and tried to fall asleep. Her nights were sleepless too, and sometimes she couldn't manage to sleep a wink until morning arrived. She asked, 'How are the children?' and Chaim said, 'Went to sleep.'

'Have you told them that she's gone away yet?'

'Not really. I'm waiting a little longer.'

'What are you waiting for? Tell them, so they'll get used to it.'

He ignored what she said.

'And how about at home? Maybe I'll ask Adina to come and help you?'

He said there was no need, and after another silence she asked, 'And have you spoken to Shalom's teacher again?'

There were things he didn't tell her, in order not to worry her, but he had told her about the incident with the teacher and she supported him and understood his outburst. He didn't say a thing about the suitcase near the nursery, because he knew if he told her, she wouldn't be able to sleep. He said, 'I didn't have a chance. We got there late.'

'Did you ask him how it was?'

'It was better,' he lied, and she said, 'You see? It's because you did some shouting. Everything only comes by shouting.'

He didn't want to talk about the incident at the nursery and asked her, 'Home's okay?' and she said, 'Hot. You won't come to finish the courtyard before the holiday?'

For a moment anger stirred in him over her asking him this. He said, simply, 'On the holiday. Stop worrying,' and she said, 'Sleep well,' and put down the phone.

Next to the bed sat a few books that he planned to look over before reading them aloud to the boys, without making mistakes. To read them quickly, and naturally. At the start of the year the teacher had asked if they read to Shalom and given Jenny the names of some books, and the saleswoman at the shop recommended another two. He saw an insult in the teacher's question, an expression of disdain for his son and, indirectly, for himself as well, and it's possible that this question may have contributed to his outburst. He didn't see why he had to read to Shalom. Chaim's own father had never read books to him.

One of the books that he bought called out to him especially. It was a story about a boy who walks on the walls at night. According to the story, after they put him to sleep the boy got out of bed, walked on the walls of the room, and entered the paintings that were hanging there. The paintings came to life and the boy spoke with the painted characters. In the illustration on the book's cover the boy walks on the wall with a straight back and his hands extended in front of him, as if he's walking in his sleep. His hair is red and his face clear. He doesn't resemble either of Chaim's children.

On the nights that passed without Jenny, Chaim was almost convinced he hadn't woken up.

He went to bed late and got up at four in the morning, in order not to oversleep. And as he'd done in his youth, he stretched sewing thread at knee height across the frame of the bedroom door, so that he would know in the morning if he had left his room. Locking the door wasn't a possibility, because of the children. Since he had met Jenny his nights were calmer. She slept lightly and woke when he rose from their bed. Sometimes that happened to him every night, but for many months it didn't happen at all, mainly when he was less tense, when his catering business was doing all right. She took him to the couch in the living room. She turned on the television, because that helped him wake up. In his sleep, she told him once, he actually talks a lot. 'What do I say?' he asked her, and she said, 'I don't understand much of it. But you talk a blue streak.'

A few of her clothes still lay folded on the shelves in the bedroom. Most of them were no longer there; nor were the two large suitcases.

After midnight, following a last visit to the children's room, he got ready for bed and turned out the light in his room, closed the shutters in their room, and left the window open only a crack because suddenly a wind was blowing. On Shalom's forehead a scab had formed over the deep scratch. Ezer was no longer on his back, in the frozen position in which he fell asleep. He lay on his stomach, his cheeks sunk into the pillow. He looked like a child again. The two of them resembled Jenny more than they resembled him, but something of him, which couldn't exactly be described, was in their faces.

Ever since they were born Chaim asked himself what the boys would remember of him. Would they remember him like he remembered his father? He hoped that nothing would happen to him before Ezer reached the age when a father is etched into a son's memory, perhaps because his own father died when he was a boy, and perhaps because he was already over fifty years old when Ezer was born. He wanted him to remember a man of strength, but without fearing him. And until a few months ago he was sure that this was how he would be burned into his son's memory.

You did not have a 'first dad', I am the only dad you've ever had, he wanted to whisper in his ear, but did not.

Chaim didn't wake up that night, or if he did he didn't leave his room. The clock struck four and he hurried to get out of bed, and with the bit of light that filtered into the room from outside he checked that the thread was still in place. He turned on lights in the kitchen and the bathroom but left the living room in darkness so that the children wouldn't wake up. He found Shalom at the end of his bed, folded up like a snail. Ezer slept in the same position as before, curled up with the blanket up to his neck as if he were cold.

He got dressed in the dark bedroom and then shaved. Before he started working he closed the kitchen door. In three pans he fried the plain omelettes and the vegetable omelettes with parsley and dill and placed them on the windowsill so that they'd cool down. The smell of the coffee that he'd made for himself blended with the smells of frying and morning. Afterwards he put the slices of yellow cheese on the table and placed next to them the bowls he'd prepared in the evening. At five fifteen he carefully opened the door to the apartment, went out, and locked it behind him. For a moment he waited outside, in order to hear if one of the children woke up, then went down to the car. He hadn't found a solution for this problem, either, but in the meantime there was no choice. He explored the possibility of using a delivery man to bring the rolls, but there was an enormous difference in price. And at this time of morning the trip lasted less than ten minutes. Even though he wasn't at peace with locking the boys in the apartment, this was a better solution than leaving the door unlocked.

And this was what he had done on the first morning without Jenny, as well.

He drove down Weitzman Street, turned left on Sokolov street, and stopped in Struma Square. Even though it was light outside, the streets were empty. Luckily, most of the traffic lights flashed orange. All the shops in the square were closed, except for the Brothers' Bakery. He went inside the bakery's rear entrance and his nostrils immediately filled with the smell of dough. One of the brothers saw him and shouted, 'The Sara order,' and a worker answered him, 'Coming,' from an inner room.

A minute later he was back in the car.

Everyone slept, while his day was already under way. Chaim loved these moments in his work even more than he loved the hours of silence in the evening. The pavements silent with only doves and cats and street cleaners, not a word to be heard. He drove down Shenkar and Fichman and Barkat streets and finally turned onto Lavon Street and passed the nursery.

In two hours he would bring Shalom here and try to avoid meeting the teacher.

Since the incident the previous week they hadn't exchanged a word. He walked Shalom inside the nursery and avoided looking at her, hurried to Shalom's personal locker and put his change of clothes inside. Quickly said goodbye to the boy. In any event, he shied away from the entrance to the nursery, and from meeting the other, younger, parents, most of whom took him for the grandfather.

The insult from his conversation with the teacher still stung, not to mention what had happened after it.

Jenny had pushed him to arrange it, even though she knew he didn't want to. He had barely managed to tell the teacher that the boy was scared to go to nursery and complained that the other children hit him. That his wife had been finding dark spots and other unrecognizable marks on his body, under his clothes. That he had come home with a scratch on his forehead. It was morning, and the nursery had been full of parents. The teacher had challenged what he said. Refused to listen. Looked at him with contempt, and he was sure that it was because of his age and the way his children looked, and sure that she behaved differently with the other children and parents. She spoke better than he did, and he lost his confidence and didn't respond, even when she said his son was lying. 'Here at our nursery we don't hit,' she said. Shalom had got the scratch because he was being wild and had fallen on the wheelbarrow. If Shalom says that the children hit him, then he's lying, was how she finished. He saw that Shalom, who stood next to him, looked frightened, so he tried again, but she insisted that she didn't have time to hold this conversation in the morning in front of the children. She also certainly didn't want the other parents to hear. When he didn't relent, she shouted, 'I told you I *do not wish to continue this conversation*, Mr Sara. Here at our nursery there are no children who hit, and if your boy complains about being hit, maybe you need to look at yourself and your wife and ask why.' He couldn't control himself and interrupted, warning that he'd remove the boy from the nursery, and she smiled at him and said, 'Go ahead. You think you're threatening me?' He had no doubt that Jenny was right, that the woman didn't want the child there. But there wasn't another nursery in the neighbourhood, and this was also the only one they could afford. None of the parents spoke up or intervened, and it seemed to him that this was because they, too, preferred that his son disappear. He left the nursery, stricken with shame and loathing, directed mainly at himself, since despite the incident he had left Shalom there. Is that what his son would remember of him? The boy had cried and he had ignored his crying and left after taking him to the Russian assistant. She had bent down and wiped his face with the palms of her hands.

In the evening he told Jenny that the conversation had gone well. And that may have been the last time they had spoken.

The children didn't sense his absence and didn't wake up when he opened the door, at five thirty.

He turned on the radio and found a station that wasn't playing music. The morning was gloomier due to the trip down Lavon Street and the memory of the incident at the nursery and the fear that had arisen in him when he saw the police cars the day before. He lowered the volume on the radio and tried to calm himself down while he sliced the rolls and filled some with tuna salad and some with egg salad. On the rest he spread a layer of mayonnaise and stuck the omelettes inside. He put slices of tomato and cucumber in all of them before wrapping each one in greaseproof paper and putting it into a bag.

Shalom woke up at six thirty and came to the kitchen. Chaim sat him in a chair and the boy watched him while he packed up the last sandwiches and arranged them in tight rows in two cardboard boxes.

A few minutes passed before the boy truly woke from his sleep and asked, 'I'm not going to nursery?' and Chaim said to him, 'You're going. Ezer is going to school, too, and I'm going to work.' The boy didn't cry. And he didn't ask about Jenny this morning, either. The sleep had done him good and he appeared at ease. He asked, 'Why isn't nursery closed today?' And Chaim didn't know how to answer. He dressed him in his own bedroom and afterwards the two of them went to the boys' room and Chaim opened the window and the shutters. Light flooded Ezer's upper bunk. His clothes were lying on the floor and Shalom pointed at them and said to his brother, 'I can help you get dressed.' Ezer woke up slowly and silently, and Chaim urged him to hurry. It was already seven. Shalom followed his brother everywhere, even to the bathroom when he brushed his teeth.

The cardboard boxes were arranged in the living room on top of each other, and the kitchen was already clean when they sat down to eat breakfast. Ezer looked at his father with the same cautious glance, perhaps because he noticed that he was irritated. They ate a roll with cheese and cucumber. Suddenly he said, 'Did you know that I woke up last night and went into your room?' Chaim was dumbfounded. The sewing thread was in its place in the morning, strung taut across the door frame.

'I think I was already working. Did you check in the kitchen?' he said, and Ezer answered, 'No. You weren't at home.'

Shalom fixed an inquisitive gaze on his father, and Chaim said, 'I was at home all the time,' and then recalled the trip to the bakery. 'Was it in the morning? Was it light outside?'

'No. It was dark. It was night time.'

Chaim continued eating. Did he wake up at night without his knowing? But the thread hadn't come loose . . . So where exactly had he gone? Even though he didn't want to continue talking, he asked Ezer, 'Were you scared when you didn't see me?' and Ezer answered, 'No, my first dad was waiting for me in the living room.'

Chaim couldn't bear to hear this.

He rose from his spot, put the plate in the sink, and turned off the radio. He asked Shalom if he had finished, but Ezer wouldn't let it go. 'Do you remember what I told you last night?' he asked.

'What?'

'That I'd tell you today who lost the suitcase next to Shalom's nursery.'

Chaim turned on the tap and started to wash the two dishes. Since yesterday he had tried hard not to think about the suitcase.

'Well, I can't tell you yet. I talked to him and he asked me not to tell.'

Chaim turned up the water. Shalom asked his brother, 'Does your first dad know who lost the bag?' and Ezer smiled and said to his brother proudly, 'I know, too. Because he told me. And he told me not to tell you, because it's top secret.'

Chaim removed Ezer's plate from the table without saying a word, even though the boy hadn't finished his sandwich and looked at him in amazement. He said, 'The meal's over, we're leaving now. And I don't want you talking with Shalom about the first father and the suitcase. Enough, that's all.' He preferred to put off going to the nursery and took Ezer to school first, like the day before. Chaim and Shalom said goodbye to him at the gate and waited next to the guard until they saw his large backpack get swallowed up in the doorway to the school. Shalom waved to his brother even after he had turned and left, and then the two of them returned to Lavon Street. It was open to traffic, and there wasn't a trace of the commotion of the day before.

3

He had officially returned to work, and because of the shortage in manpower he worked alone.

On Monday he went to Lavon Street in the early-morning hours, in order to be at the scene at the time the suitcase had been placed. At six forty-four the traffic in the street was sparse and few pedestrians were in sight. A quiet street in a quiet residential neighbourhood. The sun took its time coming up, and the morning was cloudy. A young woman walked her dog and smoked. A boy left for school. No one wore a dark tracksuit, or a hood, or limped.

His working hypothesis then was that the suitcase had been placed next to the nursery, and for a reason, and that the investigation would have to be speedy because it was possible that the fake bomb was only a warning before a more severe attack. And Uzan was his sole suspect.

The first surprise at the scene was the off licence.

The policeman from the bomb squad arrived around seven thirty and pointed out the exact spot where the suitcase had been placed, based on the photos that had been taken at the site. It was found on the side entrance path to the building at 6 Lavon Street, hidden amid the bushes. The path led to the rear courtyard – to the nursery – but to its right, about ten feet away, on the ground floor of 4 Lavon Street, was an off licence.

It was true that the side entrance path was separated from the shop by a low stone wall, but, technically speaking, the suitcase was found closer to the shop than to the nursery. Avraham was amazed that Saban hadn't said anything about this. He asked the sapper if the possibility had been considered that the bomb had been placed in that spot because of its proximity to the shop and the man shrugged his shoulders. 'We didn't speak about the suitcase. They told us there's a suspicious object next to the nursery at 6 Lavon Street, so we dismantled a suspicious object next to the nursery at 6 Lavon Street. From there it's your job.'

In the pictures of the suitcase before the controlled explosion it was clear that even though it was buried behind the bushes, the bushes' thin branches didn't hide it all that well. If the neighbour hadn't seen the man place it there, it was fair to assume that someone else would have noticed it while walking on the path.

In the picture the suitcase looked old.

A small cloth suitcase, pink in colour, made by Delonite, with a dull-green leather handle.

Before 8 a.m., parents began rolling pushchairs down the path to the nursery, and Avraham entered after them. An older man walked in front of him, and for a moment it seemed to Avraham that he noticed a limp in his right leg, but it's possible that his steps were heavy because he was carrying a toddler in his arms. The teacher refused to speak with Avraham and asked that he return in the afternoon. 'It's enough that the children were frightened yesterday. Do I really need the police here now?' she said. He could have insisted, but he let it go. There was something harsh and aggressive in her that gave rise to a restlessness in him whose meaning he understood only later in the day.

He waited for the off licence to open and in the meantime questioned the residents whom he found in their homes.

His questions repeated themselves.

'Do you know about a dispute between one of the tenants and the owner of the nursery?'

'Do you recall any recent events connected to the nursery that operates in the courtyard?'

'Were there any criminal or other types of events that you can tell me about?'

'Did you by any chance see who placed the suitcase yesterday morning?'

'Did you see in the days prior to the incident a suspicious man wandering around the area of the building?'

To these questions, which he had composed the evening before at home, he added a question about the off licence and events connected to it that might have occurred recently. The tenants answered in the negative, and at a certain point he switched the order of the questions. At the end of the questioning he presented a picture of Uzan. No one recognized him, except one tenant, a housewife, a mother of four, who lived on the second floor. She claimed that she had seen him in the area of the building several times in the past year and assumed that he was the father of one of the children at the nursery. But she hadn't seen him recently, certainly not the day before, when she woke up only after the suitcase had been blown up. He wrote her name in his notepad.

At ten thirty he returned to the off licence and questioned the young assistant at length after she told him that the owner wouldn't arrive for another two hours. We open at ten, she said, and no one was in the store when the bomb was discovered. They'd heard about it afterwards from one of the customers, and the owner couldn't be of use to the investigation because he never got to the shop before noon. Paper plates were hanging in the display window upon which various sale offers were written in marker in Hebrew and Cyrillic letters. For Rosh Hashanah, Avraham could have bought two bottles of Chilean red wine for thirty-five shekels and a bottle of Absolut vodka for fifty-five. The assistant didn't know if the owner had been threatened or blackmailed in the past. And she herself had not been a witness to any violence while she was on duty.

He ate lunch in the cafeteria with Eliyahu Ma'alul, who interrogated him about his engagement to Marianka and her coming arrival.

'She's quitting the police there in order to come and live with you here?' Ma'alul asked, and Avraham said, 'Yep. That's the overall plan.'

Ma'alul whistled. 'Major decision. And what'll she do here? Start learning Hebrew?'

'Not clear yet. We'll make plans when she comes.'

They didn't talk about Ofer Sharabi and the previous investigation. And Avraham didn't know if Ma'alul failed to mention the report that Ilana Lis had written because he was unaware of it. The senior juvenile investigator looked at him with his moist, sunken eyes, which reminded Avraham of his father's eyes, and said, 'You don't know how happy I am for you, Avi. You look like a new man, as I told you. And as soon as she lands in Israel I insist you two report for dinner at our place.'

The briefings with the intelligence co-ordinators didn't reveal anything and the policeman from the detective squad who had tailed Uzan had nothing of substance to report. Uzan didn't leave his apartment on 26 Hatzionut until eleven o'clock. Apparently he lived there by himself. Drove a black Honda Civic he owned to visit his mother at Wolfson Hospital. Made no stops on his way there. He had bought a newspaper and a soft drink at the shop in the hospital and gone up to the Oncology Unit. He had carried a large bag that he had brought from home, apparently with a change of clothes and bedding. He still hadn't left the hospital.

Avraham waited in his office at the station and debated whether or not to call Ilana Lis. Since his return they hadn't spoken, but now he had a good excuse to talk to her. He could find out what she knew about the extortion business and the protection racket in the alcohol industry. Instead of her he called Marianka. Her phone was on but she didn't answer.

He turned on the computer and from the screen a picture he had taken on the day they had first met in Brussels, at sunrise, when she had taken him for a tour of the city streets, stared out at him. Back then he hadn't imagined that the city would be his home for three months. For three months over the summer he would wake up next to Marianka each morning, in the bedroom in her apartment that looked out on a small square in the middle of which was a blackened stone sculpture of a Belgian composer whom he had never heard of. When he had gone to live with her in Brussels, Avraham had written the address in his small notepad: *Alfred Bouvier Square, Building 6, Apartment 5 (green door, no bell).*

He returned to the scene that afternoon.

'You don't have anything else to investigate? I don't understand why you are questioning me,' the teacher asked him when he entered the nursery. 'I told the police yesterday that this has nothing to do with me. And I begged them not to come in the middle of the day because it scares the children and upsets the parents. The children were scared enough yesterday when they turned up and weren't able to come inside.' She was alone in the nursery. Wooden chairs were turned over on a low table in the middle of the room.

Her refusal to co-operate immediately caused his anger to spike, but only later in the conversation did Avraham understand why he also felt uneasy in her company. She asked his permission to tidy the place while he presented his questions, and he implied that if she preferred, he could take her to the station for questioning. The room's floor was clean but it was scattered with things and messy. They sat across from each other on two plastic chairs that she brought in from the courtyard. Next to one of the walls was a tall pile of thin mattresses that gave off a smell of urine. Through the rusty bars of a small, high window very little air or light penetrated. In the evening Avraham wrote in his notepad that Chava Cohen ran the nursery and had worked there for ten years, and had been a teacher for more than twenty. She was in her forties, short and stocky, the palms of her hands wide and strong, and her face tired. She hadn't got round to emptying the large black bin that stood in the corner of the room, crammed full of nappies.

He asked if she was involved in any disputes, and she raised her voice: 'With whom? I'm the owner of a nursery school, for God's sake. For a whole day I've had to explain that my nursery has nothing to do with this.'

'Maybe not the nursery, maybe *you* have something to do with it. Are you involved in any personal or business disputes?'

'Explain to me why you think this has something to do with me. Don't you understand that the more we talk the more it harms my business? Maybe this is connected to someone who lives in the building?'

Her answers reminded him of his unsatisfactory conversation with Uzan. He said, 'I don't understand your objection to co-operating with me. We are concerned that the suitcase was maybe just a warning, and that if we don't act in time, whoever placed it will go from warnings to truly violent acts. We don't know how much time we have and we need co-operation from everyone who can be of assistance—' and she cut him off: 'But I explained to you that I'm not involved. I can't help you at all.'

And then he understood.

Suddenly he was in the building on Histadrut Street again, in Hannah Sharabi's apartment, on the second day of the investigation into the disappearance of her son Ofer. He had sat across from her in the kitchen and she served him black coffee. It was a Friday morning, his birthday, and he had tried to get her to tell him about her son who was missing. Hannah Sharabi also said that she couldn't help him. That she didn't know a thing. In contrast to the woman who was sitting before him now, Hannah was quiet. Avraham could barely hear her when she spoke. Every now and then she sobbed. And he didn't detect that she was lying. That in fact she knew where her son was. Only three weeks later, after her husband admitted to killing their son, did she break down in the interrogation room.

The air in the nursery was heavy and dizzying.

Avraham steadied his breath, placed his notepad on the floor, and looked at the woman who sat before him. If he had learned any lesson from his failure in the previous investigation, it was this: open your eyes and look. Don't believe a single word. Chava Cohen was older than Hannah Sharabi by a few years, stockier, and her hair was curly. And he still hadn't asked her for her name. He said quietly, 'I insist that you answer my questions without any skirting around,' and she pressed an open hand to her forehead. 'I'm trying. What's the question?'

'I asked if you're involved in any disputes.'

She said that she was not. He saw her hands gather up her hair and her gaze turn away from him as she answered.

'Tell me again your name,' he said, and she answered, 'Chava.'

'Chava what?'

'Chava Cohen.'

'Do you know if there were any complaints from tenants in the building who might not like the fact that you're running a nursery here?'

'What are you talking about, complaints? The nursery has been here for ten years. And everything's licensed.'

'Again, you're not answering my question, and I'm losing patience. I didn't ask if you have a licence but rather if any of the tenants in the building don't like the fact that a nursery operates here.'

She didn't interrupt again, because she saw that something in him had hardened. 'I tried to answer. As far as I know, no. Actually, I'm certain there aren't any.'

'Do you or have you ever had any disputes with the parents of the children in the nursery?'

'Not at all. I'm not in a dispute with a single one of my parents. There are no disputes at our nursery. You can go back ten years and check with all the parents in the neighbourhood. Parents bring me their children, they beg me to keep places for their children who haven't even been born.'

From a cardboard folder Avraham removed the pictures of the suitcase and asked if she was familiar with it. Afterwards he presented her with a picture of Uzan, again without results.

'I'm asking you to take a good look at this picture,' he persisted. 'You're certain that you don't know this man? That you haven't seen him around the nursery? He's not the father of a child in the nursery?'

Once more the answer was no.

'Have you received any threats recently? Letters, perhaps? Phone messages?'

He looked at her and knew that she was lying.

On the wall across from him a large drawing of a bouquet of flowers that had captured his attention since the beginning of the conversation. At the centre of each flower was a picture of a child, around which colourful crepe-paper petals were glued. He couldn't see the faces of the children from where he sat. 'What I'm asking you right now won't leave the confines of this room. I want to know if, to the best of your knowledge, the parents of one of the children at the nursery might be involved in any criminal activities.'

Chava Cohen looked at him, surprised. 'You think they tried to threaten one of the parents?'

'I'm asking.'

She was less impatient when his questions didn't deal with her. 'I don't have children from the slums and, as far as I know, all the parents here are totally fine.'

'If I were to ask you to tell me what each does for a living, would you know?'

She turned and looked at the picture that had drawn his attention. 'Don't think so. I don't see many fathers, mostly mums. Some work and some don't. And as this is the beginning of the year, I don't know everyone. I can tell you that Arkadi's father is an electrician, because he helped us with an electrical problem last week.'

Avraham got up from his seat when he asked her who else works at the nursery, and she answered, 'No one. Just me and an assistant.' And when he asked for the phone number of the assistant he noticed that she grew tense again. Despite her resistance at the start of their conversation, she invited him to return to the nursery tomorrow in order to talk with the assistant, because there was no hope of getting her on the phone. 'But what can she tell you that I haven't said? She's barely been here two weeks. I brought her in a day before the start of the year, and she doesn't know anything about the parents or the building,' she said.

He didn't speak with Ilana Lis until the following day, after he'd finished the investigation's pressing tasks.

Uzan again left his apartment at eleven and drove in the black Civic to the hospital without stopping on his way. When he got out of the automobile he was carrying the large bag with a change of clothes for his mother. He left the hospital at four, without the bag, and travelled to his home. Avraham debated whether or not to summon him for additional questioning, but there was no new information, other than the testimony of the neighbour who had identified his face from the photograph and thought that he was the father of a child at the nursery. But Uzan had no children.

He left two messages on the mobile of the assistant and, just as Chava Cohen said, she did not respond. Nevertheless, he decided he would summon her to give testimony at the station and not question her at the nursery in the presence of the older teacher, and this would prove to be the right decision.

Though he seemed to be getting nowhere, he sensed that a breakthrough was near.

For the first time since his return to work he went outside to smoke a cigarette on the steps of the station, just as he loved to do. The heat was bearable – from time to time a breeze even blew, and he thought that he ought to go shopping before Rosh Hashanah. He called Ilana from his office and she was happy to hear his voice.

'You've been in Israel for two weeks and you haven't come by yet to say hello?'

He told her that he had returned to work and that he was handling the investigation into the fake bomb that had been placed on Lavon Street all by himself.

Ilana was silent, and it seemed to him that there was doubt in her silence. 'How's it coming along?' she asked, and he said, 'Actually that's why I called,' and he told her about the off licence.

'I thought the bomb was placed next to a nursery.'

'That was the assumption,' he said. 'But when I arrived at the scene I discovered the shop, and I think we shouldn't dismiss that possibility either.'

Ilana agreed. She recommended that he check if other business owners in the area were being blackmailed, and he said he had done that already. No business owner in the area had submitted a complaint about blackmail, and to the best of the district's intelligence officers' knowledge no gang operating in the area was extorting protection money from business owners.

He listened to the familiar voice and waited for her to mention the report she had written about the Ofer Sharabi investigation.

Ilana told him that in recent months a covert investigation was being conducted on a national level, in co-operation with supervisory bodies from the Ministry of Industry, Trade and

Labour, into the practice of importing counterfeit alcohol into Israel. This was a massive industry, and apparently more than one crime family was involved in it. If this turned out to be connected, catching the individual who had placed the bomb might lead investigators to whoever was running it. 'It's possible that this is really the issue,' she said. 'But as far as I know, they push these counterfeit bottles onto the kiosks and clubs, and the owners co-operate because the prices are much lower than the prices of the real brands. It's hard for me to believe that now they're trying to push them into the shops, and by force. First thing, invite an investigator from the Ministry of Industry to check the shop. Start there.'

He waited until the last moment and Ilana still didn't mention the report, but before they got off she said to him, 'Avi, there's something I have to tell you face to face, because I don't want you to hear it by chance from someone else. Will you tell me when you have time to meet outside work?'

Marianka also sounded distant when he finally managed to speak with her, that evening.

He told her that he had been trying to catch her for the last few days, to which she offered no response. Nevertheless he told her about his first days at work and Saban's speech, and was surprised by her reaction. 'Why does he sound so idiotic to you?' he asked, and Marianka said, 'Because that's the speech of a politician, not a policeman. He's simply vapid, don't you think? Real police officers know that there aren't areas free of violence. Wherever there's people there's violence.' There was an anger in her voice that Avraham didn't understand.

When he asked her how she was doing and how the preparations for the trip were coming along she avoided answering. She asked how he was feeling at work and he said excellent.

Since he had returned he was sensitive to what was being said and what wasn't, to what was visible and to what was trying to remain hidden. Nothing evaded him. Not Chava Cohen's lies, or the fear in the voice of the assistant before she had agreed to come to his office tomorrow morning to give testimony, even though it would be just a few hours before the holiday began.

'And how are your parents?' Marianka asked, and he said that he'd see them tomorrow.

'Do you know that it's Rosh Hashanah?'

She didn't know, and he told her that it was his favourite day of the year. 'I don't know how to explain it to you,' he said. 'I suppose you just have to be there.' A sentence was echoing in his brain, but because of the distance between them he didn't say it out loud: *When the sun sets this evening, it's as if it understands that it's setting for the last time.* Before they got off, he asked her, 'Do you miss me?' and she said, 'Yes.'

The next day, at 8.30 in the morning, Natalie Pinchasov was in his office and within a matter of minutes told him about the warning call. She was twenty-two years old, and her face was pale and beautiful. Avraham thanked her for agreeing to testify on the eve of the holiday. Most of the time her eyes were lowered and her voice quiet, and she looked around as if seeking out someone else unseen in the room. In her hair were dyed red streaks. He asked how long she'd been working at the nursery and she said since the start of the autumn session, less than three weeks. He noticed that on her neck, below her hair, was a long scar.

'How did you wind up at the nursery?'

'My past employer recommended me. Last year I didn't work steadily; I was a substitute assistant at a few nurseries. A week here, a week there. There isn't a lot of work at nurseries now. But about a month ago one of the women I worked with called and said that Chava was urgently searching for an assistant.'

'Why urgently?'

'Because the assistant who was working with her quit a few days before the start of the season.'

He spoke to her in a soft voice. Offered her coffee or tea. Asked her where she lived. She took two buses to work, left her house around six thirty. The nursery opened at a quarter to eight but she needed to be there fifteen minutes before then in order to help Chava get the place ready and welcome the children. Afterwards he asked her if she had witnessed any anomalous events at the nursery and she cautiously asked him, 'What is . . . anomalous?'

'Whatever strikes you as odd. Something that looks exceptional to you and that you might perhaps connect to the bomb.'

She again looked around, and he said to her, 'I promise that everything you say will remain between us. Not a word you say will leave here.'

She touched the scar on her neck. 'There were two parents, yes. Who had an argument with Chava. But I don't think that this can be connected to the bomb.'

'It doesn't matter. I want you to tell me whatever strikes you. Parents who . . . what?'

'Who argued with her.'

Chava Cohen had told him that she wasn't involved in any disputes with anyone.

According to the assistant, one mother – Orna Chamo was her name – suspected, correctly, that her son spent most of the day separated from the rest of the children, seated in a chair in a corner of the room, without permission to move from that spot, because he cried a lot. A few days after the start of the year the mother had arrived for a surprise visit and a scuffle almost broke out between her and Chava Cohen. She had taken her child out of the nursery. And a few days ago one of the fathers, an older man whose name was Chaim Sara, had almost violently attacked the teacher because he suspected that children were hitting his son, and then Chava Cohen answered him rudely. In the meantime Chaim Sara's son continues coming to the nursery, but now only his father brings him and not his mother, maybe in order to intimidate the teacher.

'Do you think one of them could be connected to the suitcase?' Avraham asked, and she said, 'I don't think so. Don't know. Maybe there was . . .' and she fell silent.

What was she afraid to say?

'Natalie, I want to explain to you why it's necessary you tell me everything. Our fear is that the suitcase was just a warning and that whoever placed it might commit more extreme acts, which would put the children in the nursery at risk. I understand that you're afraid to lose your job, but I promise you that nothing you tell me here will leave this room.'

She spoke quietly. 'There was a phone call. A woman called on the day of the suitcase.'

He tensed and stuck the tip of the pen into the open notepad in front of him. 'And said what?'

'Said that this is just the beginning. That the suitcase is just the beginning, and that I should tell Chava.'

'The beginning of what? Try to remember the exact words.'

'That's what she said. "The suitcase is just the beginning. Tell Chava the whore that this is the beginning." And then she hung up.'

'You answered the phone? At what time exactly was this?'

'I don't remember the time exactly. In the afternoon. When the children were napping.'

'Give me an approximate time.'

'After one, maybe.'

He knew the answer to the next question but nevertheless asked her if she had reported the conversation to Chava Cohen, and Natalie answered, 'Of course, I told her right away. She said that this was a mistake for sure. That it wasn't connected to her and that it must have been a wrong number.'

'And she asked you not to tell anyone about the call?'

Her face went pale, and he was afraid that she'd burst out crying. 'She's worried that it will frighten the parents. Also, yesterday afternoon she called me and asked me not to say a word about it, because it would mean more investigations and more police and the mess would just upset the parents.'

At the time the phone had rung at the nursery, Uzan was sitting across from him, in the interrogation room, and would not have been able to telephone anyone. And was doubtful that Uzan would have been able to distort his voice to sound like a woman, even if he'd had the opportunity.

'You're one hundred per cent certain that this was a woman?'

'Yes. It was the voice of a woman.'

Nevertheless he showed her the picture of Uzan and she examined it for a long time before saying that she'd never seen him before.

He escorted her out of the station and asked the duty officer for Benny Saban's cell number. Lit a cigarette on the stairs. At the sound of Saban's voice, it occurred to him that this was the first time he had talked to him on the phone, and he didn't know what to call him. He said, 'Benny?'

'Yes, speaking. Who is this?'

'Inspector Avraham. I apologize for the disturbance on the evening of the holiday, but I wanted to update you with regard to the suitcase.'

'What case? *Who is this?*'

In the background a hammer could be heard banging loudly, and it seemed to him that someone was speaking Arabic.

'Suitcase. The suitcase on Lavon Street. Next to the nursery. It's Inspector Avraham, from the station.'

'Ah, ah, Avi. How are you? I'm happy to hear from you. Yes, what about the suitcase? The line is really shitty.'

'I wanted to tell you that you're right. It was a warning. I discovered that on the same day a woman called the nursery and announced that this was just the beginning.'

'Great, great. I'm happy to hear it. And what are you doing with this?'

He didn't understand the question. 'This means it's possible that the suspect we arrested was the wrong man. He was with me in the interrogation room at the time the warning call was made. And apparently we are looking for a woman, not a man. Or maybe a woman *and* a man. In addition, the information didn't come to me from the teacher, who tried to hide it.'

The call was disconnected, and Saban didn't call him back.

He had wanted to ask him if he should call Chava Cohen in for an emergency interrogation or wait until after the holiday.

The station was quiet and most of the doors were closed. He stayed until the afternoon, thought things over, reviewed the notes in his pad. In addition to the information about the phone call, two new names were written in his notepad: *Orna Chamo* and *Chaim Sara*, a young mother and an older father. Next to the mother's name were written the words *scuffle almost broke out*. And next to Chaim Sara's name *almost violently attacked*. It would be necessary to call the two of them in for questioning. At the bottom of the page *WOMAN'S VOICE* was written in big letters.

He decided to pick up again after the holiday, in part because the nursery would be closed for the next three days so the children were in no imminent danger. Saban got back to him that afternoon, when he was already at home, and supported his decision.

On his way home the shops were closed and he bought a six-pack of Heineken and three packs of cigarettes at a kiosk.

It was the last day of the year.

The year in which he had met Marianka.

Without knowing why, he got into his car and went back to the sea.

The beach was empty, and the sand between his toes felt soft and warm. He took off his clothes and entered the water until it reached his chest. He looked at the flat, brilliant horizon for a long time. Afterwards he floated with his eyes closed. At dusk, when he walked the few streets that separated his apartment from that of his parents, he didn't think about an old suitcase with a handle of greenish leather, or about a warning call that Chava Cohen had known of and hidden. Or about Amos Uzan, who it seemed had in fact left his home in the morning merely to breathe some fresh air and to buy a few things at a local shop.

'You're not cold in a short-sleeved shirt?' his mother asked him while he stood in the doorway. 'You didn't notice that the summer is already over?' His father kissed his cheek and said, 'With her the winter starts in July. He should wear a sweater, right? A parka!'

In the past, this sort of banter might have annoyed him, but it didn't any more.

They quickly ate the holiday meal, without prayers of any kind. As every year, his mother served chopped liver on a slice of tomato and fresh chicken soup and a pot roast with a texture that always made Avraham a little nauseous. They raised a glass to the coming year and wished one another 'only health', because you don't need anything else, and afterwards they turned on the television. When his father fell asleep in his armchair, his mother asked him questions about Marianka, when was she going to arrive, and if everything in the apartment was ready for her to come, and if they'd already decided to get married, and he answered briefly, even though he was thinking only about this, about the weeks to come, about the day Marianka would land, how they would travel home from the airport.

He recalled the day he had gone to her in Brussels.

The plane had landed at five in the morning and Marianka was waiting for him at the airport.

Only a week had passed since they'd said goodbye, but suddenly a surprising, perhaps even shocking, distance had arisen between them – and now to think that all this was indeed happening, that he'd taken leave of absence from his work and travelled to her. In the taxi to the city they'd sat close to each other but their hands didn't touch. He'd said, 'You're tired. When did you wake up?' and Marianka said she hadn't slept. He was already searching her face for signs of regret, but she'd smiled at him and said, 'I was waiting up.'

They entered her apartment on tiptoe because her housemate was sleeping. Marianka's room was wide, but when they rolled his suitcases into it and stood next to them, in the space between the bed and the wardrobe, the two of them asked themselves if two people would really be able to manage there over the course of an unspecified amount of time. He restricted his movements, sat on the bed only when she said to him, 'You can sit.' His knees were rubbing against the suitcase, and he shook his head when she asked if he wanted breakfast. When he lay on his side, in his shoes and still wearing a jacket, she pulled his arm. His face was near to hers and he thought that she wanted him to kiss her, but she said, 'I need more time to look at you.'

Obviously he didn't tell his mother any of this and a little after ten o'clock said goodbye to her and returned home.

4

On the eve of Rosh Hashanah the children fell asleep just after midnight, exhausted from many hours of playing with their cousins in the backyard. Shalom fell asleep in the living room in his holiday clothes, and Chaim moved him to the mattress and undressed him. Ezer took off his shirt and trousers himself, and his eyes closed a minute after he lay down on the sofa bed, which was prepared with a sheet for him. Both of them had got very wild, elated to be with their cousins. Ezer still appeared distant and guarded but also laughed and participated in the games. And didn't say a word about the first father or the suitcase, Chaim having forbidden him to mention them.

He looked at their silent breathing before leaving. Their hair was damp with sweat and their faces were red. They slept in the small room, which had been his room during his childhood, with the rectangular window facing the backyard and the white curtain over it. A bed was made for him in the next room, which had once been the room of his younger brother and sister.

Did he have a plan then?

It seemed he did not. For a moment he thought that he had to escape, to disappear with the children immediately, and the next moment he thought that he might as well just relax and wait. There was no reason to escape. He had to wait for the suitcase to be forgotten, and till then simply stick it out.

He knew how to do this. He had lived like this for many years. Maybe this was his only plan: that other things would happen and erase him from memory. He had no doubt he would be forgotten. When he listened to the news, he expected to hear a report about violent acts in the area. Before the holiday they had reported on the radio about an attempt to assassinate a criminal on Shenkar Street.

On the eve of the new year he still didn't know for certain if the police were continuing to investigate who had placed the suitcase, because he was only called in for questioning after it. Before being called in for questioning, he didn't think they'd get to him, in part because of the man who was arrested trying to flee and was caught right before his eyes. And even if they released the man who had been arrested, how long would the police investigate a fake bomb in a suitcase next to a nursery that hadn't harmed anyone?

He tried not to think about his bad luck, because that only wore him down. And anyway, time was his prescription for the boys as well. He had to give them time. Even if he didn't have a plan, he had a goal: to protect them. To make sure they wouldn't know a thing, so they wouldn't get hurt. To prevent them feeling pain, as much as he could, and to continue searing his image into their memory. To bring Ezer, from whom he had grown distant because of Jenny, close to him again.

The more days that passed, the more things would be forgotten.

Life taught him that things were forgotten, even if he actually remembered.

★

After he had left the children's room he told his mother to rest and straightened the living room, folded up the small tables that had been attached to the dining-room table, and stacked the plastic chairs in the courtyard. Adina washed up in the kitchen. Only once over the course of the meal had his sister asked about Jenny, and his mother had told her in their language not to talk about it in front of the children. Because he was the firstborn it fell on him to read the prayers.

After Adina had left, he made his mother a cup of tea. This was their first chance to speak, and she said, 'They look good.'

'They're getting used to it,' he said. Ezer had smiled more than he had smiled before, and had even joined the cousins when they sang the holiday songs.

She asked if he wasn't going to have something warm to drink and he changed his mind and made himself a cup of tea.

'Things are better for them. She didn't care for them like a mother. Put in Sweet'n Low, not sugar.'

He waited for the water in the kettle to boil again.

'And you're sure everything is okay at the nursery?' she asked, and he said, 'Yes.'

Again she said to him, 'It's good that you shouted at the teacher. She won't be so rude next time. And how is Ezer doing at school?' and he answered, 'Fine.' He still hadn't told her a thing about the suitcase, because he knew she'd get stressed out and increase his stress.

'Do they ask about her a lot?'

'No. They ask sometimes.'

'Children don't understand much.' She sighed. Afterwards she asked him, 'And what about money?' and he answered, 'We'll manage.'

★

The holidays were always difficult. Employees of the Ministry of the Interior and the Tax Authority in Holon, his main customers, went on leave, and even when the offices were operating normally, some of the employees were away. More people brought in food from home, whatever was left over from the holiday meals. All in all, during these weeks he prepared and sold less than half the amount of sandwiches that he sold in winter.

He had ideas for increasing income from the business, but in the meantime he hadn't implemented them. He planned to sell hot meals again, a meat dish with a side of rice and salad, as he had done when he opened the business, before the recession. He hoped that if he offered a dish at twenty-five shekels, there would still be demand. And it might also be possible to offer drinks in bottles and cans, but he would need to sell them cold and at a price below that of the vending machines. Beyond this, he wanted to check with his cousin who arranged the Ministry of the Interior account for him in Holon if it would be possible to sell at other branches, perhaps in Rishon LeZion or Ramat Gan. Another possibility was to take advantage of the available morning hours for making deliveries, but he feared heavy loads and long hours of driving. Either way, he would be forced to work more, not just during the day but in the evening as well, at home. This didn't scare him. Anyway, in recent months Jenny hadn't worked and they had been living on only the earnings from the business.

His mother said, 'Adina will come and help you with the children,' and he said, 'No need. I want to be with them more.'

'But did you see how well she gets on with them?'

He saw. His mother sat Adina next to Shalom and she looked after him throughout the evening, took the bones out of the fish for him, rinsed his hands when he got messy with oil, everything that Jenny didn't do. When he got hit by one of the cousins and cried, out of all the people there he ran to her. She was forty-five years old, divorced, with no children, and had started cleaning at his mother's place two years earlier. She lived nearby and they had become friends. She was grateful that his mother had invited her to their Rosh Hashanah dinner. 'It's a pity God didn't bless her with children. She would be a good mother,' his mother said, and he got up from his place and put the teacup in the sink.

When he lay down in bed he heard her turning the tap on and off in the kitchen and afterwards flushing the toilet in the bathroom. He thought that perhaps it was a mistake to come to her with the children for the holiday, even though he didn't know what he would do with them for four days by himself. The two of them were happy to sleep at her place, especially Shalom, the younger one. He asked what would happen if Mum came back and didn't find them in the apartment and Chaim calmed him down. He said she wouldn't come back over the holiday. But again he hadn't talked to them enough, as he had promised himself he would. He let his mother talk to them instead, as if something in her weakened him, although she herself was weak and was only trying to help. She was already eighty years old. His father was many years older than his mother and had died when he was fifty-six.

The next day, Chaim went to the synagogue that his father had attended.

He had slept well and was refreshed and more certain of his strength. His body felt younger and more energetic. He thought that it would be difficult to find a place to sit in the synagogue and prepared himself to stand during the service, but the small room wasn't full. Most of the worshippers were old, perhaps his mother's age. A few of them recognized him and greeted him with a nod or wished him a happy new year. He sat next to Shlomo Achoan's father and tried to pray with great conviction, but he lost his place in the prayer book. And missed his sons, who were still sleeping when he had left. He wanted to take them on a hike through the orchard where he had played with his father as a child. When he returned, before noon, they were on the carpet, quietly watching television. The shutters were closed against the sun and the house was almost completely dark. Ezer sat cross-legged and his younger brother was lying next to him. His mother sat on the sofa behind them, holding a saucer with shelled hazelnuts and almonds. Perhaps because of what he saw in Ezer's gaze Chaim suddenly said, 'Do you want to call Mum?' And Shalom jumped from his place and hugged his leg. Ezer looked at him with his distant eyes and he saw joy in them. Was this in fact how the plan began to unfold? He went into his mother's bedroom, dialled the number, and waited. He sat on her bed while the two of them stood next to him, their eyes fixed on the phone. Afterward he heard his own recorded voice announce, 'You've reached Chaim and Jenny Sara. We can't answer at the moment. You can leave a message when you hear the beep.'

He put the receiver down and said, 'She didn't answer,' and Shalom said, 'Why didn't she answer?'

'Maybe she's sleeping.'

'Maybe she doesn't want to talk to us?' Shalom asked, and Chaim said quickly, 'We'll call again soon.'

Ezer was silent, and in his eyes, which had actually smiled the day before, Chaim saw tears, and so he said, 'I spoke to

Mum this morning, before you got up. We'll give her another call soon.'

His mother entered the room and said to him in Farsi, 'Wouldn't it be better for you to tell them that she's not coming back?'

He didn't answer.

None of this had been planned.

And he wasn't sure that this was a good idea, even though the promise had made them so happy at first. They left the bedroom and Shalom said to his father, 'I get to talk to Mum first, before Ezer, right?' and Chaim said, 'The two of you will talk at the same time.'

They lay down on the carpet again in the dark living room.

His mother suggested to Shalom that he gather up leaves in the backyard, but he said, 'I just want to stay with Ezer.'

Even though Chaim knew that she wouldn't answer, he took them into the bedroom again and they argued over who would be closer to him when he dialled the number and he waited and instead of Jenny's voice he heard his own again. 'You've reached Chaim and Jenny Sara. . . . You can leave a message.' The next time only Shalom went with him and Ezer remained seated in front of the television.

The holiday's second day was Friday and his mother took them to Adina's in the morning. She said that Adina had prepared plates for them with sweets and apple slices in honey and filled the house with toys. She had invited her sister's son, who was a few years older than Ezer, and they'd play ball. Afterwards everyone would eat lunch at Adina's place.

Shalom was glad to go, especially after he'd heard about the plates of sweets, and Ezer went without an expression on his face and without a word leaving his mouth, as if asleep. After they hadn't succeeded in speaking to Jenny, his face had closed again. Chaim fixed the wall in the bathroom. He sanded off the damp, crumbling layer of paint in which a dark mould had spread due to the humidity, and after the plaster had dried he put on a new layer of waterproof paint. On all radio stations songs were playing and no one said a word. He wondered how he could get closer to Ezer. Afterwards he took the radio out to the courtyard and finished filling in the concrete path leading to the house. The heat was again unbearable, and he removed his shirt. His back hurt. Despite this he worked quickly and tried not to think. If it were possible, he would have chosen to remain there despite everything. Far from their shared apartment, and far from the children's small room into which the lights from the adjacent building were reflected at night. Was he less afraid here because his father's strength was more tangible, as if he were still to be found within the house's walls? He warmed up rice and chicken and ate in the kitchen by himself. And then he suddenly crashed. Without knowing why, he went to his mother's bedroom and collapsed onto her bed, but didn't pick up the phone. Afterwards he lay down on it properly and fell asleep. He didn't make it back to the synagogue, as he had hoped.

The next day his younger brother came with his children and took the boys to the pool.

It was only when they returned to Holon, on Saturday night, that Ezer suddenly spoke up.

They passed through Jaffa on the way, because the shops were open there, and Chaim bought vegetables, eggs and cheese. He called the Brothers' Bakery and left a reminder on their answering machine that tomorrow he'd need only half the usual number of rolls. Shalom fell asleep in the car because he hadn't slept that afternoon, and Chaim carried him in his arms to bed and afterwards brought up the groceries. It was early and Ezer watched television, and when his programme ended he turned it off himself. Chaim boiled eggs and chopped vegetables in the kitchen. When he walked into the living room he saw Ezer standing next to the window, looking out through the shutters. His body was small in his white T-shirt and his legs were thin and dark.

He asked him, 'Did you do all your homework?' and Ezer said, 'Mum doesn't want to live with us any more?'

Chaim felt as if someone had struck him in the face.

'She went away for a while and she'll come back,' he said, and felt that now he'd have to say more.

Ezer turned and looked with his strange eyes at his father. 'Why did she go away?' he asked.

'Because she missed her home. Her country. She'd wanted to go for a long time.' The image of his father appeared before him and he asked Ezer, 'Do you want to call her again?'

Shalom coughed in his bed. Ezer said no. The eggs were about to boil and Chaim turned off the burner in the kitchen. When he came back he put his hand on Ezer's shoulder, the way he remembered. Said that the time had come to go to bed.

'If Mum was born in another country, how did you meet her?'

Was it then that he understood that in order to protect them from pain he had to tell the truth? That this was the only way?

'She came here to work and then I met her,' he said.

'How?'

'At work. I went there, where she worked, and saw her.'

'And you decided to marry her?'

'Yes.'

This was about a year after Jenny arrived in Israel. She still didn't speak very good Hebrew. She worked for a neighbour of his mother's, a widower who had broken his pelvis and later died of heart disease. They didn't meet at the old man's house but rather at Chaim's mother's house. Jenny was invited to dinner, and he was invited the same night. The family of the widower intended to place him in an institution, so Jenny lost her job, and then her visa expired. He didn't remember what she wore, because he didn't pay attention to details like that, only that everyone was quiet during dinner and that Jenny seemed embarrassed. She didn't know he'd be there, but she understood why the meal had been arranged. And he couldn't say how and when they met for the second time. One evening a few weeks later they went out to a Thai restaurant and she explained the dishes to him. When she understood that he wouldn't have a lot to say, she talked. Quickly and with hand motions. Told him that both her parents had died when she was a child – first her mother, from some wasting disease, and two years later her father, from a broken heart – and about her sister, who had married a Turkish businessman and lived in Berlin. There was no one left in the Philippines for her. And the work in Israel, she said, was good. There was a cheerfulness in her that was foreign to him but which pleased him. She could talk and talk, and he could be quiet. They still hadn't spoken about marriage then, or about children.

Ezer looked at him, and Chaim saw in his gaze that he wanted him to continue.

Most of the light in the living room came in from the kitchen, and a little filtered in from outside, through the shutters.

Chaim could look at the faces of his two sons for hours, but not for the reason that most parents do this, or so he thought. He looked at the narrow eyes, at their foreign facial features, trying to identify exactly how they were different from his face and how they nevertheless resembled him, despite their foreignness. They always said that Shalom resembled him a bit more, but in personality he resembled Jenny. Energetic and talkative. And Ezer, who reminded him so much of himself, with his long silences and his closing into himself, actually looked more like Jenny, and sometimes, to him, looked exactly like her.

It would never be possible to erase the foreignness from their faces. Chaim understood this mainly through the eyes of other people.

Ezer asked, 'Why did you decide to marry her?' and Chaim said, 'Maybe because she laughed a lot. I liked that.'

'And when were we born?'

'You were born first. About a year later.'

He remembered the birth too. Jenny's screams, his concern that something bad might happen to his firstborn son during the birth. The doctor in the maternity ward didn't agree to admit Jenny even when she said that she was having contractions. She told them to return in a few hours, and Chaim was sure this was because of Jenny's foreignness but he couldn't bring himself to protest and brought her back home, writhing in pain.

*

Ezer peeled the hard-boiled eggs, crushed them, and mixed them in the bowl with the tuna. Chaim finely diced the onion and dumped it into the bowl. This is how it needs to be, he thought, and in time this is how it will be. The more days that passed without her, the more sure of himself he was, despite the suitcase. And Ezer was calm as well. When he brushed his teeth he asked where the Filipinos' country was and Chaim said it was far away, more than ten hours by plane. In bed he didn't lie in the frozen position that frightened Chaim but on his side instead, bringing his face close to his father. Chaim asked if he wanted him to stay in the room and Ezer said, 'You know, before I thought Mum wouldn't come back.'

He smiled and said to him, 'No, she'll come back, in a little while,' and Ezer said, 'I know now. But I checked her wardrobe and there wasn't anything there. She took everything.'

Chaim suppressed the shudder that passed through him.

He didn't remember Ezer ever entering the bedroom, and he was always with them in the apartment. He asked him, 'When did you see?' and Ezer said, 'A few days ago. And I also found the necklace that she said she'd take everywhere. I saw it in a drawer.'

Chaim didn't understand what necklace he was talking about.

'The one with the beads. That we made together. She said she'd take it everywhere, but she didn't take it.'

Chaim said, 'She just forgot,' and stroked his cheek. He wanted to kiss him and leave, but Ezer said more: 'And I also thought that she won't come back because she went without saying to me and Shalom that she was going.' His voice was quiet, almost peaceful.

Chaim said, 'That's because she thought it would be easier for you this way,' and Ezer responded immediately, 'Did you know that my first father told me she won't come back? He helped her escape with the suitcase.'

Chaim managed not to lose his cool.

Ezer realized that he had said what Chaim had forbidden him to say, and there was fear in his eyes, but Chaim surprised him and encouraged him to speak. 'He saw her?' he asked, and Ezer hesitated before he answered, 'At night. He helped her escape and told me that she won't be coming back.'

'But now you believe that she will come back, right?' And Ezer said, 'Right,' and smiled at him.

That same night, for the first time, Chaim stretched thread across the door frame of the children's room as well.

The conversation with Ezer had shocked him, though he had restrained himself and hadn't shown it. When he left their room afterward he opened the wardrobes in the bedroom and looked. Then he checked the drawers of the nightstand next to the bed and didn't find a necklace.

That didn't make sense.

He checked all the drawers. He didn't remember Jenny wearing a string of beads around her neck. Suddenly he wondered if Ezer woke up at night, like him. Walked around the house in the dark without his knowledge. He stuck the thread to the door jambs with plastic tape above knee height, so that if Shalom woke up he wouldn't run into the thread and trip. After this he tried to continue working and couldn't. He got into bed early but had difficulty falling asleep. All this was a sign of things to come, because the next day, in the early afternoon, the call from the police came.

5

The conference room on the second floor was empty when Avraham entered, a few minutes before the appointed time.

He poured boiling water from the kettle into a Styrofoam cup, made himself black coffee and grabbed his usual place, behind which was the window that looked out onto the squad cars in the car park.

He was well prepared for the first meeting of the Investigations Unit he would participate in since returning to work. Over the holiday he had read the material that had gathered in the file and analysed it in depth, and on Shabbat he drove over to Lavon Street, just to be there, perhaps to notice something he had missed earlier. And there were a few decisions up for immediate implementation that he wanted approved: to stop tailing Amos Uzan; to increase the police presence in the area of the nursery; and to add another officer to the investigation in light of its considerable urgency. In actuality, the tail on Uzan had ceased before the holiday, due to a shortage of detectives. And the investigation had moved on from him on its own.

From his perspective there were a few reasons for an increased police presence. The first was the person or people who had placed the suitcase and made the warning call. It was intended to deter them from the next attack. The second target were the residents of the neighbourhood. The presence of patrol units would increase the sense of security among them. The third target, and perhaps the most important of all, was Chava Cohen, the owner of the nursery, who had lied to him during her interrogation and hidden the warning call from him. In her case the patrol units were actually supposed to increase anxiety. He wanted her to see a patrol car pass on the street or park next to the nursery every time she left or entered. In the meantime, he decided not to call her in for more questioning.

The urgency stemmed from the warning that the suitcase was 'just the beginning'.

When Avraham rose to speak there was considerable anticipation in the room, perhaps because he hadn't participated in unit meetings for some time. But Benny Saban seemed restless. The violent blinking attacked his eyes again and he covered them with the palm of his hand as casually as he could and kept drumming on the table with a pen. First he congratulated Avraham on his return and updated those present that prior to the holiday he had begun working on the fake-bomb case at Lavon Street. That was Avraham's cue to address the group.

'As Saban has just said, we're talking about the investigation of a fake bomb that was placed in a suitcase last Sunday next to a nursery on Lavon Street in Holon,' he began. 'The searches in the area did not reveal any special findings, but patrol officers detained a suspect for interrogation based on vague testimony from a neighbour who claimed that she saw the man who placed the bomb. He was interrogated by me and released but remains under surveillance. In the absence of physical findings or intelligence, the investigation is concentrating on possible motives for placing the bomb. During the first few days, I explored a few different directions: the nursery, the building in whose courtyard the bomb was placed, and the off licence located in the adjacent building.'

'What shop?' Saban asked, and Avraham looked at him, surprised. Eyal Shrapstein also participated in the unit meeting, and Avraham saw him for the first time since his return. He had come back from a family holiday in Tuscany tanned and smiling, his hair golden from the sun. When he'd entered the conference room and noticed Avraham, he'd said to him, 'Welcome back,' and sat down, naturally enough, in the empty seat next to him.

'On the eve of the holiday there was a definite breakthrough in the investigation, and I can now say with complete certainty that the bomb is connected to the nursery. The owner of the nursery denied that she received any threats, but in my interrogation of the assistant who works with her I discovered that after the placing of the fake bomb a phone call was received from a woman warning that the suitcase is just the beginning.'

Saban stopped drumming with his pen on the table and asked, 'A woman?' and Avraham said simply, 'Yes.'

'Very strange.'

'Right, very strange. Beyond this I know of at least two disputes the owner of the nursery had been involved in, or two incidents in which parents threatened her or attacked her verbally. They will be summoned for interrogation today. At present this is the main lead, and tomorrow, after questioning the two parents, the owner of the nursery will be summoned for additional testimony.'

Shrapstein asked, 'What else do we know about the content of the threat?' and Avraham answered, 'Nothing. That's all that was said in the threatening message. The suitcase "is only the beginning". Therefore I think that it's necessary to increase the presence of patrol units on the street. That might deter the criminal, or criminals, as well as calm the parents. And in my opinion it is necessary to add staff and to move forward urgently with the investigation in order to remove the threat.'

Shrapstein smiled, and Avraham noticed that on the wrist of his right hand he wore a new watch with a golden face and a leather band. 'Have you considered the possibility that it's a fake call? We've had experience with crazies like that,' he said, and just as Avraham was about to answer, Saban cut him off. Paying no attention to Shrapstein's question, he blurted, 'Why don't we close the nursery? I don't like the idea of someone placing a real bomb when children are there hanging over my head.'

Avraham was prepared for the possibility that this would be his response. 'I don't think we should. That won't increase the sense of personal safety among the residents. On the contrary, it would disrupt their routine and increase their alarm.'

Saban looked at him with admiration. 'Right,' he said.

'Beyond that, my target is the teacher. My sense is that she knows who placed the suitcase. I want her to stew for now, to understand that we're keeping an eye on her, and tomorrow or the next day, when I know more, I'll haul her in for another interrogation.'

Only over the course of the holiday had he come to understand the situation: Chava Cohen had claimed in her interrogation that there was no connection between the fake bomb and the nursery not because she believed it or because she feared that investigating the connection between them would frighten the parents. She had said this to him only because she knew that there was a connection, because she knew perfectly well who had placed the suitcase and who had made the warning call. And had lied about it. Though he still wasn't sure whether she had done this because she feared the person who threatened her or because she had something to hide.

Saban's secretary came into the conference room, placed before him a mug of boiling water and some pretzels, and whispered something in his ear. He said, 'Good, Avi. Excellent. Excellent work. May we continue?' Avraham hadn't yet responded to Shrapstein's question regarding the possibility that the warning call was a fake. And his request to add another officer to the investigation was temporarily postponed due to lack of manpower.

In the remainder of the meeting, Inspector Erez Eini reported that he was about to close the case of the armed robbery at the Union Bank. One of the two suspects still denied everything, but the second had broken under interrogation. 'This will last another day or two, no more,' he promised. And Shrapstein was appointed head of the special investigation team that would handle the assassination attempt on Shenkar Street. The criminal who had been shot was known to everyone and refused to participate in the investigation. And from the questioning of eyewitnesses, all that was gleaned was that the assassin rode a grey Yamaha T-Max scooter whose licence plate was covered up and wore a black T-shirt on which was a drawing of a chicken and the word 'Polska'.

'What's "Polska"?' Saban asked, and one of the investigators on the team said, 'That's the thing, we checked it. It's the word "Poland". In Polish.' Saban blinked again. 'Poland? The country? How many people wear a shirt like that in Israel? Just find out where people buy shirts like that and who bought one.'

At least twice during the meeting Saban asked to hear Avraham's opinion on other cases as well.

★

Chaim Sara entered Avraham's office at twelve thirty.

Thin, straight-backed, a bit taller than average, his face clean-shaven. He was much older than Avraham had suspected, and his hair was silvery. His clothes appeared to Avraham very old: tight brown trousers with a brown leather belt and a button-down shirt whose white colour had turned grey from wear and washing and the edge of whose collar had lost its lustre. He was fifty-seven years old, owner of a catering business. Resided on Aharonovitch Street in Holon, about two hundred yards from the place where the suitcase had been placed. It seemed to Avraham that he had already seen him before, but he couldn't recall when or where.

He phoned him at noon, and to his surprise Sara said that he could report to the station within half an hour. And something else disturbed him, but he couldn't explain what it was. Sara responded to his questions with short, economical sentences. Many of them were cut off, as if he couldn't decide how to conclude them. His voice could barely be heard, and there was a tenseness in him that was especially evident in his gaze. He didn't lie, and didn't hide a thing. And only once was his answer extended and almost eloquent.

Avraham said, 'You have been summoned for questioning with regard to a bomb that was placed next to the nursery on Lavon Street. I understand that your son goes to this nursery?' and Sara said, 'Yes. Shalom goes there.'

He avoided asking how someone as old as Sara came to be the father of such young children, even though he wanted to.

'My name is Inspector Avraham and I am the officer in charge of the investigation. I am trying to clarify with parents of children at the nursery if they recall any unusual events, things that may have caused them fear or suspicion.' Perhaps because of his age, Avraham was convinced that Sara had no close ties with other parents and that he didn't know that he was the only one, for the moment, called in for questioning. And he didn't intend to reveal to Sara what he already knew about his run-in with Chava Cohen. He waited for him to report it voluntarily.

Sara shook his head. He didn't recall any unusual events. He sat straight up in the chair, aligned with the backrest as if he were tied to it with a rope, and the palms of his hands were spread flat on his thighs.

'Do you know of any disputes between any tenants in the building and the owner of the nursery?'

He didn't know of any.

'Could you tell me, please, who takes your son to the nursery and who brings him home? You or your wife?'

Sara said, 'Me now. My wife is travelling,' and Avraham wrote *wife is travelling* and made a mental note to ask him about this later on. He was looking for a woman's voice.

'Excellent. When you dropped off or picked up the child, in the days before or after the bomb was discovered, did you see a suspicious man wandering around the area, someone who drew your attention?'

The answer was 'No,' after a long silence.

'Are you certain? Nothing unusual? Maybe someone who wore a hooded sweatshirt?'

Chaim Sara's skin was smooth, with no wrinkles. And the colour of his teeth was yellow, but Avraham didn't smell smoke on his clothes. Even though he answered the detective's questions quietly, the older man who sat before him was tense and afraid. Avraham was about to ask him the crucial question but at the last moment decided to ease the tension first.

'Have you lived in the area for many years?'

Some time passed before Sara answered, as if he didn't know the answer. 'Maybe twenty years.'

'And before that?'

'Before what?'

This was strange: in response to the simplest of all questions he mumbled and had difficulty answering.

Before he moved to Holon he resided in Nes Tziyonah.

'So, tell me a bit about the nursery and the teacher. What do you make of her?'

'The nursery session just started a few weeks ago, I still don't . . .'

Sara paused.

And Avraham waited. Until he understood that Sara wasn't about to continue. And then he asked, 'Do you know if any of the parents had a dispute with her?'

'No.'

'You didn't have a dispute?'

And Sara answered this one quickly. And his answer was complete. 'I had an argument with her a few days ago,' he said. He said that he and his wife thought, it appeared mistakenly, that children at the nursery had hit his son. He had found bruises on his son's body, and one day the boy had returned with an open wound on his forehead that was caused when he'd fallen on a wheelbarrow. In the morning he didn't want to go to nursery, said that he was afraid. His wife had spoken with the teacher and she had denied everything. He had gone to the nursery in order to speak with the teacher and she had insisted that nothing had happened, and then it seemed to him that she had insinuated, in the presence of other parents, that he himself had hurt his son. He had blown up at her, but it hadn't come to violence, and, in any case, he knows he made a mistake.

In his imagination, Avraham tried to picture the conversation between the older man, whose speech was clipped and disciplined, and Chava Cohen. When he had interrogated her, she had raised her voice at him, to the point where he had felt attacked. And she hadn't stopped lying. She had lied about the threatening call, she had lied about the disputes she was involved in. Sara didn't lie.

Suddenly, for the first time since the investigation had opened, Avraham directed his thoughts to the children.

From one year to three years old.

Some of them might not even be verbal yet. Did she hurt them? He couldn't say if she was capable of that, but it seemed to him she was. It wasn't for nothing that during her questioning at the nursery he had been reminded of Hannah Sharabi. He tried to resist the image of the gaunt boy who appeared, against his will, in his thoughts. The thin young body that was slammed against the wall by his father, and which then lay motionless on the floor.

Ofer Sharabi. Maybe also because he had seen Shrapstein at the unit meeting he thought about the dead boy again.

He asked Sara, 'When was this?' and Sara said, 'When was what?'

A moment passed before Avraham regained his focus.

'Your argument with her.'

'About a week and a half ago.'

'In other words . . . before the bomb was placed,' he said, and Chaim Sara didn't respond.

Avraham asked, 'Is it possible that there were other parents who had disputes with the teacher?' and Sara said, 'I don't know. Maybe it was only my son who . . .' And, again, he didn't continue with whatever he had intended to say.

'Do you think she hurt your son?'

'The teacher? God forbid. We never thought that it was *her*. We thought that the other children . . . I wouldn't leave Shalom there if . . .' and again he stopped.

Was there a moment during the interrogation when Avraham suspected that Sara was the one who placed the suitcase? If so, that moment had passed. Now he mainly felt an overpowering loathing for Chava Cohen. There were a few more questions that he needed to ask, and he asked them.

'On the morning the bomb was placed, where were you?'

'With my sons.'

'At home?'

'Yes. I took them to the nursery and school.'

'But before eight in the morning, were you with them the whole time?'

'Yes. No. Actually no. I leave early each morning to get rolls for the business.'

'At what time?'

'Five maybe?'

Avraham looked at the clock in the corner of his computer screen, at his notes, and recalled that he had to get back to Sara's wife who was travelling. The suitcase was placed a long time after five, but if Sara left his children at five, why couldn't he have done this later? He lived a three-minute walk from the nursery, no more. He tried to imagine the older man sitting before him in a sweatshirt with a hood and couldn't do it. In addition to this, Sara was a bit taller than average, whereas the man who placed the suitcase had been short, according to the witness's description. He asked him, 'Do you want something to drink?' and Chaim Sara said no. For a moment he debated whether or not to insist that he get up from his spot to pour himself a glass of water.

He imagined Sara entering the nursery later, to pick up his son. Strange and slow among the young parents. Would he tell Chava Cohen that he was questioned by the police? Safe to assume no, though Avraham would be glad if he did. At exactly 3 p.m. a patrol would be stationed across the street from the entrance to the nursery. He didn't ask Sara to conceal his visit to the station.

'Let's continue. Your wife wasn't there that morning?' he asked, and Sara said, 'No, she had already gone. I was alone with them.'

'I would be happy to speak to her as well. Where did she go?'

'She left around two weeks ago. To the Philippines. Her family is there.'

'I see. Do you know the exact date on which she travelled?'

'Two weeks ago. I can check the date.'

'And why did she go?'

'To visit her father. He's sick.'

'When is she returning?'

'In another two or three weeks. Depending on his condition. You can call her there if you need to.'

After he had parted from Sara, Avraham wrote an additional comment on the sheet of paper: *Check if caller had an accent.*

Immediately after lunch, without smoking a cigarette, he telephoned Orna Chamo, the mother who had removed her son from the nursery. In contrast to Sara, she was talkative, and it seemed that she was only too happy to be called in for questioning. He didn't have to ask a thing. And, like Sara, she didn't hide a thing from him. He told her that he was calling in order to invite her in to give testimony regarding the bomb left next to the nursery on Lavon Street and she said, 'You have no idea how much I want to talk about that.' She couldn't report to the station at short notice because she had a month-old baby at home – so she started right there on the phone. She said, 'Before I come I just want you to understand that this teacher is a criminal and I could have killed her if I were a more violent person.' She said that from the first day she felt that something wasn't okay. Her son is only a year and eight months old, smaller than most of the children, and since he still doesn't speak he couldn't tell her anything. A week after the new session had begun she'd made a surprise visit to the nursery. With her new baby. The children were in the yard, just thrown into the sandpit with no supervision. She didn't see her son when she went inside either, but she heard him crying. When she opened the door to the bathroom she spotted him in the corner of the small, musty room. He was sitting on a small chair. Chava Cohen had arrived from the yard and tried to explain, but from the argument that had developed, and which quickly escalated to raised voices, the mother understood that her son spent entire days there on the low chair in the corner of the nursery, or in the small bathroom, not allowed to move from that spot, because he cried often and, according to the teacher's claim, had difficulty walking like the rest of the children. 'I didn't raise a hand to her, but believe me I wasn't far from it,' she said, and added that in her opinion things were happening at the nursery that the police needed to investigate. And she had no doubt that what was going on there had a connection to the bomb.

After hours of not smoking, Avraham lit a cigarette on the steps to the station.

His telephone conversation with the mother weighed on him. The thought of her son being shut into a small bathroom, without permission to leave. He also thought about Sara's son. The dark patches, and the open wound on his forehead. From moment to moment his suspicion of Chava Cohen transformed into loathing, and he had to remind himself that she wasn't the one he was looking to trap but rather whoever had placed the suitcase. Though he might ask Saban for permission to open a criminal investigation into the teacher as well.

And there was also that meeting in the morning with Shrapstein, who had sat so relaxed next to him in the conference room. As if nothing had happened between them in the last investigation. And his smile when Avraham mentioned the warning call and then asked for the investigation to be treated as very urgent. Since their meeting he had felt an irritation that he tried to suppress.

He couldn't control himself. If he had spoken with Marianka, she would certainly have convinced him not to do this, but Marianka was visiting her parents, and they had agreed to talk only in the evening, after she got home. When Avraham heard the feminine voice he only said, 'Ilana,' and she said, 'Hi, Avi, how are you? How was the holiday?' He tried hard to sound casual when he said to her, 'Peaceful. Hey, do you have a minute? I wanted to ask you something.'

A few days before it seemed to him there wasn't a person in the police he trusted more. She was Ilana Lis, his 'rabbi', the woman who had welcomed him into the Investigations Unit, who had guided him through his first investigations, who had taught him almost everything he knew. If there was a person in the world from whom he shouldn't hide something, it was her. He told her that by chance he had heard about a report she'd written regarding the Ofer Sharabi murder investigation. He didn't ask why she hadn't told him about it, or why she hadn't forwarded it to him. She was silent for a moment, and then said, quietly, 'Yes, I wrote a report. You know that when the case blew up it made a lot of noise and questions were asked.' There was no embarrassment in her voice. She didn't answer immediately when he asked if he could read the report. Finally she said, 'I'm not supposed to do this, but I'll send it to you. No problem. But I want you to talk to me after you've read it, Avi. I know you, and I'm not ready for you to disappear on me without us talking.'

He returned to the office immediately and checked his email.

Then he read his notes from the Chaim Sara interrogation and the summary of the interrogation of Natalie Pinchasov from the evening of the holiday. When an investigation into child abuse at the nursery opened, Natalie would be the first to be questioned, and he had no doubt she would co-operate. His eyes stopped on something she had said regarding the previous assistant, who *left a few days before the start of the year.* Perhaps this former assistant would know more about the goings-on at the nursery? If children were being harmed, it's fair to assume that it hadn't begun just this year. And perhaps whoever had placed the suitcase was a parent of a child who had been hurt at the nursery last year?

It was four thirty when he called Natalie Pinchasov. He caught her on the bus on the way home, and she was alarmed to hear his voice. And she didn't know the name of the previous assistant. He said, 'I have another question. Regarding the woman who called the nursery on the day when the fake bomb was placed. Do you remember if she spoke with an accent?'

Natalie Pinchasov wasn't sure. 'I don't think she had an accent. You mean Russian? No, I don't think so. But maybe there was something odd about her voice, I'm not sure.'

He hadn't thought about this before but suddenly asked, 'And, today, did you notice anything unusual?' and she said, 'Don't think so. There were police cars outside, but I didn't see anything happen.'

'But if something unusual happens, will you please let me know? Any little thing, okay? It's important for me to know if Chava Cohen speaks to you about the warning call or if one of the parents at the nursery mentions the suitcase, okay? And let me know if any of the children suddenly stop coming to the nursery, or if you see someone suspicious in the area, anything that seems unusual to you.'

Orna Chamo didn't know the name of the previous assistant either, but got back to him a short time later with the information.

Instead of travelling home he went again to the sea before sunset. Stopped at a stand on the boardwalk and bought a cold bottle of Corona. He took off his shoes and socks and sat down, in his clothes, on the beach. Not far from him, a bald, half-naked man danced a slow, strange dance, even though no song could be heard anywhere, and two older women did yoga exercises. Joggers passed by him.

Before leaving his office he'd dialled the number he got from Orna Chamo and a girl answered. He asked to speak to Ilanit Hadad, and the girl said she was out of town. He asked when she would return, and the girl didn't know. Couldn't say where her sister had gone. 'If you need her straight away, you can talk to Mum. She gets back this evening,' she said. And no email from Ilana Lis had arrived.

The sea was dark and choppy. Pinpricks of light flickered on the horizon from a cargo ship.

Just open your eyes and look, he thought. In the end, all the points will connect.

In every investigation there's a moment when it seems that the confusion before your eyes will never become clear. That the details are too numerous, too strange, distinct from one another like the people sitting on the beach. Everything is sunk in darkness or fog. But after some time the connections are clarified and the picture always grows clear. In the darkness a new point of light suddenly turns on, and it illuminates the others as well; details look different, take on meaning, connect. What looked strange turns out to be familiar. This time it was a small suitcase containing a pretend bomb without explosive material inside. And a man fleeing with a limp. A sweatshirt with a hood and a warning call from a woman. A teacher who concealed the warning call and perhaps abused children, or perhaps did not. And there were strange details that perhaps had no connection between them: a suspect who, since he was released from custody, had left his home only to go to the hospital to visit his mother, and a foreign woman who had travelled to the Philippines to see her dying father. Actually, two women had travelled: one to her home in the Far East, and the other to an unknown destination.

In contrast to his previous investigation, this time the sea was of no critical importance. But if so, why was he returning here almost every day? The half-naked dancer stopped dancing and approached the two women doing yoga, and Avraham observed the three of them from far away.

But the sea did have importance, and suddenly he understood it.

The sea continued to be important because Ofer Sharabi was still somewhere deep inside it, drowned and unseen.

Do you want to rescue Ofer from the sea? Avraham whispered to himself. And smiled.

You're a fool. Four months ago, Ofer's father had tossed the boy's dead body, folded up inside a suitcase, from a cargo ship in the middle of the Mediterranean. What's the chance that it could be found now?

At night he didn't tell Marianka that he had asked Ilana to send him the report about the previous investigation. Or about Ofer and the sea. He told her about the long day, about the first unit meeting. It was late for her when she called him and she was anxious to get off the phone, but she did want to hear what he had to say. 'So do you have a clearer direction?' she asked, and he said, 'Don't know. Maybe not.'

'And the father you questioned?'

'I don't think he's capable of placing a fake bomb, but possibly. Seems to me that he's too tall and too old. In any case, after the last time I don't intend to trust anyone. And in the meantime, he's almost all I've got.'

She was silent, and he added, 'If you saw him, you'd understand.' Actually, the only reason he didn't cross off Sara after interrogating him was his wife. She had gone away and was not available for questioning. And he was looking for a woman's voice.

Afterwards he told Marianka how from moment to moment the antipathy he felt towards the teacher was growing, and about his intention to open an investigation on her when the case of the bomb was closed, and she cautioned him that this antipathy wouldn't help him in the investigation. That was strange, the sort of thing Ilana might say – but in English, and from the mouth of Marianka, but he didn't say anything about it. It was impossible to convince him that Chava Cohen didn't know who placed the bomb and who had threatened her.

When he asked if she had bought a plane ticket yet Marianka said no. She was still looking for a cheap one.

According to their plan, the next day was supposed to be the start of her last week at work.

He talked about the preparations for her arrival, but Marianka said she needed to get off, and he didn't ask her why. Before she hung up he nevertheless said to her, 'Marianka, I feel I'm not reaching you,' and she said, 'It's always hard for us to talk on the phone, no?'

'Maybe. Are you hiding something from me?'

She didn't answer his question, just said, 'Avi, I really have to get off, okay? I promise to call you tomorrow.'

6

When he left the police station, Chaim already had a plan, although its contours were blurry and would only become clear to him in the hours and days that followed.

For a moment he couldn't remember where he had parked the car.

His body was weak from the effort of concealing his thoughts, and his hands were sweating. He felt unstable as he drove and couldn't decide which way to go. It was two o'clock, and the children needed to be picked up in about an hour. He stopped in the car park of the mall next to the station, in the shade. Ate an entire sandwich, and then another. Didn't turn off the engine. Listened to the radio.

Could he discern the faults in his plan? It wasn't the product of orderly thinking, with an eye towards foreseeable dangers and ways of dealing with them, but rather was a confused outburst born of anxiety, of impulses, some of which he understood and others he didn't, but now, because of what had happened, he simply couldn't wait.

The police inspector suspected him – of that he had no doubt. Neither did he doubt that Chava Cohen had testified against him. And to this was added the night-time conversation with Ezer and the vague things that the boy said he saw. Suddenly they were watching him everywhere. A guard in a security uniform and a baseball cap wandered out among the parked cars, looked at him through the glass, knocked on the window, and asked, 'You waiting for someone, Grandpa?'

The first step in the plan was to return home immediately and call his mother.

He remained in the car park a few minutes more, so as not to attract attention.

His mother was resting in bed, next to the telephone, and answered immediately. When she heard his voice she asked, 'Is everything okay?' and Chaim said, 'Can I bring the children to you?'

He knew that his question would alarm her, but he intended to tell her everything in any case.

'To sleep here?' she asked, and he said, 'Yes. For a night or two.'

'What's happened?'

'Not over the phone. I'll tell you when I come.'

She said, 'I'll get up and make them something to eat.'

The tiny shirts and underwear that hung on the line had dried and he folded them and placed them in the same holdall that they had taken to her house for the holiday. Ezer was surprised when he came to pick him up in the car, but until they got to Shalom's nursery they drove in almost complete silence. Chaim asked him, 'How was school?' and Ezer said, 'Good.' This was after gym, and he wore a vest and shorts and his skin was moist with sweat and warm. Chaim asked, 'Did you learn anything interesting?' Ezer said, 'No,' and he let it go.

He assumed he'd be unable to avoid running into Chava Cohen and for a moment thought of asking Ezer to go inside, instead of him, and get Shalom. She was sitting in the yard when he entered, handing out apple slices to the remaining children. And even though she saw him she ignored him, as always. One of the next stages of the plan was to talk to her, but this wasn't the time. He was sure that he'd been called in for questioning because of her testimony. She had apparently testified that he had placed the suitcase, and because of her he had been interrogated by the police. He passed her without saying a word, looked elsewhere. Inside the nursery the young Russian assistant was changing a nappy, and to Chaim it seemed that he had acted wisely when he informed her that in the coming days Shalom would not be in nursery because they were going on holiday. When he buckled Shalom into the car seat in the back, Ezer asked, 'Where are we going?' and he said, 'To Grandma's. You'll sleep there, and tomorrow you won't go to school. You'll have a good time with Grandma.'

Ezer looked at him in amazement, and Shalom asked, 'And what if Mum comes home?'

He didn't answer.

Afterward Shalom asked, 'You're not sleeping with us at Grandma's?' And Chaim said, 'I'm going home because I have to work. And also to wait for Mum in case she comes back.'

At his mother's house the children made a beeline for the living room and plopped down on the carpet, opposite the television, because it was already on, loudly, showing a cartoon. She closed the kitchen door behind them and asked him, in their language, 'What happened?' and Chaim said, 'We're going away.' In the white nightdress she napped in, which exposed her thin arms, spotted with bruises, and wearing grey socks, she looked older than she had during the holiday. The long days with the children exhausted her. The tea she prepared him was very sweet, as always, sweetened with three packs of Sweet'n Low. She waited for him to continue. He didn't tell anyone the entire truth, only parts of it, and to everyone a different part – to the children, to the police inspector, and even to her he told only a part, even though he had no one else close. He would need her for another two or three days, no more. He said to her, 'Someone put a suitcase with a bomb in it next to Shalom's nursery and the police suspect me. I was there today for questioning,' and she stared at him in disbelief.

'Why you?'

'Because of what happened with the teacher. She gave them my name. Apparently she thinks it's me. I can't imagine what she told them exactly.'

'When did they put it there?'

'A week ago.'

'And now they've called you in?'

Only she understood how cruel this was, and asked the unnecessary question because she had nothing else to say. There was a closeness between them that was unusual between a parent and an adult child, perhaps because he'd married at an advanced age and for many years she had been his sole confidante. She knew him better than anyone else. His misfortunes. The doors that always slammed in his face. 'When good luck sees us, it continues on to some other place,' she used to say to him when he was still a boy. He didn't answer her question.

She said, 'You were there today? This morning? Why didn't you call to tell me?' and he said, 'I didn't have time.'

The police inspector had called him a little before noon, when he was about to finish his rounds at the Ministry of the Interior and the Tax Authority. In the days since, he had thought about the possibility that they'd call him in, even though he didn't know for certain if an investigation was being conducted. A few sandwiches remained, and he had planned to go to garages and workshops in the area, but he had told the detective that he would come to his office immediately. Should he have tried to postpone the meeting? At that moment he'd thought that putting it off would raise suspicion and that immediate compliance was best.

The detective had said to him on the phone that he would like to gather evidence in connection with the bomb that had been placed next to the nursery.

All that he had to do was tell the truth.

On the way to the station he had again told himself that he had nothing to fear. It was just a bit of bad luck. He thought that if he were able to imagine that the interrogation was a conversation of sorts with a radio host, he would be able to answer calmly and sound relaxed.

The police detective was kind, but a few minutes after the start of the interrogation Chaim understood that he suspected him of placing the suitcase. At first, perhaps in order to confuse him, the detective had asked him general questions about Shalom's nursery – if there were any unusual events at the nursery, if Chaim had noticed a suspicious man in the area – but then he changed direction and asked for his opinion of the teacher and if he was aware of any disputes between her and one of the parents. Chaim had said no. Something in the way the detective had asked the question implied that he had been updated on the details of the incident with the teacher, and the detective's next question had confirmed this.

His mother asked, 'And what did you say?' and he answered, 'I told him what happened. He obviously knew.'

After the interrogation it seemed to him that he'd acted wisely when he hadn't denied things and had tried only to minimize their importance. He had told the detective that there was an argument with the teacher and that he had made a mistake when he had threatened her. The detective had tried to put words in his mouth, asked if he thought the teacher abused the children, perhaps abused Shalom, and he had denied it.

'So there's a chance they'll lay off you now, no?'

'He asked me afterwards about what I did on the day when they placed the suitcase. And he asked questions about Jenny.'

His mother got up and opened the refrigerator.

That had been the moment in the interrogation when Chaim had understood that it was no longer possible to simply wait.

His mother arranged four plates on the table and set a pot on the stove and he said that he wasn't staying to eat.

'And what did you say about her?' she asked, and he said, 'That she was travelling.'

'Wouldn't it be better if you'd told them that she'd died already? Perhaps they'd understand.'

Chaim brought his fist down on the empty plate in front of him and his mother was alarmed.

On the way back to Holon he again felt a weakness in his arms, and understood that this was because of his mother. The palms of his hands hung limp on the steering wheel and the road disappeared from before his eyes at times. She said little after he had told her that the detective had asked about Jenny and after he had blown up at her. The few questions that she asked had escaped from her mouth with an undertone of despair. He needed strength from her, but she no longer had strength to give. She was afraid almost like him, perhaps more. Instead of advising him, she had asked, 'So what will you do?' and he answered, 'I'll go away for a few days. Until they find who placed the suitcase.'

'That's a good idea. And what about the children?'

'They'll travel with me. I just need this evening and tomorrow to get organized.'

Afterwards he told her that he planned to call the teacher and apologize – maybe that would help and she'd get the police to lay off him – and his mother nodded. 'Talk nice to her. Maybe you should sit down with her.'

'I thought of doing it over the telephone. But if she wants to meet, I'll go.'

Before he left, she went into her bedroom and removed the brown envelope from the underwear drawer. She asked how much he needed, and for the first time in a while he didn't refuse. He just said, 'As much as you can spare.' At home he tucked the money into a leather briefcase he hid in the dresser, behind the towels. Now he had six thousand dollars and more than twenty thousand shekels.

The next stages in the plan were packing and searching.

He went up to the storage space and found the old suitcase behind the fan. Wiped the dust off it, inside and out, and arranged three pairs of trousers, three button-down shirts, three pairs of pants, two vests, and a sweater inside it. At this point he still didn't know where they would go. Afterwards he brought clothing from the children's room, for Ezer mainly short-sleeved shirts because he didn't like wearing long ones, and for Shalom some warm shirts as well. And without yet knowing why, he added to the suitcase some of Jenny's clothes that had remained in the closet.

Stickers from a previous trip were turning yellow on the suitcase, and when he removed them he saw that they were from the flight for the wedding.

He hadn't flown since, and that was only the third time he had ever flown in his life. Afterwards Jenny had flown to the Philippines one other time, when they had threatened her with separation.

She was much more used to travelling than he, and in the giant airport she seemed quite at home. The security guard asked them in English what the purpose of their journey was and she simply said, 'To get married.'* After passport inspection, she ran toward the conveyor belt in order to have time to shop at the duty-free. She bought two vials of perfume and a belt for herself, perfume for his mother, and a camera for the two of them, a wedding gift, so he would be able to take pictures of her in Cyprus. Now he opened her drawer in the wardrobe and found the envelope with the pictures. He still hadn't come across the beaded necklace anywhere that Ezer said he saw. He didn't understand why it was important to him to find it. After their conversation the night before, he had gone back and looked for the necklace in the bathroom, in the cupboard, under the bed. Jenny's passport was no longer in the drawer; neither was her temporary identification card. That was the place where she had kept the pills, before he discovered them. There was also the copy of the New Testament that she hid and the clear bag with the letters that her sister sent to her from Berlin along with two old photos of her father and mother and a shabby crucifix, plaited from bamboo. The wedding pictures were all that he found in the envelope, and he looked at them now, maybe for the first time.

* Israel's strict religion-based marriage laws mean that Jews who wish to marry non-Jewish partners must make arrangements to marry abroad and then prove to the Ministry of Interior that their marriage is authentic for it to be legally recognized by the state. Many of these couples choose to marry in Cyprus because it's close to Israel, and the market meets demand with cheap wedding packages.

A picture from the airport, a moment before the flight: he's sitting in a chair in the waiting area near their gate, with their bags gathered around him.

The flight was very short and from the beginning he had felt sick. He told her it was good that they weren't flying to the Philippines to get married, as she had wanted at first.

Outside the small airport in Larnaca, where he felt more comfortable for some reason, stood the minibus and, to his disappointment, it had become clear to Chaim that it wasn't waiting just for them. The driver was named Agapitos, and he was young and skinny and very energetic. In one of the pictures he's hugging Jenny and another woman from the group. Agapitos was a motormouth and talked mainly with the women. His shirt was open and his chest was tanned and smooth, and Chaim thought he was a homosexual but was embarrassed to ask Jenny if she thought so as well. Agapitos patiently explained to them that they were waiting for five couples from Israel. While driving he briefed the passengers: they would be taken straight to the city hall in Larnaca, and that was where their ceremonies would be held, one after the other, in the mayor's office. The order of the marriages was set in advance by the company that organized the deals and it would not be possible to change it. A Russian woman who sat behind them asked her future husband to ask if she would have an opportunity to shower and change clothes, and Agapitos said, 'Clothes, yes; shower, no,' but apart from this it seemed to Chaim that no one spoke during the short trip from the airport to the city centre other than Jenny and a much younger Filipina woman who sat in front of them.

On the back of the picture Jenny had written the woman's name, in English, in dainty letters: Marisol. After the wedding she was travelling to South America with her husband.

Chaim had taken off his trousers and shirt in a storage room in the city hall and over his vest put on the suit his mother had bought him. Jenny was in her knickers and bra when she fixed his tie for him, and for a moment he saw the part of her body that pleased him most of all: a dense, dark line of hair that started above her navel and continued to the line of her knickers on her brown rounded stomach. He waited a long time for her to do her makeup. She explained to him how to work the camera and he photographed her in the dress she had bought in south Tel Aviv. The picture came out dark and her face was barely visible in it. Marisol photographed the two of them together before they entered the office: he is taller than Jenny even though he's standing hunched; the suit fits him; and he of course looks older than her.

Fifteen years separated them.

The mayor asked if they had prepared something to say to each other before they signed the documents and he said no. Agapitos, the driver, waited for them in the office, where he functioned as witness, interpreter and photographer. And that was it. Agapitos asked them to kiss against the background of the large window that looked out onto the sands and the palm trees and the sea. In the afternoon they arrived at an otherwise deserted hotel, the Flamingo Beach, and a waiter brought, just for the two of them, a bottle of champagne and macaroni in cream sauce. They sat by themselves on the balcony. His mother called to congratulate them and Jenny said that her sister would call soon from Berlin, but she didn't. In the evening they undressed, as they had done a few times in his apartment, she before him, in the bathroom. She waited for him in bed without clothes on. He used the bathroom after her, brushed his teeth, took Viagra, returned to the darkened room, and got into bed in his underwear. The two of them had wanted children then, or at least he'd thought so. As usual, they first lay silently next to each other for a long time, on their backs, and Jenny slowly caressed his soft stomach and his smooth thighs, without looking, until something happened.

The next morning they returned to Israel, and on the flight he again was stricken with nausea.

And now he will need to get on a plane again because of her.

He completed his work early, before nine thirty. And didn't imagine that this might be the last time. He covered the bowls of fresh salad with tinfoil, cleared a place for them on the shelves in the refrigerator, and cleaned the kitchen. On the call-in talk shows a woman from Jerusalem said that her husband was in the middle of becoming religious and was growing distant from her because of her impurity, and afterwards another caller said that his wife had abandoned him with a four-month-old baby, and Chaim listened in shock to his story. The apartment was dark and silent after he turned off the radio, and he turned some lights on. But the silence didn't bother him. He hadn't been alone at night for many years. Tonight he wouldn't stretch the thin thread across the bedroom's door frame, he would just lock the door.

It was true that his search didn't turn up anything, but the packing was over. And the activity lessened the stress he had been feeling since the afternoon. There was still space in the suitcase, and he put toys, as well as two children's books, inside, and only afterwards did he call his mother. The children were already in bed. She said to him, 'They asked when you're coming. I told them tomorrow. I didn't say anything about a trip,' and he said, 'No need, I'll tell them.' She didn't ask where he planned to take them, and if she had asked he wouldn't have told her, although she apparently knew already.

'Have you made all your arrangements?' she asked, and he said, 'Almost.'

'And have you talked to the teacher?'

'Not yet.'

'Call now. Afterwards it will be too late.'

He had put off the conversation with the teacher because he didn't know exactly what he would say to her. Would he have to reveal that he had been interrogated by the police and say that that was why he was calling? Of course she already knew. When he had picked up Shalom from nursery this afternoon he had seen a patrol on the street. And should he tell her that he was taking the children on holiday for a few days? That would explain to her why Shalom wouldn't be coming to nursery when she didn't see him in the morning, and that was why he had told this to the Russian assistant, but if he was right about her having directed the investigator to him, then she was liable to inform the police that he was going away.

The thought of making the apology caused him shame, but he didn't have a choice. He wasn't doing this for himself but rather for the sake of the children. He also hadn't yet decided if he'd tell her that he had no connection to the suitcase or only that he was no longer angry with her and understood that he had made a mistake. He recalled the day he had returned from work and seen the cut on Shalom's forehead. Jenny had refused to do anything and hadn't wanted to talk about it. He had gone to the nursery the next day and confronted the teacher only because of her.

He spread out the blankets in the children's room and straightened them over the sheets. Afterwards he called the teacher and didn't get an answer.

They'd go away for a few days, and when they returned there would be no more investigation. They'd go back to their routine, and with time the children wouldn't ask him about Jenny any more. How would he make sure that the investigation was over? He thought that he could ask his mother to follow it in the papers. In any case, if they didn't look for him again, he would know that it was okay for them to return. And maybe the trip would return Ezer to him. Maybe it would make clear to his son what had really happened that night. Maybe it would explain to him who his father really was, and who his mother had been.

He waited a few minutes, then called again, but once more got no answer. For a moment he thought that she wasn't answering because she knew that he was the caller, from the number, but it was unlikely that she would know his home number.

The time between attempts got shorter and shorter, and he held the receiver for a long time before he gave up and put it down.

He called her for the last time at eleven thirty.

7

The report about the previous investigation was in his inbox when he woke up on Monday morning, a little after five. In the subject line, Ilana had written *For your eyes only* and the message was brief: I was asked to write, and I couldn't have written differently. I hope you'll understand. And please don't disappear on me. Ilana. The report hadn't arrived from a police account but from a Hotmail account under the name of *rebeccajones21*. It had been sent after midnight, probably from her home.

Avraham placed the coffee on the burner, to let it brew, and showered in water that wasn't warm enough. It was still possible to delete the report from his inbox, still possible to put off reading it. Marianka would certainly have implored him to do just that. He was in the middle of a new investigation, and it was best not to return to a case that he had left behind. His mobile started ringing while he was reading but he didn't get up to check who was calling him at such an early hour, because he thought he knew and couldn't have imagined what had happened a few hours earlier.

The threat had been carried out.

The suitcase *was* in fact just the beginning.

The first sentence that Ilana had written in the report was sharp and painful: *On the evening of Wednesday, 4 May, Hannah Sharabi, the mother of the victim, Ofer Sharabi, submitted a complaint about the disappearance of her son. At this time she already knew that Ofer was no longer among the living and that he had met his end in a violent incident with his father, Rafael Sharabi, the previous evening.*

Everything that Avraham hoped would be forgotten came back to him while reading.

The spring evening when Hannah Sharabi had arrived at his office and said that Ofer hadn't returned from school. She had sat, frightened, before him, and he had thought that this was because she feared for her son's fate. He had suggested that she ought not to submit a complaint immediately, and the next morning she had appeared in the station with a bag of photos of Ofer. Avraham was in their house later that same day. An investigation was opened. He believed every word she said to him, and everything the father told him later. He was certain that Ofer had run away from home and defended the parents even when Ilana and Shrapstein thought he ought to examine their stories and question the parents again.

The mobile continued ringing in the bedroom. He didn't intend to respond to Ilana.

Under the heading *Work of the Investigation Team – Evaluation*, Ilana had written the following lines, and he read them slowly:

> *The commanding officer of the investigation team, Inspector Avraham Avraham, committed a few errors that brought about a delay in solving the investigation and made it difficult to gather evidence against the suspects in the case. Yet it is important to point out that the analysis of these mistakes is being done after the fact and in my opinion there is nothing here to indicate concrete negligence in the management of the investigation.*
>
> *First, it can be said that the commander erred in the interrogation of the mother immediately after she reported her*

son's absence. There is a reasonable possibility that a more substantial investigation, and especially an extensive search of the apartment at this stage, would have revealed findings in the apartment arousing suspicion against the parents of the victim that would have contradicted their original version, according to which their son was missing. The backpack of the victim, who, according to the mother's claim at this stage, had left in the morning for school and hadn't returned, was still in the apartment and was only thrown away a few days later. Similarly the commander refrained from entering various rooms in the apartment, which, after the fact, it became clear were part of the crime scene. It is possible that had the commander ordered an extensive search of them in the first few days following the incident between the father and his son, evidence would have been discovered. During the substantial amount of time that passed between the committing of the crime and the solving of the case, the scene was cleaned up, and this made the consolidation of the evidence more difficult.

Second, the commander erred in managing the investigation of the father, who at the time the case was opened was outside Israel. The commander did not summon him to return immediately after opening the investigation but instead waited five days for his return, during which time the father disposed of the victim's corpse at sea and attempted to cover up his guilt in additional ways. In the absence of a body it became difficult for the prosecution to prove the exact circumstances of the death, necessitating the confessions of the parents, who finally spoke of an accident. In retrospect, it was also possible to establish that the first interrogation of the father was not sufficiently thorough, in light of the fact that he broke and admitted to killing his son during the shortest of interrogations, which was conducted by a different investigating officer on the team (Inspector Eyal Shrapstein).

The third mistake was the commanding officer's decision to ignore the unusual behaviour of one of those questioned in the case, Ze'ev Avni, a neighbour of the Sharabi family and the private tutor of the victim. Ze'ev Avni ridiculed the commanding officer over the course of three weeks, and had he not confessed of his own accord it is possible that he would not have been exposed to this day. Two days after the investigation was opened Avni called the police and left a misleading message about Ofer's location and later wrote anonymous letters to Rafael and Hannah Sharabi in the name of the victim, letters that eventually led to the case being solved. In my opinion, the investigating team did not devote adequate attention to Avni's unusual behaviour, resulting in a delay to the resolution of the case, a delay that had a material effect on the evidence.

Yet it is my desire to emphasize that in the end Inspector Avraham stood at the head of a team that solved the investigation.

Inspector Avraham is an experienced and promising investigator who has participated in many complex investigations, and I am hopeful that the errors in the management of this particular investigation will not have any effect on his advancement or on his future contributions to the police.

Avraham sat in front of the open report for a long time. Marianka stared at him from a passport photo he'd taped to the plastic frame of his monitor, and he remembered how distant she had sounded the day before. The mobile continued to ring, and he went to the bedroom and turned it off, but Ilana didn't give up and called the house line. He removed the cord from the jack. Silence prevailed in the room, though inside him a cacophony of voices roared. What especially pained him was the inescapable fact that because of his mistakes Ofer's parents had evaded serious punishment. Because of his oversights in the investigation the police did not have a body; because of them the crime scene had been cleaned before it was examined, and the prosecution was forced to base the indictment on the confession of the father that Ofer's death was the result of an accident. The father claimed that he had seen Ofer sexually assault his sister in her room and that in his effort to defend the daughter Ofer had been injured and died, and there was no way to contradict his version because the mother kept silent. But wasn't that his fault? Yes, of course it was, and he acknowledged it. More than anything Avraham wanted to respond to Ilana. But what could he write? He didn't understand who he was most angry with. Ilana? Ofer Sharabi's parents? Himself? He wanted to ask her who had read the report besides Benny Saban, and when it was written, and why she hadn't sent it to him to review. He wanted to explain and accuse and apologize all at the same time.

He opened a new message and wrote *Ilana*. But didn't continue.

'It's not important now,' he whispered to himself. 'Not important at all.'

Now a new investigation was waiting for him, and it was an opportunity to prove, mainly to himself, that the failures of the previous case had been accidental. He deleted the message with the attachment from his inbox. Had he managed to commit any fresh errors since the new case was opened? Had someone again ridiculed him, as Ofer's parents had done?

Chava Cohen's lies he had identified from the first moment. His eyes were open and he didn't believe a word of what she had said.

He got dressed quickly. Perhaps precisely because Ilana had urged him not to disappear he didn't turn on his mobile even when he entered his office, late, with no one noticing him. There were sentences in her report he already knew by heart: *The commander erred in the interrogation of the mother immediately after she reported her son's absence. In retrospect, it was also possible to establish that the first interrogation of the father was not sufficiently thorough, in light of the fact that he broke and admitted to killing his son during the shortest of interrogations, which was conducted by a different investigating officer on the team.*

Benny Saban opened the door to his office hastily, without knocking, at eight thirty. He was surprised when he saw Avraham sitting behind his desk, immersed in the investigation file open before him. Saban said to him, 'You're actually here? Ilana Lis has been looking for you since six this morning. Have you forgotten that your holiday is over?' Avraham looked at him in amazement.

Did Saban know that Ilana had sent him the report to read? He was still convinced that that was why she had called.

Avraham said, 'I didn't notice that the phone was off. Sorry. Did she tell you why she's looking for me?' and was astounded to hear the answer. Saban said, 'Your teacher. Chava Cohen. They beat her almost to death. She's in hospital, unconscious at Wolfson. Ilana's been at the scene since seven this morning, and she wants you there ASAP.'

★

The streets to Tel Aviv were jammed, and for the first time in a while Avraham turned on his siren. He drove quickly and against the direction of traffic on Kugel Boulevard and from there to Jaffa, via the run-down neighbourhood of Kiryat Shalom. Ilana picked up immediately. And didn't say a thing about his disappearance during the morning. She heard the wail of the siren and asked, 'You on your way?' and he said, 'I'll be there within five minutes.' She had already returned to her office at the Tel Aviv district headquarters.

She checked to see if he had received a preliminary report and he said that Saban had updated him verbally. Chava Cohen had been found shortly after 3 a.m. She was lying in a ditch under a pedestrian bridge on the boardwalk, precisely on the border between Jaffa and Tel Aviv, not far from the Etzel Museum. She had trauma to the ribs and chest – but worse to the head. Three Sudanese men had found her unconscious and called the police. Saban had no idea how long she'd lain in the ditch or what her condition presently was. The Sudanese men were interrogated and were being detained even though they weren't suspected in the attack. Avraham asked, 'And we know with certainty that this is the same woman?' and Ilana said, 'Yes. No mobile or any identification was found on her, but we identified her from her car. At five this morning.'

'What do you mean, "from her car"?'

'Her car's in a car park. The patrol officers called the guard and went over the images on the security cameras. They identified her arriving and getting out of a red Subaru Justy at one thirty a.m. We called her at home and woke her son. He didn't know that she had gone out at all. He checked the bedroom and saw she wasn't there. A patrol vehicle took him to Wolfson and he identified her in surgery.'

Why was he surprised when he heard that Chava Cohen had a son? Perhaps because until this moment in the investigation she was only a teacher who, apparently, abused children. She had blown up at him during her questioning and concealed the threatening telephone call. He hadn't asked her if she was married or if she had children. He also didn't ask Ilana how old her son was. He asked, 'Will she come out of it?' and Ilana said, 'Hard to know, she's still in surgery. But she received very serious blows to the head. With a rock. I understand that the entire left side of her face was smashed in.'

Chava Cohen's stern face appeared in his imagination covered in blood. And her son, looking at her over the doctors' shoulders. Every time he recalled that face he was filled with hatred. Ilana said, 'Avi, I understand from Saban that threats were made to her. Did we do anything about them?' And a moment passed before he understood what she was actually asking.

Benny Saban had referred to Chava Cohen as 'your teacher'.

He said, 'No, Ilana, that's not correct. She received one threatening call and she concealed it and insisted that the bomb had no connection to her. I questioned her for hours and I asked her if she had received any threats, and she denied it. And we've had patrol units around the nursery area since yesterday.' From afar he saw the small wooden bridge and the ditch beneath it. Patrols blocked the street. He asked, 'So what now? Do I continue with the investigation?' and Ilana said, 'I want to hear what you've got and then we'll proceed. Forensics has been working in the area for a few hours already, but you're familiar with the background and the threats and perhaps you'll see something we missed. I want you to come here afterwards and tell me what you know. And we'll analyse the findings from the scene together. Can you be in my office at eleven?'

The first thing he wanted to do was see Chava Cohen at the scene of the attack.

She entered the deserted car park in a red Justy at 1.36 and circled it a number of times before parking close to the empty guard booth. Was she looking for another car? Waiting for someone? No other vehicles entered the car park between 1.00 and 2.30. The time of Chava Cohen's arrival seemed strange to him, because it wasn't a round number. Was she early for a meeting, or maybe late? She had been wearing jeans and a short green shirt and was carrying a small cloth bag in her hand. She had locked the car and looked around, and afterwards glanced at the watch on her wrist. She did not appear anxious. Avraham had no doubt it was her: her steps were small and quick as she walked towards the boardwalk and left the camera's range. Avraham circled the old car and didn't see anything exceptional. An old beaten-up car that hadn't been washed for a long time. In the dust on the rear window a finger had drawn a crooked heart with two arrows through it. Even though she had driven it alone the Subaru was part of the crime scene, and he entered it carefully, his shoes covered with plastic booties and his hands enveloped in gloves. The smell permeating the car's interior seemed familiar to him. On the passenger's seat was a plastic bag with a pair of Adidas, size ten, inside, probably the son's, and at the foot of the seat a blue towel had been thrown. In the glove compartment were old road maps, fuel receipts, two CDs and a *Yellow Pages* booklet.

He moved to the back seat, where he discovered nothing of value. In the boot he found an old crate with tools, a large, half-filled bottle of water, as well as a cardboard box with objects that appeared to be related to the nursery: packages of paper, new boxes of paint and a few jars of glue. Under the boxes of paint he discovered something that drew his attention: a small Philips cassette case without the cassette in it.

His brief phone call with Ilana on the way to the scene increased his unease. Had she implied that he should have done more to protect Chava Cohen? Since the attack had occurred in Tel Aviv it was fair to assume that the investigation would be conducted by the District Investigations Branch under her command. And if Ilana decided that he should stay with the investigation, he'd need to work closely with her again. Despite the report. He measured the distance from the car park to the ditch. About three hundred metres. The meeting place could have been the old structure of the Etzel Museum, which was lit at night as well. Ilana had asked him to look, and he looked. And it seemed to him that he had already seen everything. From moment to moment the story of the attack was written out in his thoughts. He scribbled a few details with a black pen in his notepad while an officer from the forensics team walked him carefully through the scene of the attack. The rock with which Chava Cohen was beaten had been found next to her in the ditch and taken to the lab. It weighed nine pounds. And the place where Chava Cohen had been found was apparently the place where she was attacked. There were bloodstains on the stones at the bottom of the ditch and no signs of dragging. In two of the bloodstains the investigators identified partial shoeprints and hoped that they didn't belong to any of the Sudanese men who had found her. The cloth bag that she had carried from the car had disappeared.

A few metres away, a surprisingly tall wave exploded on the rocks and Avraham suddenly understood that, once again, he was by the sea. He went up onto the small wooden bridge above the ditch to take in the entire scene at a single glance, as he always did.

Just last evening he had sat by himself on the sandy beach, two or three kilometres north of here, and thought that the sea was of no importance to this investigation.

The ditch led to the beach. At night the beach provided an excellent escape route. Dark and empty. It was possible to walk its length, north to the centre of Tel Aviv, or south, to Jaffa, without being seen.

He recalled the man who had walked with a suitcase before morning a week ago on Lavon Street. He had placed the suitcase with a fake bomb inside it next to the nursery and fled. The same man had attacked Chava Cohen at night and again fled, perhaps along the beach. Chava Cohen had come to a meeting with a man she had said she didn't know. The man with the suitcase. What was strange was that she wasn't afraid of meeting him in the dead of night in a dark, empty place. Perhaps because it was a woman. The forensics officer argued that this possibility was inconceivable. 'No way,' he said. 'When you see her you'll appreciate how brutal it was. They shattered her jaw with a rock, like an animal.'

Perhaps because Ilana didn't mention the report during their brief phone call on the way to the scene, Avraham was surprised by the way their conversation unfolded.

He froze before knocking on her office door. And waited. Heard a chair's movement from inside the room, and then the door opened.

This was the first time they had met since he returned, but they settled on a handshake. Ilana opened the window facing the street and placed his glass ashtray on the table. 'It waited for you in the drawer,' she said. As every other time he saw her, it seemed to him that her red hair had greyed a tiny bit. She wore a dark suit and a black shirt underneath, and around her neck was a string of small pearls the colour of ivory. At first glance it seemed to him that nothing in the room had changed, other than the position of the round Seiko wall clock, which had been hanging over the door and now stood on the floor in a corner of the room at a strange oblique angle, as if it had been punished and demoted. Avraham put the investigation file on the table and she said to him, 'In a moment, Avi. Do you want coffee or something to eat? I haven't managed to drink anything all morning.'

Actually that's how it always is, he thought.

Every meeting began with an enormous distance between them, which only working together was able to close. This time it was different, because the work itself now created a distance between them – that is, the report did. Ilana returned with mugs of coffee and he opened the investigation file, but again she sought to stop him. 'How are you? We haven't seen each other in over three months, no?' she said, and her blue eyes looked at him with such directness that he had to lower his gaze. He answered, 'I'm okay,' and she said, 'Okay? You're getting married. Has your girlfriend arrived yet?'

He didn't answer. And wondered why she didn't say Marianka's name.

'I know that you were avoiding me this morning, and I also know why.'

Suddenly Avraham noticed that another thing in the room had changed. The photograph on her desk, surrounded by a black frame. Ilana appeared in the picture with her husband and four children at the foot of Sacré-Cœur Basilica, at the top of Montmartre, in Paris. It had been taken a few weeks before her oldest son was killed in an army training accident and had stood on the desk ever since, facing her. Now it wasn't there. 'What did you think of the report?' she asked, and he tried to evade the question: 'Wouldn't it be best to talk about that another time?'

'It would be best to talk about it now, precisely because we're about to work together again. We'll get to the case in a bit.'

He forgot that the questions she asked could be as direct as her gaze.

She said, 'Explain to me what insulted you,' and he said, 'I wasn't insulted, Ilana.'

'So what made you angry?'

Was it so hard to guess? The fingers of his right hand stretched out over the investigation file. He knew her well enough to understand that there was no hope of him postponing the conversation.

'It's quite clear, no? It made me angry that you wrote a report about my last investigation without saying a word to me. That you blamed me for destroying the evidence in the case and for the parents of Ofer Sharabi eluding the punishment that they probably deserved and you didn't even tell me. And we were in touch, Ilana. We even spoke on the phone a few times when I was in Brussels.'

'Are you angry because of what I wrote or because I didn't tell you?'

Avraham couldn't answer that question. He lit a cigarette and was surprised when she took the pack from his hand and removed a cigarette for herself. 'You're back to smoking again?'

he asked, and she said, 'Not exactly. I'm back to smoking with you.'

When they had first met, Ilana had smoked more than he did, and staff meetings in her previous office in the Ayalon District took place in a cloud of smoke. She had stopped on the day her son was killed. Standing beside the grave, she had held out a half-pack of Marlboro Lights to Avraham and said to him, 'Here, take these.'

Ilana asked, 'Can I explain to you what happened exactly?' He nodded and for the first time raised his eyes to hers. He never smoked those cigarettes, and the pack of Marlboro Lights that she had given him at the cemetery was still in one of the drawers in his office.

'A few weeks after the case was closed, when you were already in Brussels, a complaint arrived from the attorney's office. As you know, they settled on a plea agreement with Rafael Sharabi, claiming that they had no choice because there wasn't enough evidence to prosecute him owing to our negligent investigation. It reached the commissioner, and he asked for an external probe. The district commander suggested that I write the probe's report. He knows that we're close, and I told him that I was involved in the investigation, but he persuaded me that I should write the report so that the investigation wouldn't go to someone from outside. What I'm saying is, it could have been worse. His stipulation was that you were not to be involved in the writing and that I was not to inform you of the report.'

She stopped for a moment in order to check his expression and again searched out his gaze. He remained silent. She had actually protected him: that was what she was trying to tell him. This was a conversation between two people who were close and who had known each other for many years, but also between two seasoned police detectives who knew what to say and how and when to say it in order to realize an objective.

'Therefore I had to write what I wrote, Avi. It wouldn't have gone through if I'd covered up the mistakes that were made in the investigation. And you know very well that we made mistakes. So I put it down in black and white, and in the same breath I wrote that you solved the case and that you have an excellent record. Which reassured everyone.'

In the report she hadn't written, 'We made mistakes.' All of them were attributed to the 'investigation team's commander'. But maybe that's what she'd had to do. And maybe that indeed was what had happened.

He lit another cigarette and looked out of the open window. He wanted to ask her why the family photo had disappeared from the desk. Ilana said, 'Avi, thanks to that report, no one in the police talks any more about Ofer Sharabi or the plea bargain with his father. It's over. And when we solve this assault case we'll go to the media with it and no one will remind you of Ofer. Now you have to put it behind you – and I know that you haven't, I know you – and concentrate on the investigation. Let's lock it up by Yom Kippur. What do you say?'

He still didn't say a thing.

Did no one remember Ofer Sharabi? Was he the only one who still hadn't put Ofer behind him? He recalled Chava Cohen shutting down the red Justy's engine in the dark car park at 1.36. Showing no fear as she got out of the car and looked around. Someone was waiting for her beyond the camera's range. Didn't rush to attack her, just waited. And between 1.36 and 3 a.m. he beat her in the head with a rock. Avraham said, 'I'm sorry about this morning,' and Ilana replied,

'Forget it, nothing happened. And I'm happy you're here again. Shall we get started?'

He updated her on the details that had accumulated in the case before the assault.

She knew about the fake bomb, because they had spoken about it a few days before, but she didn't know the details of the warning call that Chava Cohen had hidden during her interrogation. She listened to him with interest and wrote a few sentences on a piece of paper. Afterwards she added information about what had taken place that night – from the son's interrogation and from analysis of findings at the scene. Chava Cohen hadn't informed her son that she planned to go out. Too early to tell if that was because she hadn't planned to go out or because she hadn't included him in her plan. He was fifteen years old and had lived with his mother since her divorce. And she never went out without telling him. Her mobile had not been found in the apartment; neither had her wallet. Apparently she carried them in the cloth bag she had held in her hand when she got out of the car. They had been not found at the scene, and the phone company was unable to locate the device. But a list of her most recent calls was expected at any moment. Her debit card had not been used since the previous afternoon. The amount that had been taken out was normal – two hundred shekels – and it was fair to assume that this was all the money she had had on her at the time she was assaulted. Avraham asked, 'Does the son remember when he went to sleep?' and she said, 'Between eleven and eleven thirty.'

If so, Chava Cohen had left her house for the meeting with the assailant between eleven thirty and one fifteen at the latest. She had waited for her son to fall asleep before leaving – unless she had arranged the meeting with the assailant only after he had gone to sleep.

Ilana asked him to stop. She said, 'Are you sure there's a connection between the suitcase and the warning call and her arranging to meet with the assailant? In a second you can convince me. But let's ask first if there's any chance that this was an assault during the course of a random mugging.'

How well he knew her. This was the first rule of Commander Ilana Lis, the first female officer in the history of the Tel Aviv District's Investigations Unit: one must leave all possibilities open, especially when one of them appears more likely than the rest. And tell as many stories as possible about every incident. The story richest in details will usually be the correct one, but only usually, and not necessarily. He said to her, 'No chance, Ilana. At one thirty in the morning she voluntarily arrives at a completely deserted place far from home. There's nothing for her there at a time like that, unless she had arranged to meet with the assailant,' and Ilana said, 'Why? Maybe she went to look at the sea. To meet a girlfriend or a boyfriend. The assailant sees her and can't resist the temptation – a lone woman in the middle of the night, in an empty car park. He tries to snatch her bag and she resists. A struggle ensues. He picks up a rock, beats her, flees. You know things like that happen every day.'

'But not every day does the person assaulted receive threatening calls – and hide them. And not every day is a fake bomb put outside their workplace. There are too many details missing in your story. Where is the boyfriend or girlfriend she was supposed to meet? Why haven't we heard from them? And why didn't she tell her son that she was planning to go out? Beyond that, I think she went to the meeting with a recording device.'

Avraham suddenly thought of the Hotmail account from which Ilana sent him the report: *rebeccajones21*.

Did Ilana sometimes go out in the middle of the night by herself for a meeting with a boyfriend or girlfriend, as she supposed that Chava Cohen could have done? He recalled that a few days earlier Ilana had told him that she needed to tell him something when they met – before he heard it from someone else.

'Why do you think that?' she asked, and he said, 'Because I found a cassette case for a tape recorder in her car boot. And the cassette was missing. I think that the assailant arranged a meeting with her and that she intended to record it, because he blackmailed her or threatened her. And then something happened.'

Ilana studied him. 'He didn't plan to hurt her in advance,' she said.

'No. She was attacked with a rock that was in the ditch. An argument developed that boiled over into violence. Maybe the assailant discovered the recording device.'

'And why did he take the wallet and mobile with him?'

'Why? Either so it would look like a mugging or because she had something in her bag that might expose him. It's likely there was an exchange of text messages or phone calls between them. They had to have co-ordinated the meeting somehow.'

Ilana wasn't yet convinced. Perhaps she just wanted to be hard on him. 'I think you're going in the right direction but are running too fast. And there are two details in your story that are hard for me to accept. The first is that the phone threat she received at the nursery was from a woman while the assailant, apparently, was a man. And the second is actually connected to this. It's hard for me to believe that Chava Cohen would go out in the middle of the night to meet someone who had threatened or blackmailed her. Unless it was a person she knew well. We checked – her ex has an alibi, and there seems to be no conflict there. And I don't believe it could have been her son, although if there's one person she would go to meet regardless of the time or place, it would definitely be her son.'

He looked at her, amazed: that was exactly the detail that was tough for him as well. The only detail in the story that didn't sit well with the rest.

He was searching for a woman's voice. And Chava Cohen hadn't been afraid of coming to a late-night meeting perhaps because she'd thought she was about to meet with a woman and not a man. But her assailant had been a man, without a doubt.

Ilana looked at the wall clock sitting on the floor and called the hospital.

Chava Cohen was in surgery, and it was too early to know when she would get out, or in what condition. Avraham lit another cigarette and paced around the room while Ilana spoke with the forensics lab. 'And there's another possibility,' she said after she'd put down the receiver. 'I understand that the main direction of your investigation before the assault was parents of children at the nursery. So perhaps we're looking for a man *and* a woman. The man placed the suitcase and the woman made the phone call. And Chava Cohen planned to meet the woman but ended up meeting the man.'

The exchange of thoughts and words with her always caused something in him to come alive.

He looked at her and smiled. 'That's a brilliant idea,' he said. It had crossed his mind too since the investigation had opened.

She asked, 'Do you have someone in mind?' and he said, 'Perhaps.'

And it was exactly then that the list of phone calls arrived.

A young policeman Avraham didn't know entered the room and Ilana introduced Avraham to him as the commander of the investigation. Sergeant Lior Zaytuni shook his hand and extended the fax to him. 'There are no incoming or outgoing calls near the time of the attack, but look here – from ten at night she had more than ten calls from the same number that went unanswered. But at eleven thirty she answers that number and speaks for four minutes.'

Avraham immediately knew that he had seen the number before.

He opened the notepad and leafed through it but Zaytuni beat him to it. 'The number belongs to a man by the name of Chaim Sara, who lives on Aharonovitch Street in Holon,' he said, and Ilana looked at Avraham. He nodded but wasn't able to add any details because Natalie Pinchasov returned his call just then.

He asked if she knew what had happened during the night and she said she did. When Chava Cohen hadn't arrived at the nursery she had called her and hadn't got an answer. Afterwards she had called her son and he told her about the assault. In the meantime the nursery was still open, because there were parents who insisted that they couldn't drop everything to come and get their children, but she hoped that by noon everyone would have been and she'd close it. Avraham asked, 'Did Chaim Sara's son come to the nursery?' And the assistant said, 'No. Maybe I should have called you but I forgot. The father told me yesterday that the boy wouldn't be coming because they're going away.'

★

When they were again alone in the room, Ilana asked him to tell her about Sara, and Avraham went over the details of the testimony he'd collected in his office.

Actually he didn't know much about him. Yet.

An older father of two young children, fifty-seven years old. No criminal record. Presented himself during questioning as the owner of a catering business. There were signs of anxiety evident in Sara throughout their conversation. His answers were brief and clipped, as if he had difficulty speaking.

Did he arouse suspicion in Avraham? Maybe for a moment, as when he prolonged his answers of all things. What disturbed Avraham was the gap between the stammering in his answers to seemingly simple questions and the fluent and complete story he had told about the incident with Chava Cohen. As if only that answer had been prepared in advance. 'But most of my suspicions at that stage were directed towards Chava Cohen's lies, and it could be that I wasn't attentive enough,' he conceded. If Sara was indeed the assailant, his motives were clear: he suspected that Chava Cohen had hurt his son. Sara claimed that his wife wasn't available for questioning because she had travelled to the Philippines and he didn't know when she'd return, and this response also disconcerted Avraham. After all, she hadn't flown to the Philippines on a one-way ticket. But Sara also inspired trust in him, perhaps even pity, and perhaps it was exactly because of this feeling that Avraham was now quite certain that they had to arrest him immediately.

Ilana put down the pen in her hand.

For a few moments they didn't speak. They looked at one another in silence, which he was also very familiar with. The silence before a decision. The report was no longer a barrier between them, but were it not for Avraham reading it that morning, he might not have seen what he saw. Finally Ilana said, quietly, 'I want to locate him but I don't want to arrest him yet,' and Avraham said, 'Come on, Ilana, he called her more than ten times before the attack. And she left home after a conversation with him, or with his wife. Give me a few hours with him and the investigation will be over.'

Ilana smiled. 'I see that your confidence has returned. That's good. But we have time, Avi, and we have a lot to do before then. This time I want us to be prepared for the arrest and interrogation so we can submit a perfect case to the attorneys, without a single loose end. Let's wait for the results from the lab. The scene was very messy, and it's likely we'll have finger- and shoe prints and DNA. And don't forget that if we're lucky Chava Cohen could regain consciousness at any moment and simply tell us that he was the assailant. I'm with you on your feeling, but to arrest him on circumstantial evidence would be to shoot ourselves in the foot. I'll request a sweeping gag order. Not only on the name of the victim but on the attack itself as well. And in the meantime we'll locate him and put him under surveillance. Look into this information that he plans to go away. And check what vehicle he owns and if he moved it during the night. Go over all the cameras on the way from Holon to Tel Aviv. I want to see his car on the way to the scene of the assault. And try to find out if his wife went away or not. If he lied and she's in Israel, then another detail in our story lines up and we'll be able to assume that Chava Cohen arranged the meeting with her. When we have direct evidence we'll arrest him. Only, in the meantime let's make sure he doesn't escape, okay?'

8

He thought about Jenny from the moment he woke up in the morning, and in his thoughts she had unexpected vitality.

He must have dreamed about her – that was the only explanation – but Chaim didn't remember the dream or what had happened in it. Blurred shards of memory floated in his body: the thick soles of her feet, her brown thighs, the line of hair running from her navel down her abdomen. Her face was hidden by a pillow. It seemed to him that in the dream he saw the smiling face of Agapitos, the driver. And one other dull memory retrieved from the night: a wide rectangular window, with a wooden frame, looking out on a small courtyard from beyond which came screaming voices.

Had he already known when he woke up that the reason for the trip wasn't only to avoid the police's interrogation? The questioning at the station had scared him less the day after. When he had left the station, his hands trembled on the car's steering wheel, but since he had started carrying out the plan, the shaking had ceased. He was frightened not because of the questions the detective had posed to him but rather because of those he had not. And he had no reason to panic. At night he'd spoken with Chava Cohen and the conversation had gone well. The investigation had certainly turned away from him, or would do so in the days to come. He could have cancelled the trip – and in retrospect, if he had cancelled it, it was possible he wouldn't have been caught – but he already wanted to get away for other reasons. He wanted to get away for the sake of Ezer and Shalom, in order to bring Ezer back to him, and to let him understand what had really happened. And in some way that wasn't entirely clear to him he also wanted to get away in order to prove something to Jenny, or in order to bury her once and for all.

Out of habit he looked in on the children's room. The beds were empty and the room cool. Perhaps because he was by himself, for the first time in a long while without Ezer and Shalom, he woke up with those thoughts of Jenny. And maybe it was because of the searching he had done the night before, and the wedding pictures. He moved the transistor radio from the kitchen to the bathroom so he could listen to the Voice of Israel while he shaved, but the raised voices got mixed up in his thoughts with his own voice and he turned it off. When he got dressed in the bedroom he noticed the suitcase. And was that perhaps the reason Jenny was able to penetrate his thoughts? Everything was carried out according to plan. And from moment to moment it filled up with details. In the suitcase there was still room for the clothes that were drying on the line, and then the idea came to Chaim to buy Jenny a present.

He fried the eggs and placed them on the windowsill, so they'd cool off, and left for the bakery. This time he didn't drive quickly, and on Sokolov Street he slowed almost to a stop and could look into the windows of the travel agencies and the closed clothing stores. He didn't know where Jenny bought clothes. He recalled that she once told him that they were more expensive at the malls than in the city.

At the Brothers' Bakery it was a morning like any other. The smell of baking dough rose from the ovens and the flour-covered floor. Chaim told the younger brother that he was going away for a few days with the boys and that he'd let them know when they were coming back so as to restart his daily order, and he was surprised by the ease with which the story flowed out of him. Exactly like it had gone last night, in the conversation with the teacher, he thought. The younger brother patted him on the shoulder and wished him a pleasant vacation, and Chaim wished him an easy fast on Yom Kippur.

On his way back home it was already daylight and the roads were no longer empty. This was exactly how he had driven on the morning he hid her body. He had returned home then and still didn't know what he'd say to the boys, and he hadn't thought about the police at all. He had called his mother once the sandwiches were wrapped up and stacked one on top of another in the crate. The children hadn't woken up yet, and he saw before his eyes their sleeping faces, sunk into their thick pillows in the same room where he had grown up. His mother asked him immediately, 'Did you call the teacher?' and he answered, 'Everything's okay, don't keep worrying. How did they sleep?'

'Shalom had a hard time getting to sleep, but they didn't wake up during the night. What did you say to her?'

'I told you already, everything's okay. We had a good talk. Don't keep on about it.'

She didn't ask any more questions.

From the exhaustion in her voice he guessed that she hadn't slept well, her thoughts turning her over in bed. He said, 'Maybe call Adina and ask her to help with the kids,' and his mother said, 'I already have. I think she'll come this evening, after work.'

*

Perhaps he should have called his mother last night after talking to the teacher to reassure her, but it had been late.

Chava Cohen hadn't answered him until eleven thirty. She hadn't recognized his voice, and even when he had told her his name she didn't immediately remember.

At the start of the conversation she was impatient, just as she had been at nursery, but afterwards she softened. She asked, 'Did you just call me a few times?' and he said, 'Yes. I'm sorry to bother you.' She asked him how he had got her phone number, and he said from the nursery's contact list. Then she asked what he wanted and he answered her directly, as he had decided. 'I want to apologize for what happened. We're celebrating a new year, so I wanted to wish you a good year and to turn a new leaf.' She didn't answer right away, and he listened to the sound of her breathing. Was she not certain it was him? She asked, 'Why would you call me at this hour, Mr Sara?'

He responded, 'As I told you, to ask for your forgiveness. And also to say that I have no tie to the suitcase with the bomb that they put by your nursery. I would never do a thing like that. If you knew me better, you'd know that's not me.'

Again he heard her breathing. And in the background, voices from a distant television. She asked, 'And you called only for that?'

And he confirmed this and said, 'Now we're in the Days of Forgiveness, no?'

By then he already felt their conversation was going well. His anger with her had dissipated while he spoke.

She asked him suddenly, 'Did someone from the police question you about the suitcase?' and he said, 'Yes, they called me in for questioning at the station today,' even though he wasn't sure that this was what he should have said. She was silent again. Subsequently when she spoke her voice was more polite, less aggressive.

'Can you tell me what they asked?'

'If we had had a dispute, and if you have disputes with other parents at the nursery.'

'And what did you say?'

'That what happened wasn't a dispute, and that there aren't any disputes at the nursery.'

'They didn't ask you about people who worked at the nursery?'

He didn't understand her question and said no.

'Are you sure? They didn't ask anything about the assistant who worked for me last year?'

Afterward she asked additional questions about the police interrogation and he answered, emphasizing all the good things he'd said about her. She ended the conversation after wishing him a good year and he said he'd see her at the nursery, not the next day but rather after the holidays. Before this, she said to him the sentence he had hoped to hear: 'I didn't think that you had any connection to that suitcase, Mr Sara. That suitcase has no connection to the nursery, either. But thanks for calling. And give little Shalom a kiss from me.'

He started his rounds at work early that day, before eleven, although business was always slow at this time of year. He wanted to get home before one and continue with his plan.

Most of the work was at the Ministry of the Interior building. In the large hall where they renew passports and issue identity cards, the line was short, because of the holidays. He moved on to the small hall of the visas department, where most of the work took place. Dozens of foreigners and their spouses or employers crowded in line without knowing when the clerk would call them. Some of them had been standing there without food since 7 a.m.

Chaim himself had gone there for the first time with Jenny, to extend her visa, which had expired before they got married, when she lost her job.

Luckily for him, he hadn't had to queue. They were received by the clerk immediately upon their arrival, because Ilan, his cousin, worked there. Jenny by chance had seen Marisol, the Filipina woman whom they'd met before the wedding in Cyprus, and got excited. Her husband, a plumber, was much younger than Chaim and already twice divorced. They still planned to travel to South America and were trying to extend Marisol's visa, but the Ministry of the Interior was creating difficulties, because they were sceptical of the marriage's credibility, despite the pictures from Larnaca. Jenny had urged Chaim to say something to his cousin on their behalf, and he did. He wasn't selling his food there then, not until five years later, when the high-tech firm for which he was catering hot lunches closed and a second company cancelled its contract for budgetary reasons, and after two months without work the idea of selling there occurred to him, or, actually, to his mother. She spoke to Ilan, and together they arranged it. Since then his cousin had been promoted and appointed director of the Department of Population Registration. Chaim knocked on the closed door to his office and didn't get an answer, and one of the clerks told him he was on vacation until after Yom Kippur. Chaim told the clerk that he too was going away for a few days, and she said, 'How nice. With Jenny and the kids?' He said yes and smiled.

After work he returned home and took an afternoon nap, and at three thirty he walked into town.

*

He bought the airline tickets at the Magic Tours travel agency in Holon's Weitzman Square at four thirty.

The wide square was quiet and grey, surrounded by old, tall, empty-looking residential buildings. Most of the travel agencies presented signs in Russian and landscape shots from Russia and the Ukraine, so he chose Magic Tours, but the agents there were Russian too. The agent who invited him to sit opposite her typed with one finger of her left hand. She was around fifty, short and wide, wearing a suit and narrow glasses but no wedding ring. While waiting for the search results she tried to start a conversation with him and asked, 'Do you do business there?'

He said, 'My wife is there. I'm travelling to her with the children.'

Next to him an older couple booked a guided group tour of Spain and Italy. Chaim was prepared for the next questions as well.

'It's good that you say that two of the travellers are children. What ages?'

'The older one is seven and the other is three.'

'So that's almost full price,' the agent said, and Chaim imagined the moment at which he'd present Ezer and Shalom with the tickets. He planned to do this only the day before their trip. Maybe he'd first show them the packed suitcase and ask, 'Can you guess where we're going tomorrow?' He assumed that they'd know the answer, but if they didn't, he'd say to them, 'We're going to visit Mum.' The agent apologized for the computer's slowness and added, 'Not a lot of Israelis are travelling to the Philippines right now. Not during this season – it's hot there, like here, but with a lot more rain,' and he thought he'd better pack umbrellas.

Ezer and Shalom would bound down the stairway from the plane and he would have to stop them running through the airport to find Jenny. They would stand outside the airport, in the rain, under their little umbrellas, and wait. And they'd have no one other than him. They were already used to being disappointed by her, and this would be the last, and final, such disappointment.

The search results appeared on the computer screen and the agent said, 'I have a flight after Yom Kippur. Sunday evening. With a stop in Hong Kong. Departing from Tel Aviv on El Al at nine p.m. and landing in Manila with Cathay Pacific at six forty.' Chaim immediately asked, 'You don't have anything before Yom Kippur?' and the agent brought her face close to the screen and tapped the keyboard again with the same one finger of her left hand. She shook her head, no, but then said, 'There's a flight just before Yom Kippur. With Korean Air, via Seoul. Leaves Tel Aviv on Friday and lands in Manila on Saturday. Also in the morning. With a six-hour layover in Seoul. But the tickets are more expensive and you'll be in the air on the holiday.'

Chaim didn't want to wait. He asked, 'Are you sure you don't have anything before that? Tomorrow or the next day?' She shook her head.

That was the flight.

She asked, 'Three tickets, yes?' and he said, suddenly, 'On the way there, yes. But on the way back we'll need four. My wife will be with us.'

He didn't know Jenny's passport number but the agent had no need for it. She only wanted to know how her name was spelled in English. 'Jenny. Jenny Sara,' he said.

'Do you know if on her passport it says Jenny or Jennifer?'

He didn't know.

'I'd better write Jennifer. With two *n*s and one *f*. I don't think there will be a problem with that.'

Only when she asked him about the hotel room in Manila did he falter. She thought that they'd have no need for a hotel, but he explained that Jenny had been living in Israel for many years, and that she had no relatives in Manila, and no apartment to stay in there. He didn't take into account that they would need a hotel for so long and was suddenly busy calculating the cost of the room. When she found them an inexpensive hotel, she said, 'So, a room for four, or two rooms?' And he said to her, without thinking, 'For three. Why four? Me and the two children.'

She observed him with a look full of amazement from behind her glasses. 'And what about your wife?'

He apologized and said he'd got confused, and she said, 'The price is the same in any case. It's a standard family room with a couch that opens into a double bed and two small children's beds.' Again, when he paid her cash, in two-hundred-shekel notes that he removed from an envelope, she looked at him amazed.

On his way home, on foot, before evening, it seemed to Chaim that someone was following him. He lingered at a corner. Didn't cross the street even when the light for pedestrians changed to green. The woman who passed him with a pushchair was taller and thinner than Jenny. Maybe the fear rose in him again because of the mistakes he'd made at the travel agency. At the clothing store he made no mistakes. He slowed the pace of his walking. Tried to think different thoughts. The woman with the pushchair continued walking until she disappeared from his sight.

He thought that in the past twenty-four hours he had spoken to more people than he spoke to in a normal week of his life. There was the good talk he had had with Chava Cohen at night, and the conversation with the young security guard at the entrance to the Tax Authority building, and the exchanges with the clerk at the Ministry of the Interior. In the afternoon he talked about their trip twice, to the Russian agent at the travel agency and to the saleswoman at the clothing store Bella Donna. He recalled what Jenny used to say to him: 'People can only talk to you in your sleep.' But even when he spoke, she didn't listen. Sometimes he would turn to her in the evening and she would ignore him, focused on the glowing television, or rereading old letters from her sister. As if she hadn't forgiven him for having the children, as she hadn't forgiven them. And even on the day he had come back from work and saw the welts on Shalom's face, he had tried to convince her to speak to the teacher, but she wouldn't listen. He remembered that Ezer looked at him, and when he noticed his gaze, the boy took off, walked to the living room, as if he were ashamed of his defeated father. That was their last conversation. The saleswoman in the clothing store said to him, when she examined the picture of the children, 'Such beautiful boys. And how much the two of them look like you,' as if Jenny's death intensified the resemblance between them and brought them closer to him. He had entered Bella Donna after going past all the clothing stores on Sokolov Street because only there did he see clothes that looked to him like the clothes Jenny wore. The saleswoman first scrutinized him with a reserved look, perhaps because men rarely visited the store and perhaps because he hesitated for a moment at the entrance, opposite the display window, before going inside. In the entrance to the store, on the right side, were thin colourful dresses, short tricot shirts, and buttoned shirts on hangers. Inside the store were evening dresses and suits.

Chaim told the saleswoman that he wanted to buy a gift for his wife and presented her with the picture Marisol had taken in Cyprus: Jenny in a white dress and he in a suit just moments before entering the mayor's office. 'That's a picture from a few years ago, but she looks the same, in terms of sizes,' he explained, and the saleswoman said, 'Terrific. I think size thirty-eight will do it,' and suddenly he didn't understand why he had brought a picture that he himself was in to the store, or a picture at all. Jenny wouldn't wear the clothes anyway.

'What does she usually like?' the saleswoman asked, and Chaim said, 'She wears colourful clothes.'

'And is this a birthday present?'

'No. I'm travelling to see her with the children. She's in the Philippines and we're flying to her on Friday for a holiday and then we're all coming back together. We'll surprise her with the gift.'

'How nice. So let's see, do you want something more for the evening or something for everyday?'

After thinking it over, he said, 'Maybe we should get one of each.' He hadn't thought about it earlier, but it was an excellent idea. The presents would be from the children: one outfit would be from Ezer and the other from Shalom.

On the counter the saleswoman placed two dresses and two shirts and three pairs of pants. She put the dresses and the shirts against her body so he could see. She was younger than Jenny and thinner, but the difference between them wasn't great. She asked him how many years they'd been married and Chaim answered over eight, and she laughed and said, 'And you still buy her presents! I should be so lucky.'

In the end he bought a purple silk shirt and white jeans and she wrapped them separately in festive paper.

When he went to place the black shopping bag in the suitcase in the bedroom it seemed to him that someone had opened it in his absence. The children's clothes weren't organized like he remembered organizing them, stacked on top of each other like the sandwiches in the crate. Also the door to the bedroom wardrobe was open, and he couldn't remember if he had closed it the day before, after his search.

He went from room to room and listened.

The window in the children's room was open and he closed it. Had he opened it himself before going out? It was also possible that he had got up during his afternoon nap and done it. And yet he felt that someone was in the house, or had been until a few minutes earlier. He tried to recall if the key had turned once or twice in the lock before the door opened. Afterwards he looked at the street and didn't see a woman who looked like her. As this morning, Jenny penetrated his thoughts, and he removed her from there. And maybe it was natural that she hadn't disappeared entirely, and wouldn't disappear until they went. On Friday they'd get on the plane to Manila with a stopover in Seoul. For Ezer and Shalom this would be their first time on a plane. They'd sleep another night in the room he grew up in at his mother's house before he got them. And only on Thursday would he tell them about the trip and include them in the preparations.

He saw in his mind's eye the smile spreading over and lighting up Ezer's dark face when he told them that Mum would be waiting for them at the airport.

Avraham hung up the phone and paced back and forth inside the small room. When he returned and sat down, he gazed at the lists he had prepared since that morning with a black pen. It was nine thirty and he was still at his office.

A moment before the border police called, it seemed to him that the points were connected and the picture was getting clearer, but now one detail didn't sit well with the rest. Jennifer Salazar had left Israel on 12 September and still hadn't returned. The exit register in the computers of the border police confirmed that she had left Israel a few days before the suitcase with the fake bomb was placed on Lavon Street and before the warning call was received at the nursery. And she hadn't returned since.

Avraham removed the black pen from his shirt pocket and drew three black points on a clean piece of paper, like the corners of a triangle without sides. Next to one point he wrote *Holon*, next to the second *Tel Aviv*, and next to the third, a bit further away from the other two, he wrote *Philippines*. He continued gazing at the sheet of paper for a while, then took his notepad and went out to smoke on the steps to the station.

It was a long day that began early with the report about the previous investigation and the phone calls from Ilana that he hadn't wanted to take. Afterwards, Benny Saban had burst into his office and informed him of the assault and he had rushed to the scene, and from there gone to his meeting with Ilana. He'd wanted to arrest Sara and interrogate him immediately when they'd received the list of Chava Cohen's conversations and it had turned out that Sara called her multiple times and briefly spoken with her before she left for the meeting in which she was cruelly attacked. But Ilana refused on the grounds that it was necessary to first collect additional evidence against Sara. Which, in the meantime, was piling up more and more.

Even though a team of division detectives had observed Sara's every move from the moment he returned to his home from work in the afternoon, Avraham followed him as well, at some distance, on his way from Aharonovitch Street to the city centre. He saw him when he entered the Magic Tours travel agency in Weitzman Square. Maybe he shouldn't have done it; he wasn't an experienced detective, and Sara knew his face, but if he couldn't interrogate him he at least wanted to observe him. And perhaps he wanted to make sure himself that Sara didn't flee. He waited a few minutes in the empty square after Sara continued on his way, then entered the travel agency. This was a mistake as well. At any moment Sara was liable to retrace his steps.

The travel agent hesitated before giving Avraham the flight details. First she called the manager of the office, who had already gone home.

Sara had purchased three tickets for flight KE 958 from Tel Aviv to Seoul and for connecting flight KE 623 from Seoul to Manila. His flight would take off from Ben-Gurion Airport on the eve of Yom Kippur, Friday, at 8.30 a.m. This was the first flight on which she'd found seats, and Sara wanted to fly as soon as possible. On the return flight to Tel Aviv, his wife would be joining him and their two sons. The travel agent said that Sara's wife was waiting for him and the boys in the Philippines, but she didn't know when she had flown because she seemed to have purchased her plane ticket somewhere else. Avraham asked her to inform him if Sara contacted her, even though it was reasonable to assume he'd know about this regardless, because they'd already received the court's approval to tap Sara's phones. Upon leaving the travel agency Avraham called Ilana and told her that Sara was planning to flee and that airline tickets to Manila were in his possession. She weighed the possibilities before instructing him nevertheless to refrain from making an arrest. 'That means we have until Friday morning to gather as much direct evidence against him as possible and bring him in for questioning, right? So let's wait a bit longer,' she said.

Avraham didn't want to wait.

And he had no doubt he could break Sara in a brief interrogation.

Sara had a motive. He had had a violent disagreement with Chava Cohen at the nursery and suspected – justly, it seems – that she was harming his son. He resided two hundred metres from the nursery next to which the suitcase had been placed. And when he was questioned, signs of anxiety had been evident. He had called Chava Cohen and conversed with her before she had gone out at night to a meeting where she was attacked. And even before this he had made it known that his son would not be coming to the nursery the following day. After the assault he had ordered plane tickets for himself and his two children in order to flee Israel. Avraham had no doubt that he was the man with the suitcase – and the one who had waited at night for Chava Cohen outside the range of the cameras in the car park next to the beach then beaten her in the head with a rock and left her unconscious in a ditch.

He had observed him from a considerable distance when he entered the Magic Tours travel agency that afternoon.

Just like during the interrogation at the station, Sara's clothes looked old. He wore the same brown trousers, fastened with the same brown belt. Before entering the travel agency Sara had sat on a bench in the square for a few minutes and scattered some dry pieces of bread he found for the pigeons. Was the urgency Avraham felt related only to the report about the previous investigation he'd read that same morning? From the need to prove to himself, and to Ilana, that he had learned from his mistakes and could head a team investigating a serious crime and solve the mystery within a few hours? During their discussion Ilana had said to him, 'When we solve this case no one will mention Ofer to you. But you have to put him behind you and focus on the new case.'

But the problem wasn't only Ofer Sharabi.

Chava Cohen had been lying in a recovery room in a hospital since noon, still unconscious. And he hadn't visited her room yet. In the days before the assault he had cast doubt on everything she had said and sensed his disgust intensifying each time he heard her name. He still thought that she had lied to him and that she knew who had placed the suitcase, and who the assailant was – but now he also felt a sense of duty towards her, almost a desire to apologize. She was the victim of an assault. And she had a son who hadn't even known that his mother was leaving in the middle of the night, not to return. The day had been so packed with events that Avraham almost hadn't thought about the report from this morning, but now he recalled the urgent calls from Ilana, wanting to inform him of the assault. Like a child, he had sat at his office desk and refused to answer.

And Marianka hadn't called, even though she had promised.

Suddenly Avraham felt the pen continue on the sheet paper in front of him as if on its own and connect the black point next to the word *Philippines* to *Holon* and *Tel Aviv* with a continuous line. Even if Sara's wife was abroad, that didn't mean he was mistaken. His and Ilana's working hypothesis was that they were looking for a man and a woman. The man had placed the suitcase on Lavon Street and the woman had called to make the threat. The woman had arranged the meeting with Chava Cohen and the man had shown up in her place. But the first phone call, at least – which they knew with certainty had been made by a woman – could have been made from anywhere. They hadn't succeeded in locating its source, but it was certainly possible to ascertain if it had been made from Israel or abroad. He thought about calling Ilana to share the idea with her but knew that she wouldn't change her mind with regard to the arrest and the interrogation. And, anyway, they were supposed to meet in her office tomorrow morning.

A young patrolwoman in uniform sat by the door of Chava Cohen's room in the Trauma Unit.

On a bench in the corridor outside the room sat a stocky man in a vest, his arms tattooed, and next to him slept a tall, thin youth. His head was resting on the man's shoulder and his body, folded up below, was covered with a blanket. Avraham thought that the man was Chava Cohen's ex-husband, and only later on did it turn out that he was her brother. The sleeping youth was her son. The son who had been called into the operating theatre and looked at his mother over the shoulders of the surgeons in order to confirm her identity for the police. He hadn't gone home since. Avraham presented his ID and the policeman opened the door to the room for him.

'Do you want me to call one of the doctors?' she asked, and he said no.

He wanted to be alone with her.

But it was difficult to see Chava Cohen in a room that was lit only by a small, weak light above the bed. Her face was bandaged and her body was covered with a blanket. The right side of her head, which wasn't bandaged, was shaven. Dark signs of the injuries stuck out on both her neck and the exposed parts of her face, on her right cheek and forehead. Her eyes were closed.

Avraham didn't see anything that he didn't already know after the phone call with the doctor who operated on her. Nevertheless he sat next to her for some time, as if he hoped that she would wake up while he was there. The doctor said on the phone that Chava Cohen might open her eyes at any moment, but was also likely to remain unconscious for many days. And there was no way of knowing in what condition she'd wake up because it was impossible to measure the severity of the damage.

When he left the room Avraham introduced himself to her brother as the commander of the investigation team. The son didn't wake up even though they spoke loudly next to him, and Avraham wondered if the son could ever forget the picture he had seen in surgery. He asked the brother a few routine questions, even though he wasn't interested in the answers. The brother didn't know a thing about the nursery his sister ran, or about Chaim Sara. He lived in Haifa and had last seen Chava Cohen on Rosh Hashanah. Before he said goodbye to him, the brother asked, 'You still don't know who did this?'

Avraham shook his head because the contents of the investigation were confidential, but he was convinced he knew.

Only upon his return home did he find a message from Marianka.

It was after midnight, and Avraham took off his shirt and poured himself some cold water, and after that he opened his inbox and his eyes froze.

He'd had a feeling that she would write to him, because she hadn't called, but he hadn't imagined what she'd write. The lines were short, like a mourner's notice. Marianka had written:

Don't wait for me, Avi.

Not now.

I know that the timing isn't good and that you're in the middle of an investigation. Try to concentrate on it as much as you can and don't think about me.

Maybe one day it will be different.

I will call to explain when I can.

PART TWO

9

That night autumn arrived.

The heat stored over the summer in the narrow spaces inside and between the walls of the buildings didn't dissipate, but strangely dark clouds spread out in the sky and before morning cool drops of rain began falling on the protective nylon tarps that covered the scene of the assault.

Avraham couldn't sleep, though he tried.

When the night turned blue and he understood that sleep was beyond him, he rose from his bed and got dressed. He searched all over the city for an open café because he wanted to be among people, but he couldn't find one. For some time he continued driving with no specific destination, until finally he understood where he had to go.

The police radio that morning was mainly reports of traffic accidents. At five thirty a truck slid on an oil stain that the rain had loosened from the asphalt and struck a motorcyclist travelling in the opposite direction.

Avraham suggested to the policewoman sitting in front of Chava Cohen's room that she should take a break. She said, 'Are you sure? Because if you're serious, I'm going home to wash and see my kids. I live here, close by,' and he said that he could stay until eight thirty. A meeting of the investigation team had been set for nine at the Tel Aviv district headquarters.

After she left, he opened the door. Chava Cohen lay in her bed, unconscious. Her face looked more peaceful than it had the day before. Outside the room, on the bench in the dark corridor, her son still slept. Avraham didn't see her brother anywhere. He bought instant coffee from a machine and returned to his place across from the son. He didn't actually have any reason to be there. He no longer thought that she'd feel his presence and wake up. Suddenly it seemed to him that he had come to the hospital to watch over not Chava Cohen but rather her son sleeping with his body folded up, alone, outside her room. And there, of all places, facing the sleeping son, his eyes slowly closed.

The corridor was silent and dark, and only at its far end, at the nurses' station, a light glowed.

He woke up when one of the nurses tapped him on the shoulder and asked if he would like something to eat. The bench the son had been lying on was empty, and he saw him coming out of the bathroom after washing his face.

In Conference Room C at the Tel Aviv district headquarters Sergeant Lior Zaytuni, the young detective whom he had met in Ilana's office, was waiting. He had been the first to arrive at the investigating team's meeting, and the hems of his trousers were soaking wet, as if he'd skipped through a puddle on the way to headquarters. His face was youthful and smooth, and to Avraham he looked too young to be a police detective – perhaps in his early twenties. During the meeting he barely opened his mouth, and when he spoke, a flustered quiver could be heard in his voice. He had difficulty connecting his laptop to the projector by himself and had to beg the assistance of Ilana, who arrived exactly at nine and asked, 'Why the hell isn't Eliyahu here yet?'

Ma'alul arrived a bit late, as was his habit, owing to the traffic the sudden rain created. Avraham asked Ilana to add him to the team, even though for now the file didn't contain interrogations of children or teenagers, and Ilana agreed when the Juvenile Division responded that Ma'alul wasn't involved in any pressing investigations. He put a brown leather holdall on the table and asked for their permission to eat during the meeting, since he hadn't had any breakfast at home. Ilana's secretary served everyone weak coffee in paper cups.

Before setting out an egg salad sandwich wrapped in tinfoil and a peeled cucumber, Ma'alul polished the area of the table in front of him with a white handkerchief that he removed from his bag. When he saw Avraham waiting for him in order to open the meeting he said, 'Start, Avi, start. Don't wait for me. I eat through one ear and hear with the other,' and Avraham looked at him with searching eyes, though Ma'alul couldn't have known why.

It was the sentence that Marianka wrote to him.

Don't wait.

Ilana laughed out loud, and Ma'alul apparently noticed something being crushed in Avraham's eyes and whispered voicelessly to him, just moving his lips, 'You okay?'

A slideshow of images from the night of the assault was projected onto the screen. Chava Cohen in the ditch under the bridge among empty plastic bottles and rags. She had been left lying face down, and the forensics investigators who had analysed the scene determined that she had sustained the final blows to her head while laid out like this, motionless. She had looked so sure of herself when she got out of the red Justy in the car park, about an hour before she was found in the ditch, and Avraham thought about the difference between the before and the after. How a person's life can change in a moment. Ilana said to him, 'Come on, Avi, let's move it along, we're running late. Go ahead and explain to us what happened.'

He was still trying to understand.

That night, immediately after reading the message, he had called Marianka, even though she had asked him not to. The telephone in the small apartment in Alfred Bouvier Square in Brussels rang but she didn't answer. If he could have walked on foot or driven to her in a car, he would have. Knocked on the door and demanded an explanation despite her request. In the end he wrote her an email, just one line: Why aren't you answering me?

For a moment he thought that perhaps he hadn't communicated with her enough in recent days, because of the investigation, but he knew that wasn't the problem. He had felt her disappearing on him, and even asked her if something had happened, but she had avoided answering. She had been in his apartment for just one week back in June, more than three months earlier, but he felt her there in every corner: on the porch, which was his and Marianka's porch, in the living room, whose walls were supposed to be painted white and light blue, in the bedroom, where the wardrobe was half empty and the old wooden shelves were awaiting her clothes. Before morning, prior to going out to the hospital, he again checked his inbox. No answer to the email he had sent her.

Ma'alul patiently chewed his sandwich and covered his mouth with his hand, and Avraham said, 'Chava Cohen, a forty-two-year-old resident of Holon, a teacher by profession, was assaulted at night between Sunday and Monday near the beach in Tel Aviv. As is visible from the pictures, it was a brutal attack and was carried out with a rock found at the scene. Threats preceded it, apparently, as well as a fake bomb that was placed next to the nursery that the victim runs on Lavon Street. The scene is messy, and it looks like we will have numerous findings from the forensics lab. There will be fingerprints as well as shoe prints. So when we arrest a suspect in the assault we'll have something to work with.'

Ma'alul put his roll on the table and wiped the tips of his fingers with his handkerchief. He said, 'Excuse me interrupting you, but what does this mean that the assault was apparently preceded by threats and a fake bomb?' and Avraham said, 'There *was* a fake bomb, not apparently, and there was also a threatening call to the nursery. We haven't located the person or persons who placed the bomb or made the phone call, but we're certain there's a connection between the crimes, even though the victim concealed the threat from us and claimed she had no information about the identity of whoever placed the bomb.'

This time Ilana stopped him. She said, 'I would like to emphasize that this is Avi's assumption, not ours. And even if it seems reasonable to me as a working hypothesis, I don't want the connection between the bomb and the assault to become indisputable fact in the framework of the investigation. Rather, I think we should also explore other avenues,' and Ma'alul asked, 'For instance?'

Despite his age, Ma'alul looked to Avraham like a schoolboy during lunch break, with the half-eaten sandwich lying on the crumpled tinfoil in front of him.

'For instance, a random assault. Or a mugging. Her phone was stolen along with her wallet. We know for certain there was no rape, but it's impossible to rule out the possibility that there was an attempted rape, or maybe a sexual assault that got complicated.'

Avraham waited for Ilana to finish, then continued without responding to what she'd said. His head was heavy with exhaustion despite his brief nap across the hall from Chava Cohen's son at the hospital. 'Our primary suspect is Chaim Sara, a fifty-seven-year-old resident of Holon,' he said. 'He has a motive I can elaborate on in what follows. He has no prior criminal record. His son attends the nursery run by the victim, and apparently he came to suspect that she had harmed his son. It's also possible that the motive was expressed in the manner of the assault. The victim was struck on the head, and the suspect said in questioning that his son returned from the nursery with injuries to the head, so perhaps there is a parallel here that needs to be taken into consideration. The main evidence gathered against him is circumstantial but strong. On the night of the assault he called the victim and held a conversation with her before she left her home. The day after the assault he bought plane tickets for himself and his children. He plans to flee Israel on Friday morning.'

Emotion was evident in Zaytuni's face and voice as he asked, quietly, 'Have we taken out a stay order to prevent him leaving Israel? If not, maybe it would be a good idea to contact the courts.' Only he looked and behaved as if this investigation into Chava Cohen's assault was the investigation of his life. For Ilana, of course, it was one investigation among many for which she was responsible, and for Ma'alul a break from his work routine in the Juvenile Division. And Avraham had to prove something to himself and to Ilana, but it seemed to him that the closer he tried to get to the investigation the more it retreated from him, and the letter from Marianka only distanced him from it further. Ilana answered Zaytuni instead of him. 'If we need to, we'll take out a stay order on Thursday,' she said. 'We have two days until then, and I hope that we'll have results from the lab and that we'll be able to bring the suspect in for interrogation and take finger- and shoe prints from him and confront him with the findings from the scene. And, more than that, I hope that the victim will wake up and be in a condition to tell us who assaulted her, or provide a description of him. If she saw him, of course.'

Zaytuni hurried to write something on the notepad lying in front of him. Ma'alul, having finished his breakfast, smoothed out the tinfoil that the sandwich had been wrapped in with the palm of his hand, folded it into a neat square, and put it back in his bag. Avraham said, 'There is another issue with the suspect that I've been trying to clarify since yesterday. Our assumption – or mine, as Ilana said – is that a man and a woman were involved in placing the bomb and the assault. The warning call to the nursery was made by a woman, and it seems to us that Chava Cohen would not have arrived at the place of the assault in order to meet a man who had threatened her, but perhaps she would have come to a meeting she had arranged with a woman. According to the records of the border police, the wife of the suspect, a Filipina citizen by the name of Jennifer Salazar, who holds a temporary ID card, left Israel on September the twelfth and has not returned, but something is fishy here. I checked with most of the airlines departing to the Philippines and there was no passenger by the name of Jennifer Salazar on any flights. Not on that date or any other. I will try to reach the Philippines police in order to clarify whether or not she entered the country and if she has a criminal history.'

Ilana looked at him curiously. He hadn't managed to tell her about the calls to the airlines before the meeting.

Did her scepticism concerning Avraham's story stem only from her way of working? Maybe it was somehow connected to a loss of faith in him because of the mistakes in the previous investigation. In fact, the idea to call the airlines had occurred to him when he recalled things she had said to him during the search for Ofer Sharabi. More than a week after the search had begun, in a moment of frustration, Avraham had suggested to her the possibility that nothing at all had happened to Ofer. Maybe he had got onto a plane to Rio de Janeiro and was lying on a beach there. Ilana said to him then, 'You know that he's not in Rio de Janeiro, or at least you certainly could know. You can verify with the border police if he left Israel or not. And if he did, you can check with the airlines that fly to Brazil and see if he was on one of the flights that departed to Rio or to destinations along the way. He didn't get on a plane with a fake passport, right? He's not a Mossad agent, he's just a high school kid.'

Now Ilana asked him, 'And what if she travelled to some other place?' and Avraham answered, 'The suspect stated in questioning that his wife had travelled to the Philippines to take care of her sick father, and this is also what he told the travel agent from whom he bought the tickets for himself and his children. But maybe you're right. In any case, if he lied about the travel, it'll be additional evidence of his involvement in the assault and the placing of the suitcase, no? Otherwise why would he lie?'

He didn't think about Marianka until the end of the meeting, and only twice checked his mobile under the table to see if he'd received any new messages. Ilana kept on insisting that Sara should not be the only direction of the investigation, and Avraham didn't bother to object. He and Ilana drank another cup of coffee and at ten thirty divided the tasks among the team. Ilana instructed Zaytuni to continue investigating the assault as if it were a robbery. He'd explore links to incidents of assault that occurred in the area in recent months, go back and question the Sudanese men who had found Chava Cohen in the ditch, and regularly monitor whether her credit cards were being used or if the stolen phone was turned on or sold. Ma'alul was put in charge of investigating the parents at the nursery. He was supposed to confirm the suspicion that Chava Cohen hit the children and verify whether or not any other parents had a motive for assaulting the teacher. Avraham would continue conducting surveillance from afar, as well as his silent investigation into Sara and his wife. Since the previous evening, after he had bought the plane tickets, Sara hadn't left his apartment and hadn't made a phone call. 'And, most of all, let's cross our fingers that the victim will wake up and make our lives easier,' Ilana summed up. 'If it doesn't happen by then, we'll meet here on Thursday morning and decide how we want to bring Sara in for questioning before the flight.'

Ma'alul again asked for permission to speak. He turned to Avraham and said, 'Avi, before we start working, I'd like you to explain to me why you're so sure it's Sara. Because you're sure of this, yes? And I respect your gut feelings.'

Was there a need to explain again?

He was sure because of the phone call and the motive and the plane tickets. Because of the strange travel story. And there were additional reasons, that he managed to explain to himself only retrospectively, once the case had come to an end. Ilana examined Ma'alul's facial expression and large eyes while

Avraham spoke. He wasn't convinced, and she asked him why.

'I would be convinced if this were a spontaneous attack,' Ma'alul said. 'At the nursery, for example, or immediately after it was closed. But if there actually is a connection between the suitcase and the assault, there appears to be a clear pattern of criminal activity here – placing a fake bomb and making a phone threat after that and then a meeting late at night in an empty place. It all attests to a criminal plan and not to violence stemming from a loss of control. It's hard for me to believe that a fifty-seven-year-old man, without a criminal past, would, or could, carry out well-planned acts like these. Guys like him resort to violence spontaneously, and sometimes unintentionally, out of a loss of control. On the other hand, I didn't question him or see him, and I'm willing to go with Avi's gut feelings.'

Zaytuni wrote hurriedly in his notepad again. This time the words that caused Avraham to respond to the doubt that had been cast on his investigation were 'guys like him'. He said quietly, 'Did any of us think that Ofer Sharabi's parents were capable of hiding his death and fabricating a sophisticated cover story for his absence?' and was immediately sorry he'd said that.

This was the first time that he, Ma'alul and Ilana had gathered together since the day that case was solved. And the first time that he addressed aloud the lessons he'd gleaned from that same case. To look with eyes open. And not trust anyone. The two of them considered him with a strange look, and Ilana said, 'This isn't the same case, or the same people, Avi. And I tend to agree with Eliyahu. But let's see.'

They walked together down the long corridor on the way to the lift, Zaytuni and Ma'alul first, Avraham and Ilana after, and Ilana said to him, 'You look like you haven't slept. Everything okay, Avi?'

And Avraham said only, 'I had a very short night.'

When they reached the lift, Ilana asked, 'Did you hear what happened at the hospital?' And Avraham turned to her, surprised, because he feared that something had happened to Chava Cohen's son – or that someone had reported his unexpected nap. Ma'alul held the lift door open while she told them.

It turned out that a city beat policeman had arrived at an accident site where a truck had collided with a motorcycle and noticed that under his leather jacket the rider lying in the street was wearing a black T-shirt with the word 'Polska' on it. He had quickly reported this, even before the rider was taken away in an ambulance. Shrapstein was waiting for the injured man in the hospital with an arrest warrant in hand and shortly afterwards he had in his possession a documented confession, and the assassination attempt on Shenkar Street had been solved.

And all this had happened while Avraham dozed in a chair in front of Chava Cohen's room, not far from the emergency room? He didn't tell Ilana that he had gone there to check on her because he hadn't been able to sleep at home, and that of all places his eyes had closed opposite her sleeping son. Ma'alul said, 'The sages would say about this, "To the righteous goes the luck", no?'

He managed to avoid thoughts of Marianka also later that day, until he returned home, before evening. He went back to the station and heard a brief report about Sara's activities. His preparations for the trip continued: at eleven he went out and again walked into town, this time in order to buy a suitcase. His children still weren't with him and his wife was nowhere in evidence. And he didn't meet anyone. A representative of Royal Jordanian, the last airline with which Avraham had to check on Sara's wife's travels, confirmed that Jennifer Salazar had not flown with them to Manila via Amman and Hong Kong.

He ate an early lunch in the cafeteria and returned to his office.

According to the World Clock website, when it was noon in Holon it was exactly six in the evening in Manila. He was surprised when he heard the deep masculine voice that answered him at the Manila Police Information Centre, and he said in English, 'My name is Chief Inspector Avraham Avraham of the Israel Police. Can I speak to an officer from the Inspections Division?'

At first the Filipino man didn't understand his request, or why he was asking to speak in English with the Inspections Division, which they called the Department of Criminal Investigations and Surveillance, and Avraham was forced to explain that he needed the assistance of the local police in the investigation of the placing of a fake bomb and an assault that had occurred in Tel Aviv, even though he didn't intend to reveal too many details of the case. He thought that perhaps he should try to make contact with the Aviation Security Department or simply speak with the Philippines police through the Unit for Foreign Relations. He said again, 'My name is Chief Inspector Avraham from the Israel Police and I'm investigating an attack and a dummy bomb,' and added that the matter was urgent. The man asked him to wait on the line.

The website of the Philippines police was rich in information about the organization's structure and the positions within it, but there wasn't a photo on it of the police headquarters and thus he couldn't picture what kind of building the man who answered him was sitting in or what the room looked like where in another moment an officer from the Department of Criminal Investigations and Surveillance would pick up the phone. In the many pictures on the website the Filipino policemen appeared smiling and meticulously dressed. All of them were slender and many wore glasses, which gave their faces a refined, sophisticated appearance. The truth was that Avraham knew little about the Philippines – only that the country was located somewhere in Asia and that its economic situation must be somewhat difficult if so many Filipinos came to work in Israel. And what did the street views from the windows of the police headquarters in Manila look like? He was sorry that he hadn't done more research before calling the police, and tried to open the 'Philippines' page in Wikipedia, but he then heard another voice come on the line, thin and almost birdlike.

Brigadier General Anselmo Garbo, head of the Department of Criminal Investigations and Surveillance, asked him in quick English, 'With whom do I have the honour of speaking?' And Avraham hoped that he wouldn't be disappointed when he introduced himself again as only chief inspector. The name of the Filipino officer had immediately given rise to envy in him. 'I understand that you are phoning in regards to an explosive device,' Anselmo Garbo said, and Avraham said, 'Yes, definitely.'

'In Manila?' asked Garbo, and Avraham suddenly understood that the Filipino telephone receptionist had made a mistake and assumed that he was calling in order to avert a terrorist attack and said, 'No, no, I'm not calling about a terrorist attack. I'm from the Department of Criminal Investigations.'

Avraham read the rest of what he had to say from the paper resting in front of him in order to avoid a misunderstanding. 'We are in need of your assistance in locating a citizen of the Philippines who lives in Israel. According to the information given to us and the records of the border police, she left Israel on the twelfth of September en route to the Philippines, but we have not succeeded in finding the flight that she boarded. We would like you to help us confirm that she is in the Philippines, and also to locate her.'

Garbo listened patiently to his words and asked Avraham for his name, rank and phone number and apparently wrote them down. He had no apparent reason for thinking this, but it seemed to Avraham that the inspector he was speaking with was brilliant and shrewd. His words were brief and his voice was ear-piercing. 'Are you trying to inform me that a citizen of the Philippines is missing in Israel?' asked Garbo, and Avraham said, 'No. I want to clarify if she entered your country and when.'

'Could you tell me from which date she is missing and who submitted the complaint?'

'No one submitted a complaint. We simply need to summon her to give testimony.'

Garbo wouldn't relent, and Avraham was forced to tell him that he wanted to summon the absent woman for questioning with regard to an assault that had taken place in Tel Aviv. He explained that she was not suspected of involvement in the assault but that her testimony was essential, and for some reason he sensed that Garbo did not believe him. After receiving Jennifer Salazar's passport number from Avraham, Garbo said briefly, 'I will update my supervisors and the Department of International Co-ordination and respond to you soon,' and hung up.

On Wikipedia Avraham read that Manila is the most crowded metropolis in the world and that more than fifteen million people live there. He couldn't understand how a police inspector there could locate an anonymous attacker or a person who had placed a fake bomb and disappeared into a mass like that.

When he Googled the name of the Filipino officer he was astounded.

Brigadier General Anselmo Garbo was the most decorated inspector in the Manila police. Four years earlier, according to a story that he read in the *Daily Tribune*, he had caught a serial killer who had terrorized the residents of the city for more than six months. The man had murdered eleven people, carved up their abdomens, and placed amid their internal organs a rare flower – a *Michauxia campanuloides*. Afterwards he had sewn up their abdomens with a surgeon's precision. Garbo joined the investigation late because he was on a year of study at the Academy for Criminal Investigations in Paris, and two weeks after his return was on the murderer's trail, after deciphering the meaning of the deadly symbol.

Avraham felt as if he had spoken with a character out of a movie or a novel.

A picture was included in the story and Avraham saw that Garbo's face was small and narrow with a hawklike nose, and that he wore round glasses. Also he was bald.

He called the hospital after a cigarette break and spoke with a rude doctor from the Trauma Unit. Forensics promised him that by tomorrow analysis of the findings from the scene of the assault would be completed. When he opened the door to his apartment, in the early evening, he heard a ringing from inside. He had a feeling that the telephone had been ringing between the empty walls of his apartment for some time, and that Marianka was the caller, and he hurried to pick up but was met with silence at the other end of the line. He waited for it to ring again. Afterwards he sent Marianka another email: Will we never speak again?

She didn't reply to this one, either.

That night he slept for a long time, but the investigation wouldn't let go of him. He dreamed that he was falling and spinning around and that nothing he tried to grab hold of could keep him from falling. Marianka was supposed to be waiting for him at a bus stop.

The ringing of the mobile, which he had left next to the bed, woke him. An international number appeared on the screen and he answered because he thought it was her, but it was the sharp voice of Anselmo Garbo: 'Inspector Avraham? This is Brigadier General Garbo from the Department of Criminal Investigations and Surveillance of the Manila Police. Is now a good time for you to talk?'

He said yes and sat up in his bed.

'We performed a check according to your request yesterday, and a few moments ago I sent you by email a detailed report with the results. But I wanted to tell you in short that Jennifer Salazar last entered the Philippines eight years ago and has not visited since. And another important thing: you said that her husband testified that she travelled to the Philippines to care for her father, but both her parents died many years ago. Can you hear me, Inspector Avraham? The Philippines Police is troubled by the information you conveyed to us and asks that you provide us with updates continuously throughout your investigation into this matter.'

Avraham didn't remember telling Garbo that Jennifer Salazar had travelled to visit her father, but maybe he had. Or perhaps the illustrious inspector had simply read his mind? He thanked Garbo and promised to be in touch with him soon. And then he immediately woke up.

For some reason he felt that the information the Filipino inspector gave him had filled him with strength. That his fall had come to a halt. He went to his work room to read the report that Garbo had sent him and to update Ilana. But before doing this, he phoned Ma'alul, and the senior investigator, who the day before had been less than convinced, said to him, 'Okay, Avi, looks like you were right.' He was going to ask Ilana if he could finally arrest Sara now and bring him in for questioning, but before he could even manage to open his mouth she stunned him: 'Very good that you called, Avi. Right on time. I need you to go to the hospital immediately. Five minutes ago they called from the hospital to report that Chava Cohen woke up last night.'

He was there just a few minutes later, after travelling at a dizzying speed, and nearly ran through the corridors of the Trauma Unit, but the doctor on call wouldn't let him enter her room. According to the decision of the medical team, the police would not be allowed to see Chava Cohen before she was fully recovered. He asked the doctor on call if she was able to speak, and the doctor said, 'At this moment the patient isn't speaking, just crying. You will need to wait until the afternoon at least.' Ilana announced that she wanted to take part in the questioning, even if it took place in the middle of the night, and instructed him to have a videography team on call to document it. He told her about his conversation with Garbo and she said,

'Excellent. So if Chava Cohen confirms that Sara is the assailant, then we'll be able to confront him with that, too, during questioning.'

Chava Cohen's son and brother had been allowed to enter her room for a few moments, and he searched for them in the hope of learning whether or not she'd said something regarding the circumstances of the assault, but he didn't see them in the corridor. One of the nurses told him that they had gone to eat, and he waited. The doctors rarely went into the room, so that Chava Cohen could remain undisturbed, and from short conversations with them he understood that permission to question her could be received only once the head of the department arrived.

At eleven thirty in the morning Avraham saw Chava Cohen's brother talking on the telephone in the corridor and waited for him to finish the conversation. He, too, reported that his sister hadn't said a word, only cried. But she had recognized both of them and hugged her son when he bent down to kiss her, and this was regarded as a hopeful sign. Ma'alul called to ask if Avraham wanted him to come to the hospital, and Avraham answered that for now there was no need. In any case, he didn't know how many investigators would be permitted to enter the room during questioning.

He ate an omelette and cream cheese sandwich in the café at the entrance to the hospital. He had no doubt that in a few hours he'd be leading Sara into the interrogation room, but there was something else, too. It seemed to him that something was burning in him again. The head of the Trauma Unit arrived at two in the afternoon and, after examining Chava Cohen, gave instructions to allow her two more hours of rest, and Avraham updated Ilana about the delay. It was premature to determine her condition and what kind of serious damage, if any, she had sustained, but the preliminary examination showed that she would be able to communicate with the investigators. He smoked two cigarettes before the videography team – a cameraman and a sound recordist – arrived and began to prepare their equipment outside the room. And Ilana arrived at a quarter to five. She asked for the head of the department to be present at the interview and requested a clipboard with paper and two pencils from the nursing staff, in case Chava Cohen wasn't able to move the muscles of her mouth.

At 5.10, more than ten hours after she had regained consciousness, the department head went inside to examine Chava Cohen, after which he opened the door and signalled with his head for the investigators to enter.

Ilana entered the room first, with Avraham behind her.

The video team crowded in front of her bed and the cameraman asked for all the lights to be turned on, because the lighting was poor. Ilana sat on a chair next to Chava Cohen's bed and Avraham stood behind her, next to the IV machine she was connected to. On the other side of her bed stood the department head.

Chava Cohen's eyes were open but didn't look at him. Her mouth was open as well but didn't move. He didn't know if she noticed him, and if so, if she recognized him. Ilana bent down towards her and in a soft voice said, 'Chava, my name is Ilana Lis and I'm from the police Investigations Unit. First of all, I want to tell you that I'm very glad you've woken up. All of us were waiting for you to wake up. The doctors told me that you would be able to answer a few questions for me now about the assault. Do you feel that you can talk to me?'

The eyes didn't move, nor the mouth.

Ilana looked at the department head and he signalled for her to continue. She said, 'Chava, we found you at night between Sunday and Monday in a ditch in south Tel Aviv. Do you remember how you got there?'

Now Avraham noticed a slight movement of the head. Chava Cohen remembered. And her eyes closed. He heard the crying that the doctors had described earlier, a sort of muffled whimper that didn't emerge from the mouth, which still didn't move.

Ilana placed a hand on her mouth and waited. Soon she asked again, 'Chava, do you remember how you got into that ditch and who attacked you?' And again Chava moved her head – and again the muffled whimper could be heard. It seemed to Avraham that she was straining to raise her head off the pillow.

The department head held her arm and said, 'Chava, can you write for us on this board? You showed me before how well you can move your hand, right? Let's move it together. I'll help you.' He placed her hand on the board. Avraham didn't see the letters being slowly drawn on the sheet of paper, because Ilana hovered in front of him, only the slow movement of Chava Cohen's hand, as the department head supported her arm.

'"Uzan"? Is that what you wrote? You wrote "Uzan"?' And again the whimper was heard, this time deeper and more muffled, as if it was the moan of her entire wounded body.

Ilana turned to him. 'Does that mean anything to you? Do we know who this Uzan is?' she asked.

Avraham advanced towards the bed in order to see the letters. He wanted to be sure that that was what she wrote, and still didn't believe it. He nodded, and Ilana again faced Chava Cohen and asked, 'Chava, can you write for us here the full name?'

And Chava Cohen wrote it.

10

Everything was ready when the children woke up – except him.

In the centre of the living room stood the old suitcase and next to it the holdall that he had bought the day before, which they'd take with them on the plane. On the sofa, next to the blue cushion, which was still there, he had put the paper bag from the Bella Donna shop with the gifts inside. He spread the plane tickets out on the table like a fan. Even breakfast was ready, and on the children's plates cheese sandwiches and tomato slices had been arranged, with mugs of chocolate milk next to them.

As Chaim drank coffee facing the open window he heard stirring from their room and guessed that Shalom was awake and sitting up in his bed.

He lingered another moment in the kitchen with his coffee and listened to his son, who called out by name to Ezer, who was sleeping in the bed above him.

Even though he had seen this moment in his imagination many times over the last few days he didn't feel completely ready, mainly because of the conversation with his mother. During the conversation he had spoken firmly and aggressively rejected her arguments, but nevertheless she left him with a bitter taste in his mouth and weakened his sense of confidence. Tomorrow at this time there would be no room for hesitation. They'd already be at the airport. Would they be sitting on the plane? Maybe waiting for the announcement about the gate opening for passengers to board? He imagined himself and his children being swallowed up in the dark corridor leading to the plane. Their final day at home had been planned to the last detail.

There were, however, some details in the travel plan that Chaim still didn't know. Where would they go immediately after landing in Manila, before the hotel? Also, what would they do together in the foreign city for almost two weeks after the search for Jenny bore no fruit? At a bookstore in town he bought a travel guide for the Philippines and started reading it at night so that he'd be able to answer the questions the children would ask after he told them about the trip. If they were going for only two or three days, that would be easier. He already wanted the three of them to return and be at home. He imagined their new life without Jenny, when the children wouldn't ask him about her any more, because they'd know what had happened.

Ezer slept in his pants and had taken them off to pee, so he was completely naked when Chaim led them into the living room. Shalom was in his pyjamas. They stopped in the centre of the living room, in front of the suitcases, and Shalom asked, 'Why is there a bag here?'

Chaim said, 'You have to guess. When do you use a suitcase?' And Shalom looked at the slender body of his big brother, who said, 'When you take a trip.' Shalom was still staring at Ezer. He asked him, 'But who's taking one?' and Chaim said, 'We are. You have to guess where.'

He was surprised when they didn't succeed in guessing straight away.

When he had run through the conversation in his head the two of them knew the answer and shouted it out together.

Shalom said, 'To Grandma's?' and Chaim said, 'No. You get one more guess.'

Ezer stood silently in front of the suitcases and didn't participate in the guessing game, maybe because he still hadn't woken up entirely.

'To Aunt Adina's?'

Chaim shook his head again.

'So where are we going?' Shalom asked, and Chaim said, 'Do you want me to show you?'

If he could have banished from his mind the things his mother had said the evening before, he wouldn't have hesitated before revealing the answer to them. In their language his mother had said to him, 'Why are you lying to them and dragging them there? You can tell them here, too, that they won't be seeing her any more,' but Chaim didn't explain to her that their trip was the opposite of a lie, that they were going in order to discover the truth. Shalom jumped up and down, and Chaim thought he saw a small smile on Ezer's sealed-off face when he said to them, 'We're going to meet Mum. We're flying to her in a plane tomorrow morning.'

They were truly happy, and Chaim knew that their happiness would turn to disappointment and despair, but that was exactly what he intended. The first days would be sad but he'd cheer them up, and by the time they returned to Israel the pain would have faded. Certainly with Shalom. It would take more time for Ezer, but he too would understand. And he'd return to his father because he wouldn't have anyone else. He gave each of them a plane ticket and explained that the seats were already reserved. Ezer would sit next to the window and would be able to watch the plane take off into the sky and over the clouds and Shalom would sit next to him, between his big brother and his father. Shalom protested and said that he wanted to sit next to the window, and Chaim promised that the flight would be long and they'd be able to take turns. Ezer turned his ticket over and over and looked at the tickets remaining on the table, and Chaim said, 'There's a ticket for Mum, too. When we come back home, she'll sit next to you on the plane.'

After they had got dressed and eaten breakfast Chaim showed them what he had packed in the suitcase. He explained that it's hot in the Philippines but sometimes rains so they'd take jackets and umbrellas. Shalom tossed a plastic lion and elephant into the suitcase and Ezer placed two toy cars inside. Afterwards he showed them the packages from Bella Donna and the boys decided that Ezer would give Jenny the jeans and Shalom the shirt. He sat them at the table and placed before them the paper and markers that he had bought at the bookstore. Shalom asked, 'But what should we draw for Mum?' And Chaim said, 'Draw her pretty pictures and give them to her with the presents, so she'll be surprised.'

He sat next to them while Shalom filled the paper with thick blue lines, between which he drew a crooked square, black in colour, and he said, 'I'm drawing Mum a plane.' Ezer didn't want to draw and Chaim said to him, 'So maybe you'll write her a letter?' This was the first time he had sat like this with the children and watched them while they drew. Exactly like the young parents whom he saw at the nursery, he thought, like the father with the glasses and his son, between whom he had observed such a natural closeness. The children were excited about travelling on a plane, but perhaps also about the fact that someone was sitting next to them and watching them while they drew, which Jenny never did. How many times had he asked her to sit with them and draw? 'Do you think they'll be artists?' she once asked him, with contempt. 'They'll be like you, they'll make egg sandwiches.' He tried to teach Shalom how to draw a plane – between the blue lines of the sky he drew a long narrow shape in black, and on its side the horizontal lines of the wings and in it a row of squares that were supposed to be the windows, but Shalom was jealous of Ezer, who wrote letters on his paper. He wanted to write a letter to Jenny too. For a while Shalom drew unclear marks on the paper and pretended that they were words, and when he gave up he asked Chaim to write for him and Chaim added in red at the edge of the page, *Dear Mum, This is the plane we're flying to you in after so long*, and signed the boy's name.

Ezer continued writing large letters, slow and focused, and he refused to show his father or brother what he was writing. Chaim suddenly thought that when they returned from Manila he'd sign him up for a drawing class after school, or, if Ezer preferred, a writing class – regardless of the cost. He asked him, 'Ezer, do your friends at school take classes after school?' and Ezer nodded. 'Maybe you'll take one too when we get back from the flight. Would you like to?'

Before noon he left them alone in the apartment for a few minutes and went down to buy minced beef. He made spaghetti bolognese and Shalom ran to him in the kitchen every few minutes and showed him another drawing.

The quietest hours on that last day before the trip were in the afternoon.

He put Shalom down for a nap in his bed and afterwards returned to the living room and sat on the couch next to Ezer, who was quietly watching cartoons. He placed his hand on the boy's head and Ezer moved his body closer to him and let his head fall onto his father's shoulder. The distress that the conversation with his mother had left in him gradually disappeared. He knew he was doing the right thing for them, even if no one would understand it, not even his mother. The proof was this morning, these hours, which he knew he would never forget. He never had felt a greater closeness to his children; neither had they been so calm in a long time. Ezer no longer had a need for another, imaginary, father, and his sitting up close next to him was calm, like when he was a baby, before he had drawn away from him because of Jenny and the things she had said about him.

He asked Ezer if he could read him a story, and when Ezer nodded yes, Chaim went to their room and brought back the book about the boy who walks in his sleep. He turned off the television and read aloud to him, as he had done a few days earlier, but this time, without planning to in advance, he changed the story's plot. His son raised his dark eyes and looked at him when he changed the name of the story's protagonist from Itamar to Ezer – and afterwards his look was full of surprise when Chaim told of how Ezer gets up while sleeping and walks on the walls of the room and enters a picture hanging on one of the walls that has a colourful aeroplane painted on it. In the story Chaim made up, the boy flies with his father and his brother in order to find his mother who has disappeared inside another picture hanging on the wall in a distant country.

Chaim felt Ezer's warm breath on his shoulder as he approached the end of the story and understood that he had fallen asleep.

The boy didn't find his mother in Chaim's story, but he found his father, who had been searching for him.

That was exactly what he felt, without formulating the words in his head, that for the first time he himself was entering the picture of his life and crafting his own story. So many times he felt his fate wasn't in his hands, but this time it was different. And when they returned from Manila the children's lives would also be new – they'd be painless.

He waited for Ezer's sleep to deepen before carefully getting up and letting his sleeping body gently settle onto the sofa. Afterwards he removed a clean sheet of paper from the pack of drawing paper that he'd bought for the boys and a pen from a drawer in the living room and went to the kitchen to write the letter that Jenny had left for them.

What would his mother say about this if she knew?

A day earlier, when he had gone to pick up the boys from her house, he had told her that they'd be flying to the Philippines for two weeks, ostensibly to be with Jenny and return with her to Israel, and that the plan was that they wouldn't find her and would return by themselves. Before this she only knew that they were taking a trip in order to avoid the police investigation. His mother looked at him and said, 'Why there?' And he wasn't able to explain because of what he'd told her about Jenny's death, and because he knew that she wouldn't understand. He said only, 'This is how they'll have their farewell from her,' and she looked at him without understanding and said, 'It would be better for them not to have a farewell like that. You'll destroy them.' He had kept quiet, not intending to answer her, but she continued doubting him and undermining his confidence. For a moment he had thought that she was simply afraid that on their trip the boys would see children who looked like them and would think that their place was in fact there. His mother said, 'The police haven't called you again for more questioning, so enough, enough with the trip. It might be that they found who did it. A farewell like you're talking about isn't good for them,' and he had exploded because of her stubbornness and the firm tone in which she had spoken to him and screamed, 'Again you're telling me what to do? You know better than me what's good for them?'

She didn't know that according to his plan the children would think Jenny would be waiting for them at the airport in Manila and that this was intended to be the first disappointment.

They'd come out to the greeting area at the airport and look for her.

He'd tell them that she must be running late or got confused about the time of their landing, and then they'd wait at the airport for a long time, and in the meantime maybe they'd buy something to drink or eat if they were hungry. Afterwards they'd go to the house where she supposedly lived and he'd call her on the way and there'd be no answer, and even when they arrived there she wouldn't answer. They'd wait, helpless, in front of some random house, and finally they'd take a cab to a hotel and stay there until they could figure out why she hadn't come to greet them at the airport and why she wasn't waiting for them at the house, and he'd continue calling Jenny from there but she would continue not answering and Chaim wouldn't understand why. The next day they'd return to the house Jenny was living in and again she wouldn't be there but she'd leave a letter for them. That was one possibility, and there was another possibility: that the letter wouldn't be there but instead would be sent to them at the hotel.

When the children had said goodbye to his mother, still not knowing they were taking a trip, or where to, Chaim didn't even say goodbye to her. He had waited outside the house, on the cement path that he had paved, while she hugged and kissed them in the doorway. She cried and tried to hide her crying, but Shalom asked, 'Grandma, why do you have tears in your eyes?'

And she had said what she had always said to Chaim when he was little: 'Because I was cutting onions.'

He worked on Jenny's farewell letter in the kitchen for a long time.

He stared at the words he had written and then went to the bedroom and buried the letter in the suitcase and again opened Jenny's drawers, and for some reason removed the pictures of the wedding in Cyprus and the letters her sister had written from Berlin and looked at the cramped handwriting on the lines of the pink paper, full of hearts and exclamation marks.

Suddenly an idea popped into in his head: the house they'd go to from the airport where Jenny was supposedly staying – which they'd stand in front of, making pointless phone calls – wouldn't have to be a random house in Manila. They could go to the house where Jenny had grown up. He remembered that she had said once, at dinner with his mother and sister and her husband, that she'd grown up in a poor quarter of Manila that made Holon look like New York City by comparison. Chaim was pretty sure that the name of the quarter was Tondu, because she mentioned it another time as well. The building she had lived in with her family was close to the train station where her father was a steward. Her mother worked in a laundry. And he also remembered that a few times she'd said the name

Tutuban – maybe this was the name of the street she'd lived on as a child. Maybe he could find the address in one of her documents, he thought. He imagined the three of them standing in front of the station and saying goodbye to Jenny without her being there. A shudder passed through him, because he understood that they were travelling to Manila in order to perform a funeral of sorts for her, and again he realized just how fitting his plan was. Jenny hadn't had a funeral, and never would. He had buried her at night, by himself, in great haste, and done everything he could not to look at the body. Even his mother hadn't been with him. If he could succeed in finding the station and the street she'd grown up on, and if they went there to say farewell to her, that would be a sort of reburial. He thought how something had changed in their lives even before they went – ever since he had conceived the plan and began to execute it. The police inspector hadn't contacted him, and Ezer had drawn closer to him and trusted him and put his head on his shoulder, as if all the insults the child had heard Jenny hurl at him, because of which his image had been so diminished in his eyes, had been erased. He burrowed into the drawer, searching for Jenny's Philippines identity card but couldn't recall if he had ever seen it. Afterwards he opened the rest of the drawers and got distracted, because for a moment it seemed to him that Ezer's passport was missing. His and Shalom's passports were in the documents drawer but Ezer's wasn't there, and he tried to remember if he had removed it in order to check if it was still valid or if he'd taken it to the travel agency. That was the only thing that bothered him throughout the afternoon, but he didn't say anything to the children because he was convinced he hadn't lost the passport, and indeed, after they woke up, he discovered it on the sofa in the living room, hidden under the blue cushion, of all places.

The afternoon was peaceful as well, even though the boys fought and Shalom cried because he'd changed his mind and wanted to give Jenny the jeans and for Ezer to give her the shirt. In the end, Ezer agreed and they attached the drawings they had made and the letters to the presents' packaging with pins, and put the paper bag into the suitcase and closed it. In the holdall they'd take with them onto the plane they put two bags of crisps and colouring books and wet wipes and a change of clothes. Chaim said he'd spoken to Jenny at noon, when they were sleeping, and that she'd be waiting for them at the airport. Shalom asked to speak to her in order to tell her what he had drawn and he said that in the country where she is it's late and she's sleeping, but despite this he tried calling. They ate an early dinner and showered, and afterwards together chose the clothes they'd wear tomorrow and arranged them on the chair in their room. At seven in the evening the two of them were already in bed and Chaim explained that tomorrow he'd wake them up even before the sun was out because the cab that was going to take them to the airport would be waiting outside their place at five. A long time passed before they fell asleep. He sat next to their beds in silence and waited for them to close their eyes, and recalled that only a few days earlier he had been scared that they'd ask him why Mum didn't put them to sleep like always. Now they no longer asked why only he put them to bed each night, and he was certain that when they returned they'd never ask him again.

When he was cleaning the kitchen for the last time the phone rang. It was a little after 8 p.m.

He had no doubt it was his mother, but he thought she was only calling to say goodbye. She said, 'Are you watching the news?' And when he answered that he wasn't she said, 'Turn on channel two.'

His hands were wet and he wiped them on a kitchen towel before turning on the television, and immediately turned down the volume – and was astounded.

There was no longer any investigation that he needed to flee from.

On the screen he saw a man and a woman, their hands bound in handcuffs, getting out of a police car, and policemen in civilian clothes leading them into the courthouse. He didn't see their faces because the woman lowered her hood-covered head and the man had lifted his shirt and stretched it up over his face. Because he missed the beginning of the story he didn't hear the names of those arrested but understood that the two of them had been caught that afternoon in Eilat after a chase, and that they were suspected of the assault on and attempted murder of Chava Cohen. The assault, which was made public only that evening, had occurred in Tel Aviv late on Sunday night, and Chava Cohen was still in Wolfson Hospital, in a critical condition, but her injuries were no longer life-threatening. 'The teacher's brutal assault was preceded by the placing of a fake bomb, threats, and efforts at extortion,' said the news announcer over images from the courthouse, 'apparently as a result of the firing of the woman, whose spouse is a criminal known to the police.'

Chaim closed the door to the children's room.

Sunday night had been the night he had spoken to Chava Cohen. He had called her numerous times, and she had answered him a little before midnight – at least that was what he remembered. A short time after that she had been attacked.

Even though he was supposed to feel relief, the images of the man and woman whose faces were hidden chilled him.

He could have been in their place.

The thought he had at the sight of those first images returned to him: there's no more investigation. Had the nursery been closed since Monday? He didn't really know. He hadn't been summoned for additional questioning, apparently because the identity of Chava Cohen's assailants had soon become clear, and it must also have become clear that they had placed the suitcase next to the nursery. He didn't see the detective who had brought him in for questioning at the station among the police surrounding the arrested couple. The telephone rang again and he knew what his mother would say. 'Did you see?' she asked him, and he only said, 'Yes.' Nevertheless, he didn't for a moment think about cancelling the trip. On the contrary, he was sorry that they weren't at the airport yet. The two of them were quiet before his mother asked, 'Do you know them?' and he said, 'How would I know them?' He was tense and waited for her to suggest that he give up the trip, because they had nothing to flee from, and he stopped her right away when she said it. 'Enough. I explained to you that we're going for them to have a farewell,' he said for the last time.

'But what farewell? And I'm scared about you travelling on Yom Kippur. It's bad luck. It's forbidden to travel on Yom Kippur, Chaim – at least wait a few more days. Nothing will happen if you wait.'

He didn't respond to these words. He finished the conversation and returned to the kitchen in order to continue cleaning. Packed toiletries up in a black cloth bag and remembered to take some towels. At eleven thirty, less than ten hours before their flight, he called Golden Cabs and ordered a car to Ben-Gurion Airport for five in the morning. Afterwards he opened the door to the boys' room and made sure that the two of them were sleeping.

The nights were already cooler, and Ezer slept shirtless and held the thin blanket close to his body. Once they returned, he'd switch their summer blankets for warmer ones, he thought.

He made sure for the last time that the passports and plane tickets were in the right place, next to his wallet, and turned off all the lights in the apartment.

11

The quick arrest of Amos Uzan and Ilanit Hadad was the result of the combined efforts of the Tel Aviv district's detectives under the leadership of the head of the Investigations and Intelligence Units, Commander Ilana Lis, and the Eilat Regional Police.

Immediately after questioning Chava Cohen in her room at the hospital, Ilana had convened a meeting of the investigation team in an office provided for them in the Trauma Unit. Eliyahu Ma'alul and Lior Zaytuni were called in from their homes. At this stage all they had were two names, written in pencil by an injured hand with the help of the head of the Trauma Unit: *Amos Uzan*, the name that Chava Cohen had written first, and *Ilanit Hadad*, which she had added after the questions that Ilana had asked at Avraham's request. He felt as if someone had struck him forcefully in the chest when he saw the name Amos Uzan, the suspect who had been released at the start of the investigation, on the sheet of paper lying before Chava Cohen, but he still believed that Chaim Sara was involved in the attack and wanted Ilana to ask the injured woman directly about this. Ilana refused but asked Chava Cohen if additional people were involved in the assault, and after repeating the question a few times she had written the second name.

Avraham was forced to say yes again. He was familiar with the second name as well.

And the second name told an entirely different story of the assault than the one Avraham had told himself. Yes, he had been correct when he assumed that a man and a woman were involved in the assault, and also correct in the assumption that the teacher knew her assailants. But Sara was apparently not the man who had placed the suitcase with the fake bomb next to the nursery, or the man who had waited for Chava Cohen near a car park in south Tel Aviv and struck her on the head. Ilana asked Chava Cohen twice if she could say why she was attacked and she moved her head from side to side on the pillow. The weak crying stopped and her eyes closed, and the chief of the Trauma Unit said, 'You've got what you wanted. Please turn off the cameras and the lights and let her rest.'

Upon leaving the room, Ilana said to him, 'So tell me who those two are,' and Avraham told her.

Ilana stopped in the corridor and turned to him, and he stopped opposite her.

So you're telling me that he was in your custody before the assault and was released? And that you didn't question her at all even though you knew that Chava Cohen fired her? These were the words he read in her eyes, but she didn't say anything. She continued walking. He explained that he'd had no choice but to release Uzan from custody. He had presented Chava Cohen with his picture and she claimed that she'd never seen him before. And Avraham didn't know about the connection between Uzan and the assistant who had been fired from her job a week before the start of the year. He had tried to call the assistant in for questioning but was told that she was away.

'And that's it? She was away? So nothing could be done?' This sentence Ilana said quietly, as if in despair.

But what could have been done? The detectives had trailed Uzan for a few days and they then were needed on other assignments. And after the assault, Sara had obviously become the primary suspect and drawn most of his attention. He didn't mention Sara during their short conversation even though he couldn't get him out of his mind, because it wasn't the right moment. For a few minutes he followed Ilana through the corridors of the hospital while she looked for an available room, and afterwards, even while she spoke on the phone, until she asked him, 'Avi, please give me a few minutes,' and disappeared into the office provided for them.

Avraham left the hospital to smoke.

It was seven in the evening and darkness had fallen, and he knew that tonight would be another night without sleep. From a distance he saw Ma'alul step off a bus and walk towards the hospital, wearing the grey windbreaker he had worn at the start of the summer, during the investigation into the disappearance of Ofer Sharabi. What took place inside him was strange and inexplicable: he certainly understood that he had made a mistake in this investigation as well, but nevertheless he wasn't weakened. He felt some embarrassment over Uzan's early release, but also an inner certainty that precisely because the assault case was close to being solved he would be able to concentrate on the real case, the case that no one besides him had yet identified. Less than thirty-six hours remained to arrest Chaim Sara before he'd get on a plane and escape to Manila with his children, but now he no longer had a reason to arrest him.

And something again burned inside him, exactly like before.

Even though she didn't announce it explicitly, from that moment on, Ilana managed the investigation herself. She updated Ma'alul and Zaytuni about the results of the questioning in the hospital and determined the sequence of pressing investigative activities that the three of them would carry out. Even though the chance had been slim that Uzan was waiting at home for the police to come, Zaytuni was sent there with officers from a Special Operations Unit and would be left there to perform a thorough search of the empty apartment. The model and licence-plate number of Uzan's car were broadcast to all mobile units and traffic police throughout Israel. Ma'alul was sent to question Uzan's mother, who was three floors away, in the hospital's Oncology Department. She didn't know where her son was and only said that on Sunday, the evening of the attack, he had informed her that he wouldn't be visiting her for a few days because of issues at work. The week before he had come to visit her almost every day with his girlfriend. This, then, was their meeting place, and the reason that the investigation team hadn't discovered the tie between Uzan and Ilanit Hadad. They met at the hospital, in the mother's room, where they arrived separately, and which they left separately. Avraham was thrown the task of investigating the family of the fired assistant, and he left in his car for their house without informing them of his visit in advance. The parents were surprised by his visit but co-operated, because he minimized the importance of their daughter's involvement in the assault and focused on Uzan.

The first time he mentioned Uzan's name Avraham already understood that this was a sensitive subject.

The parents lived in one of the towers that were crowded together in Kiryat Ben-Gurion. The lift didn't work so he walked up to the sixth floor. They were eating dinner when he arrived and invited him to sit by the table located between the kitchen and the living room, on which were a loaf of bread, a bowl of salad and a cup filled with sour cream. Ilanit Hadad's sister, with whom he had spoken over the phone a few days earlier, wasn't there, and the father, in his early fifties, though he looked much older, went into the bedroom and got dressed.

He had come to question them with regard to the assault of a person whose name he was not able to reveal at this time, he said.

Amos Uzan was suspected of involvement in the assault and, according to information that had reached the police, there was a romantic tie between him and their daughter. He wanted to know when had they last seen Uzan or heard from their daughter of his whereabouts, because according to suspicions Uzan had fled and the police were hoping to arrest him for questioning.

The mother broke out crying even before he had finished speaking.

She was also in her fifties, but looked much younger than the father. She wore black tights, a white sports shirt and trainers, and Avraham assumed she had just returned from a health club or a Pilates lesson. She said, 'Ever since the day she met him she hasn't been the same girl. You don't know how much we tried to convince her to break it off with him. Ilanit's a good girl, she's not involved in anything, but when they met I lost my girl.' The father's participation in the conversation was minimal. He placed his hand on his wife's shoulder while she spoke.

Avraham asked the mother in a soft voice, 'Where is Ilanit now?' and she said to him, 'I swear to you I don't know. She hasn't been home for four days and hasn't called. She said she's going away with him to see some friends but didn't want to tell me where.' She had taken her mobile with her but it was turned off and they hadn't managed to reach her, and she hadn't responded to their text messages. Avraham sought to deepen her fear for her daughter's fate when he said, 'You're correct that Uzan is a dangerous person, and this is an additional reason why we want to locate him and Ilanit as soon as possible,' at which she broke down and explained to him that after Ilanit had visited them at their home and told them about the trip, she had discovered that one of her credit cards was missing. She suspected that Ilanit had taken it out of her wallet, and when she checked with the credit-card company they informed her that it had been used at a supermarket in Eilat. She hadn't cancelled the card.

Avraham still had not revealed to her that the victim of the assault was Chava Cohen. He asked her to tell him about Ilanit.

She was twenty-three years old, born in February 1990, and before she had met Uzan, the previous winter, she had still lived at home. Since then she had slept at his place, sometimes for weeks straight, and returned home only when they fought or when Uzan was away. She hadn't been accepted for active service in the army because she had a birth defect in her leg, a slight disability, but she had volunteered and served in the Education Force as a teacher. After she was discharged she started studying early-childhood education and worked at nurseries, but suddenly ended her studies, under Uzan's influence, and only informed her parents of this after the fact. She hadn't kept in contact with most of her friends from high school or the army, and she didn't speak about her relationship with Uzan. She had met him at a club, and he was her first serious boyfriend. They didn't know who her friends were now, and hoped that she wasn't using drugs. And mainly feared that Uzan would get her pregnant. Avraham didn't hold back and asked, 'And where does Ilanit work now?'

And the mother said to him, 'She's not working. They fired her from a nursery just before the start of the year.'

He asked her why her daughter had been fired and she didn't know.

Before leaving, he asked to see Ilanit's room, and the mother led him down a short hallway and turned on the light in an almost empty room.

Avraham entered but didn't know what to look for.

There were no sheets on the bed, and the writing desk was devoid of papers and books. Apart from these things there was only a television, hanging off a metal arm, and a wardrobe, and the mother said, 'We kept the room for her, but she took almost all her things.' Afterwards he asked for a photograph of Ilanit and the mother took a picture off the refrigerator in which Ilanit was in uniform holding an M16 rifle. It had been taken during basic training, she said. He felt an uneasiness, because he hadn't revealed to them that their daughter was also a suspect in the assault and that she would be arrested as soon as she was found, but he couldn't have acted otherwise. The mother promised to inform him if Ilanit contacted them, and wrote down on his notepad the number of the credit card that had been stolen.

Upon leaving the neighbourhood Avraham stopped his car and called Ilana.

'They're in Eilat,' he said to her, and she asked, 'How do you know?'

He told her briefly about the conversation. Ilana said that she herself would update the Southern District, and he added,

'We need to inform the terminal in Taba so that they won't cross the border into the Sinai.'

'And do you understand better now what happened there?'

'No. Her parents have no idea why she was fired and they don't know anything about the assault.'

She asked what he planned to do and he said that he would return to the station in order to scan the picture and pass it on to the Eilat police, and would wait for updates. He carried out all the urgent investigative activities, and even succeeded in tracking down the suspects, but the feeling that he was wasting time on the wrong case wouldn't let go of him. Uzan and his girlfriend hadn't been caught yet, but the case was as good as closed and he hadn't dealt with the burning investigation, though time was running out. At 10 p.m., from his office, he called the detective overseeing the surveillance of Chaim Sara and heard that the suspect had driven to his mother's that afternoon and brought his children home. But he was no longer a suspect, and Avraham should have ordered the tracking to be taken off him. He did not do this.

Did Sara's children know where their mother was?

Sara had told him during questioning that his wife had flown to the Philippines in order to take care of her father, but she wasn't in the Philippines and her father had died years ago. And if he wasn't involved in the placing of the bomb or the attack, why had he lied? And why was he travelling with his children to the place where he said his wife was even though she wasn't there?

He didn't know anything about Sara's children, just that one was seven years old and the other was three and went to Chava Cohen's nursery on Lavon Street. He didn't even know their names. Did they know where they were flying to on Friday morning? He wanted to see them, and it seemed to him that if he looked at them, he'd understand something he hadn't understood until now. He could simply knock on Sara's door and ask, 'Why did you lie about your wife and her whereabouts?' He could also have called Ilana and asked for permission to continue the investigation, but he decided it was better to wait.

In the meantime he opened the email that he received from Anselmo Garbo and read that Jennifer Salazar had been born in Manila in September 1970.

At the top of the brief report, the logo of the Philippines police was displayed: a sun of sorts inside which was a man with a club in his hand.

Jennifer Salazar did not have a criminal record and had never been investigated by the police. When she was twenty she had got married, but her marriage to Julius Andreda lasted only four years. In 2002 she had travelled to Israel for the first time and stayed there for a year, and after an additional period of time in Manila returned to Israel. The last time she had entered the Philippines was on 11 July 2005, and she had left two weeks later. According to Garbo's report, Jennifer Salazar did not have children, apparently because she hadn't informed the authorities in Manila about the birth of her sons in Israel, just as she hadn't informed them about her marriage to Sara. And since 2004 she hadn't paid income tax in the Philippines.

Avraham looked at the old picture that was attached to the report and had been taken more than twenty years ago.

Jennifer Salazar's hair was long and black and her face was wide. It seemed to him that he saw a mole under her lower lip. He tried to imagine the young Filipina woman in the company of Sara and was unable to – perhaps because in the picture she was so many years younger than he was.

A little before midnight Avraham received a final report from the credit-card company: two hours earlier the card stolen from Ilanit Hadad's mother had been used again, at a restaurant on Seagulls' Beach in the tourist section of Eilat. They had indeed fled to Eilat, but other than that it seemed they were doing everything possible in order to get caught, and Avraham recalled Uzan's smugness during the interrogation, the constant smile below his well-groomed moustache. Uzan was simply too arrogant. He had joined those gathered around the suspicious suitcase next to the nursery, taken off running from the beat policeman who had asked him to identify himself, waited patiently long hours in the interrogation room, and hadn't revealed any fear. While he had sat in the police station, Ilanit Hadad had called the nursery she had been fired from and declared that the suitcase was 'just the beginning'. And all that time the smile had barely left his face.

When Avraham was on his way to the station again, the following morning, after a short sleep at home, he was informed that Uzan's black Honda had been identified on Barnea Street in Eilat.

Uzan continued being reckless. At the restaurant where he paid with the stolen credit card he spent time in the company of Ilanit Hadad and two male friends, one of whom was known to the police. Eilat district detectives had discovered this after a short questioning of the restaurant's owner, and before morning, when they arrived at the building where the man known to the police resided, in the Palm neighbourhood, they had discovered Uzan's Honda. It wasn't even covered up. Did his smugness stem from his certainty that Chava Cohen wouldn't regain consciousness? Maybe he was also convinced that even if she did wake up, she wouldn't reveal her assailants, just as she had lied in the matter of the suitcase. Something about the violent connection between Chava Cohen and her assailants wasn't clear to Avraham, but that morning, word from the hospital had come that she still couldn't be interrogated. He had hoped that the arrest would be carried out soon, mainly because he wanted to speak with Ilana about Sara and his wife and thought that after Uzan and his girlfriend were caught she would be available to listen to him, but the Eilat detectives didn't break into the apartment immediately because they didn't know how many people were staying there and if they were armed.

In the meantime, Avraham called the border police to ask the question that wouldn't let him go during the night, before he had fallen asleep: 'Is it possible that Jennifer Salazar didn't leave Israel, even though on the police computers there appears an exit registration?' The clerk was adamant. She said that 'There's no way that's possible,' but afterwards added that entry and exit records were also maintained by the Population and Immigration Authority of the Ministry of the Interior and that he should check there as well.

A clock ticked inside him, like the clock that had been lying inside the suitcase found next to the nursery.

Though in his imagination it was a stopwatch and was connected to the picture of Jennifer Salazar that he had seen last night, and to Sara's face, and to the plane that was getting ready to take off for Manila tomorrow with Sara and his two children.

Ma'alul had come into his office in order to get an update on what had happened in Eilat and just then Ilana had called to tell him that Uzan had left the apartment on Barnea Street, accompanied by Ilanit Hadad. The district detectives had driven after him in their Citroën, and when they got onto Highway

90 leaving the city, three mobile units blocked the way after the Eilat Interchange. At eleven Ilana had called again to announce that the hunt was over. Uzan had tried to turn the car around and flee when he saw the police barricade but was caught after a short chase.

'That was quick. We did great work,' Ilana said, and Avraham asked, 'Can I come and see you in an hour?'

She had asked if he wanted to talk about the next step in the investigation and he'd said yes, though that wasn't what he wanted.

And Ilana looked at him with amazement, like the day before in the corridor of the hospital, when he told her why he had come. She was eating a salad when he entered her office. The family picture with her husband and children again wasn't in its place on the desk and the wall clock was resting at an angle on the floor. Her mood was improved, perhaps because of the quick arrest, before Avraham told her that he wanted to arrest Sara and bring him in for urgent questioning.

'Arrest him for what, Avi? We arrested the assailants two hours ago. And there's already a match between Uzan's fingerprints and prints we found at the scene. What do you want to question Sara about?'

He'd known this was what she'd ask, and he didn't have a clear answer.

He wanted to question him because the stopwatch connected in his imagination to the picture of Jennifer Salazar was ticking fast and because Sara had lied to him during questioning. And also because he couldn't succeed in resolving the contradiction between the exit registration and the report Garbo had sent him, according to which Jennifer Salazar hadn't entered the Philippines since her brief visit there in 2005. And perhaps mainly he wanted to interrogate him because he couldn't bear the thought that tomorrow Sara would get on a plane to Manila with his children before he could manage to find out what he was hiding and why.

Ilana ate the salad from a red plastic container and listened to him. At the beginning of their conversation she was still patient. She said, 'It's impossible to arrest him because he lied to you during questioning, Avi. He's not a suspect at present for any crime, and besides that, I'm considering sending you to Eilat to interrogate Uzan and Ilanit Hadad. They're keeping silent and you know the story better than anyone else – maybe you can get something out of them. Or at least out of her.' She stopped and examined the surprised look on his face, then added, 'I also want the resolution of this case to be in your name. From beginning to end. And it still isn't closed. We don't know what the motive was for the assault, and why Chava Cohen hid the fact that Uzan and his girlfriend placed the fake bomb, or why she agreed to meet them. Do you remember that we said we'd close the case before Yom Kippur? We're almost there. And I want this victory to be all yours.'

He had no intention of flying to Eilat. Or of interrogating anyone other than Sara, at least until he had clarified where Sara's wife was. And the 'victory' in the assault case didn't interest him.

'What do I need to fly to Eilat for?' he asked. If he could succeed in persuading Ilana that he was focused on the assault investigation but that he had a few spare hours, maybe she'd agree to allow him to question Sara, he thought suddenly. He said to her, 'Why don't we bring them here? And you know what? If they don't talk and we want to get a confession out of them, despite the fact that we have enough evidence, we could use the accident trick on them on the way from Eilat,' and she looked at him and smiled.

'That's not a bad idea. Is it possible Uzan doesn't know about it?'

Ilanit Hadad definitely didn't know about it.

And it was possible to change the trick a bit: to switch it from an accident trick to an infiltration trick, for example.

Ilana picked up the phone but didn't dial.

It was necessary to give Uzan and his girlfriend the feeling that the police in Eilat didn't know what to do with them. To extend their arrest in Eilat and tell them that they were not being interrogated because enough evidence had accumulated against them regardless – but that they wouldn't see any detectives until after Yom Kippur. On Sunday morning they would be put in separate police cars and transported to Tel Aviv, and then the trick would be pulled on them on the way. Ilana spoke to the commander of the Southern District Investigations Unit and Avraham waited. She asked him for a cigarette during her conversation and he lit one for himself as well. He tried to sound relaxed when he said to her, 'So I don't have anything to do until after Yom Kippur, right? It's impossible to question Chava Cohen. Does that mean you're authorizing me to bring Sara in for questioning?'

But she again refused.

She said to him, 'When you're capable of explaining to me what crime you suspect him of and what you want to question him about, we can talk again,' and he responded without thinking, perhaps because of the things said in his phone conversation with Garbo, 'Suspicion in his wife's absence. Is that a good enough reason?'

Ilana was no longer smiling.

She said to him, 'No one submitted a complaint about an

absence,' and put out her cigarette, and Avraham added, 'Ilana, I have a feeling he's going to harm his children.'

Did he understand what he said and how she was interpreting his words? Perhaps he did, because he didn't say anything else. They were silent for a few moments, and finally Ilana said, 'I'm not letting you do this, Avi. I think we both understand what's happening here, and I won't be a party to it.'

'Be a party to what?'

'To the fact that you're inventing another missing-persons case in order to make amends for what happened to you with Ofer Sharabi. You know full well that this is what you're doing, I see it in your eyes. Maybe I shouldn't have sent you the report I wrote. Yes, you're inventing another missing-persons case and another father who's going to harm his children in order to make amends for what you may have done wrong back then. But Sara isn't Ofer's father, and his children aren't Ofer. There's no saving Ofer, you understand that, don't you?'

The ticking of the stopwatch paused for a moment when she fell silent.

There was quiet in the room.

Was Ilana correct when she said he was aware of the connection between the two investigations? He said, 'That's not what I'm doing, Ilana. I'm not trying to save Ofer Sharabi. I'm trying to save these children.'

'But save them from what? From a trip to see Mum in the Philippines? Have you considered the fact that Sara didn't lie to you during questioning? Because of your prior investigation you're completely unable to comprehend that this, too, is a possibility.'

He didn't understand what she was saying. Sara had lied about the place his wife had supposedly travelled to.

'No, Avi, it's possible he didn't lie. It's possible she lied to him and he has no idea. You didn't consider that possibility? Maybe she told him that she was travelling to the Philippines to take care of her parents and in fact she went to a different place in order to meet her lover? That's a very possible scenario, and much more likely, no? That way you have an exit registration but you don't have an entrance registration to the Philippines. And she's a grown-up, it's her right to lie to her husband – agreed? She's even allowed to lie to her children. That's still not a violation of the law.'

He looked at her, stunned.

She was correct when she had guessed that this possibility hadn't occurred to him at all.

Was Sara simply in the dark about his wife?

And why should that possibility occur to her, while he himself never gave it a thought? He recalled the private Hotmail account – *rebeccajones21* – from which Ilana had sent him the report. And thought about the family picture that had lately disappeared. Had she, too, lied to her husband and children and gone to an assignation when she told them that she was at work? And was this what she wanted to reveal to him when she said she had to tell him something before he heard about it from others? This was the first time Marianka appeared in his thoughts all day, but he pushed her away. He said, 'No, I hadn't thought about that, Ilana, and you could well be right. But there's the possibility you're mistaken and something else has happened.'

'What, for example?'

He had no intention of telling her everything that he thought had happened, because he knew how she'd take his words.

*

When Avraham left her office, after 2 p.m., it was without Ilana's approval to question Chaim Sara. And he didn't know how to proceed. He called Marianka again and again, but she didn't answer. He ate lunch in a Persian restaurant near the market and prolonged his time there because he had no reason to hurry. Amos Uzan and Ilanit Hadad's detention had already been extended for a week by the court in Eilat, and according to the plan, they wouldn't reach Tel Aviv until Sunday. The stopwatch again ticked in his thoughts, but because of his conversation with Ilana, the pictures the ticking evoked were switched and he saw before him not Jennifer Salazar's young face but instead other faces, faces he'd hoped to avoid. Had he not succeeded in conducting the investigation with open eyes and truly seen what was happening? He felt this was exactly what he had done. Sadly, he thought that he had no one else to consult with, not even Ma'alul. Only a few hours remained before nightfall, and then it would be too late.

Tomorrow would be Yom Kippur eve.

He thought about the streets emptied of people, and afterwards about the phone conversation with Brigadier General Anselmo Garbo. The Filipino detective who had impressed him with his sharpness had asked Avraham to keep him updated as the investigation continued.

Perhaps he could ask Garbo to arrest Sara and question him himself when he landed with his children in Manila. Maybe that was his only option. But would the illustrious detective agree to question Sara?

If he didn't find a pretext for questioning Sara by the evening he would have no choice but to call Garbo and inform him that Sara was on his way to him.

12

It was only in the departure hall that their trip became real, and for a moment Chaim was struck with fear at the sight of the masses of people and suitcases and luggage trolleys.

Terminal 3 was more crowded than he had expected.

The last time he was here was when he flew to Cyprus with Jenny. Back then the terminal was almost completely empty, maybe because winter had already begun, and that was likely why he was surprised by the sight of long queues winding everywhere in the hall that morning. He instructed Ezer and Shalom to hold on to the luggage trolley so they wouldn't get lost, because they looked confused at the entrance to the giant hall bathed in light. Shalom had already cried that he wanted to go home.

In the days following, Chaim often thought about that moment at the entrance to the airport. True, he quickly suppressed his weakness and began searching for the Korean Air counter, but wasn't there a shred of hope in him that a higher power might cancel their trip? Perhaps he even wanted to tell his story, though maybe not just yet. On the departures board suspended from the hall's ceiling he saw that flight KE 958 hadn't been cancelled and that the plane would leave at its appointed time.

What else would Chaim remember from that morning? The clothes the children wore. The silence in the dark streets during the drive to the airport. And Ezer.

His son was different that day, and Chaim noticed it, even though he was focused on his tasks. He thought that the closeness between them created the day before was probably a part of it. As if Ezer had matured a good few years within that twenty-four hours. He was still quiet and cautious, but he tried to help Chaim and handled his younger brother with an adult sense of responsibility. He swiftly got out of bed when Chaim woke them, at four fifteen in the morning, and was alert and purposeful, as if he had been up for a while. He immediately took off his white pyjama bottoms and pulled over his thin body the clothes that were seared into his father's memory: the red pants and the tracksuit bottoms and the knitted top with the picture of the boat that Jenny had bought him for his birthday.

Manila was still far off, and the way there would be complicated by small tasks that came one on the heels of another. Waking the kids and getting them dressed. Taking them and the suitcases downstairs and into the taxi. Making sure that all the windows were closed and disconnecting the gas tap. Not forgetting anything at home. Arriving safely and on time at the airport.

Not forgetting anything at home.

The taxi driver showed up at three minutes to five.

Ezer stood next to the big window and looked out through the blinds when the telephone rang and a number Chaim didn't recognize appeared on the screen. The driver said to him, 'Good morning,' and he turned to the children and said, 'Let's go, Ezer, the cab's here,' and Ezer turned around and in an excited voice said, 'I see it down there.' Chaim carried the suitcase and placed it outside the apartment, and Ezer insisted that he'd manage to drag the large holdall down the stairs by himself.

When he closed the door for the last time he didn't notice the dark living room shrinking before him or his own fingers turning the key in the lock with a quick and natural motion. The light in the stairwell went off and he turned it on and saw Ezer hauling the holdall down the stairs.

When they got out to the street, Ezer wanted to put the bag into the taxi's boot himself and afterwards lifted Shalom into the back seat and put on his and his brother's seatbelts at the request of the driver.

There was almost no traffic in the streets.

When the cab passed Lavon Street, Chaim recalled the morning when they had discovered that a suitcase with a bomb inside had been placed next to Shalom's nursery. Their trip to Manila had actually begun then, even though they hadn't known it. Were it not for the man and the woman who were arrested yesterday in Eilat and brought to the courthouse with their faces covered they wouldn't be on the way to the airport now. The radio in the cab was on and the five o'clock news was being broadcast when the driver asked, 'Do you mind the window being open? Is it too windy?' Afterwards he asked them where they were travelling to. He was younger than Chaim, maybe forty-five or fifty, but he looked like an entirely different kind of person. His right ear, the one closer to Chaim, was reddish and swollen and in the thick lobe was a small, golden earring. Chaim said that they were flying to the Philippines, and the driver said, 'Never been. First time?' And he said that they were going to see his wife, who'd been in Manila for a few weeks with family and would return with them, and the driver said, 'Ah, so that's why your children are like that. Smart move. I almost got married to a Russian woman about six months ago but changed my mind at the last moment.

Twenty years I was married.' On the highway a southbound train raced alongside them in the opposite direction. And in less than twenty minutes they arrived.

Jenny had walked quickly in front of him and he had struggled to push the trolley behind her because one of the wheels was crooked, he remembered.

He had forgotten what she was wearing but could recall that over her shoulder she carried a small brown bag in which they kept the documents and wedding rings, and that she knew exactly where to go and which document to present at each stop. She had carried the wedding dress on a hanger, hidden under a blue cover. His grey suit was folded up inside the suitcase.

Perhaps it was already possible then to know that this was how it would end. He had got used to life alone and hadn't dreamed of getting married, but longed to have sons, and his mother knew that even though they didn't talk about it, and she thought that Jenny wanted children as well, or at least that what Jenny had told her. Had she lied? At their first meeting, the dinner at his mother's place, no one had mentioned children, but the question hung in the air, and by their third or fourth meeting the details were finalized. When Jenny didn't get pregnant his mother suggested that he search the cabinets, and he did in fact find the pills she had hidden in a drawer in the bedroom. He confronted her but that didn't help, and when his mother intervened she spoke with Jenny face to face and threatened her that they'd get divorced immediately and that she'd lose her visa. Jenny travelled to the Philippines for a short holiday, and when she returned she stopped taking the pills.

And there was a measure of compatibility between them, though they didn't consciously work at it. Jenny was organized and loved to work, like him, and her talkativeness compensated for his reticence. Even at the airport on the way to Cyprus she was the one who spoke, in Hebrew, with the security agents and flight attendants.

The fear that had seized Chaim for a moment when they entered the hall passed.

They had to find the Korean Air counter and queue for the security check, and after that hand over the suitcase and receive their boarding passes. Afterwards they would look for the passageway to the hall where carry-on bags and travellers were checked by metal detectors, then on to passport control, and finally they'd locate the gate for the plane indicated on the ticket. Shalom sat down on the trolley because he was tired of standing. While they waited at the end of the long queue for the security check in Area E behind a group of foreign tourists, a young security agent approached them and asked, 'Israeli passport?' in both Hebrew and English.

Chaim said yes, and the security agent asked them to step out of the queue and follow him.

Should he have reacted differently? He was so focused on the children and the tasks he had to perform that his reactions were quick, automatic. Shalom complained that he was hungry and Chaim promised that after the check was over and the luggage checked in they'd sit down to eat. And every time he was asked, he simply told the same story he'd been telling for the last few days to whoever enquired. The security agent was polite and cordial. He stroked the hair on Shalom's head as he checked his frowning face and compared it to the picture in the passport. Chaim said, 'That's an old picture, we should have replaced it,' and the security agent said, 'You can see it's him, no problem.' Afterwards he asked, 'All of you are flying to

Seoul?' and Chaim was surprised and said, 'Not to Seoul, to Manila.'

The security agent laughed.

'For that flight I'm no longer responsible. In Seoul they'll check you again before you get on your connecting flight. Just don't forget to tell the agents at the counter that you're going to Manila so that your bags arrive there.' When he checked the picture on Ezer's passport the boy turned red and looked at him with a serious expression. He asked him, 'Are you sure you are you, young man?' and Ezer looked at Chaim, confused, until the security agent said, 'I'm just joking with you, son. Your picture's fine.' He asked about the purpose of their trip, and Chaim answered him with the same explanation that he had given the cab driver this morning on the way to the airport.

'Your wife lives there?'

'No, she lives here. She went there to take care of her father.'

'And does she have an Israeli or Philippines identity card?'

'She has a temporary card, yes. Israeli. All her papers are in order.'

'And I understand that she is the children's mother?'

He was tense, even though he had prepared himself for the questions that would be asked. The security agent checked how long Jenny had resided in Israel and how long they had been married, then apologized and went away, and Chaim saw him walk over to the luggage-scanning machine, where he spoke with another security agent, older, before returning. He said, 'I apologize that the checks are longer today, but those are our directives. Could you give me the address where you'll be in Manila or the name of your hotel, and also your wife's phone number?'

Chaim felt Ezer's warm hand crawl into his hand as if he knew that something had happened.

He pulled his hand away from his son's and located among the documents he'd received from the travel agent the printed page with the hotel confirmation. The address of the hotel and the telephone number appeared at the bottom of the page. His voice cracked when he asked, 'Why do you need this?' And the security agent answered that it was a routine check they made in a queue in which many foreign workers were travelling. 'I can give you the phone number but I don't think she'll answer. Her phone is off. I spoke to her half an hour ago,' Chaim said, and the security agent answered, 'No problem. Does she speak Hebrew or English?'

Ezer followed him with his eyes when he walked away from them again and conferred privately with the older agent, who wore an electronic device in his ear. Shalom complained again that he was hungry. Chaim opened the holdall and found the plastic container in which he had put the cheese sandwiches and offered one to each of the boys. Ezer didn't want to eat.

Chaim said that Jenny spoke English and Hebrew.

And stood in the middle of the giant departure hall with his two sons and a trolley loaded with a suitcase and a large holdall next to them.

Because they had arrived at the airport early, there remained more than two and a half hours before the flight.

He assumed that they wouldn't prevent them from flying because Jenny didn't answer, but said to himself that even if that did happen, it wouldn't be so bad. Since the police investigation was over, they could return home. And perhaps he even felt relief when he thought that this was liable to happen. A slice of cheese slid out of Shalom's sandwich and when Chaim bent down to pick it up he saw the security agent returning to them with a mobile in his hand. There was a wide smile on his face. He spoke with someone on the phone, and when he approached them Chaim heard him say in English: 'Yes, of course they're here, they're wonderful. You want to talk to them? Okay, thank you very much for speaking with me, Jennifer. I'll pass them over to you.'

He didn't understand who he was speaking to and what exactly he had heard, but the security agent said to him, 'Take it, talk to her. You have an amazing wife.' And after he had handed the phone to him he started affixing stickers to the suitcase confirming that it had been checked, and even managed to ask Chaim, 'Are you checking in the holdall or is it going on the plane with you?' Ezer looked at his father without saying a word, and when Chaim brought the device close to his own ear, Shalom screamed, 'Is that Mum? I want to talk to Mum too!'

Jenny's phone was in the shed at his mother's house, without a battery, along with her passport and other documents that he had put there a few days after he had brought her body and buried it in the yard.

The security agent stood next to him while he spoke, without looking at him. Chaim said quietly, 'Yes,' but the voice that emerged from the device spoke to him in Hebrew.

'Chaim? Can you hear me?'

He said, 'Yes,' and the voice continued, 'Chaim, how are you? Are you ready for the journey? How are the boys?'

A tremor of weakness passed down the length of his legs when he said quietly, 'Fine. How are you?'

Now he was certain that it wasn't his mother. But the voice wasn't Jenny's either, though if he had to describe how it was different from her voice he wouldn't have been able to. Indeed, he recognized the accent, and in a strange way the foreign voice spoke like Jenny as well, with great quickness, but it wasn't her voice.

'Okay, Chaim. You won't forget to buy me what I asked for from the duty-free, right? Do you remember? Don't forget.'

For some reason he again said in English, 'Yes,' and heard the voice say to him, 'Chaim, can I talk to the boys for a moment?' but he didn't answer.

He returned the phone to the security agent, who said, 'Okay, Jennifer, thanks again for . . .' then removed the phone from his ear and said, 'She already hung up.'

The security agent pointed towards the luggage-scanning machine and Chaim pushed the trolley there. Ezer and Shalom walked behind him but he couldn't see them. In front of him a young couple with backpacks and a baby in a carrier waited.

When his turn came he lifted up the suitcase and inserted it into the mouth of the machine, then he waited until the man working it instructed him to move to the other side. Shalom sobbed that they hadn't let him talk to his mother and Chaim heard Ezer say to him, 'But maybe we'll see her in a little bit, Shalom, after we get off the plane.' The suitcase slid out of the machine, Chaim grabbed it, and they continued on to the airline counters.

He didn't ask himself then who it was he had spoken to but rather why he hadn't immediately returned the device to the security agent and told him that the voice coming out of it wasn't Jenny's. Because of the shock? Or the presence of the security agent and the looks of the children?

Midway through the conversation the possibility occurred to him that his mother had turned on Jenny's phone, understood what was happening, and impersonated Jenny – and therefore he wanted to hear that voice again. It couldn't be that his mother had taken the phone out of the shed, inserted a battery, and turned it on, but more impossible was the dim feeling that perhaps it truly was Jenny's voice, a feeling that he understood later was tied to the story he had told to his children, and also to the police detective, a feeling he would have many more times afterwards. He'd held the old phone receiver in the bedroom at his mother's house and dialled Jenny's number in order for her to speak with the children, but there was no answer. This was on Rosh Hashanah. And later he had done it from their house. A few days ago it even seemed to him that he sensed her walking behind him on the street and visiting the apartment in his absence. Perhaps that had been hope? He heard the counter attendant say, 'Passports and tickets,' and extended them to her distractedly. Afterwards he loaded the suitcase onto the conveyor belt and accepted the tickets from her. She circled the details with a pen: 'Gate B9, and boarding begins at seven forty-five.'

And maybe there was an additional reason he didn't immediately return the phone: the feeling that he had been caught. And that nothing could change that.

He waited for something else to happen, but nothing happened.

They stood a few minutes in the departure hall, without the suitcase that they had checked in, and waited for someone who didn't come. Ezer said to him, 'Give it to me, Dad, it's heavy,' and took the large bag from him. For a moment he thought it would be a good idea to leave the hall and breathe some air outside, and if they had indeed left, perhaps they wouldn't have returned.

Thousands of travellers moved all around them and no one paid them any attention.

He searched the crowd for a suspecting eye and didn't find one.

Suddenly from a distance he saw the young security agent questioning two young men. He took their passports from them, walked off and again conferred privately with the older agent, then returned to them with the phone up to his ear. Again and again he could hear the strange voice asking him, 'Chaim, can you hear me? How are you?'

Jenny had never asked him how he was, and wouldn't have asked even if she were in the Philippines now.

Ezer said, 'Dad, aren't we going?' and he answered yes, but then decided to call his mother and ask her if someone from the airport had contacted her. She said no, and asked him why he called, and he said it wasn't important. Then he asked her, 'Where is Jenny's phone?'

She answered him in a whisper, surprised, 'Where should it be?'

He could have asked her to check in the shed but didn't.

'Are you on the plane already?' she asked, and he said, 'Yes. Taking off any minute.'

They continued on their way as if nothing had happened, but Chaim already knew that, in the end, there would be no plane waiting for them. The voice of the woman who wasn't Jenny continued to speak inside his head, cheerful and smiling, like a voice from a life that wasn't his. In the passage to the hall where carry-on bags and travellers were checked with metal detectors they were asked to present passports. He held them out to the clerk, who looked for the stickers that the security agent had put on and allowed them to continue onwards without looking at their faces. He held the children's hands tightly when they stood at the end of the long line of travellers waiting to be checked. It was precisely because nothing had happened since the phone conversation more than half an hour ago that the recognition that someone was waiting for them at the end of the road deepened inside him. And he thought about the children, only about them. Would they try to separate them from him? He could call his mother and ask her to come to the airport in a cab in order to be with them if something happened. Then he thought for the first time that if he were to be caught, he'd have to tell them the truth about Jenny.

Ezer placed the holdall on the conveyor belt of the X-ray machine and passed through the metal detectors without a peep. Chaim was asked to take off his shoes and remove his belt. He took his key chain and mobile out of his trousers pocket and placed them with the documents folder and his wallet on a tray that was itself passed through the X-ray machine. And still nothing happened. The keys and wallet and phone and documents were returned to him and another woman said to him, 'Have a pleasant flight.'

Even the young policewoman at passport control performed her work with indifference. She checked the passports and asked, 'Who is Ezer Sara?' and Ezer stood on the tips of his toes in front of the high counter and said, 'I am.' She was forced to get up off her chair where she sat in the glass booth and bend forward in order to see Shalom, who stood next to his father.

Chaim waited to hear the sound of the stamp smacking the passport, but the policewoman paused.

When she rose from her place, opened the door to her booth, and said to him, quietly, 'Could you come with me for a momen?' he knew that this was what he had been waiting for.

The end of the road.

He called to the children to walk behind him in the direction she indicated, and Ezer asked, 'Dad, what happened?'

The policewoman walked behind them.

And he said to his son, 'I suppose there's another checkpoint.'

The distance to the closed door they were walking to was short, maybe fifteen or twenty steps, but Chaim carried Shalom there in his arms.

When they stood in front of the door, the policewoman said to him, 'Could you put the child down, please? I need you to go inside here. I'll remain with the children.'

He already understood where he was entering, but did Ezer understand as well? Chaim said, 'I want to go inside with them,' and the policewoman answered, in a more forceful voice, 'Sir, I suggest you go inside without arguing. The children will be fine right here.'

Shalom again cried when Chaim set him down, and there was fear in Ezer's eyes. He said to his son, 'Watch Shalom for a minute, okay?' opened the door and immediately turned back to them, because he recognized in the room the detective who had questioned him at the station. But the policewoman closed the door behind him and he only got a glimpse of Ezer holding his younger brother's hand.

13

When the case was closed and Jennifer Salazar's body had been found, Avraham thought how close Sara had come to evading them that morning, and returning from Manila without his children.

He detained him for questioning at the last moment, but that had only happened thanks to a sudden breakthrough, and in spite of Ilana's fierce opposition. And even during the interrogation at the airport there had been moments when it seemed to Avraham that he was wrong and would have to release Sara. At one point his confidence was shaken to such an extent that he had been about to stop the interrogation, and were it not for the burning sensation that he might be leaving Sara's children in truly life-threatening danger, he might have done so.

But something inside him had refused to give up.

The day before the arrest was nerve-racking, and in the end he again hardly slept a wink.

Until the evening hours he hadn't found a solution to the problem of a pretext for the interrogation and he saw before his eyes Sara and his sons disappearing into the tunnel leading them to the plane the next day. The tick-tock in his ears wouldn't stop. He recalled Sara sitting in his office during the previous interrogation. The first time they had met. Sara had been questioned then as a witness and in connection to a different matter. To Avraham it had seemed that he volunteered the information that his wife had gone to Manila, without being asked. That same evening, Marianka had asked him if he thought that Sara was involved in placing the bomb, and he had hesitated. He couldn't say. He told Marianka that he didn't intend to trust anyone. And he was right. But then he hadn't suspected that Sara had harmed his wife, or that he was planning to harm his children. Only at eight thirty, when he was sitting in Cup o' Joe, outside the mall next to the station, and eating dinner, did the solution to the problem of the pretext appear to him and he rushed back to his office and called Anselmo Garbo.

In Manila it was two o'clock and Avraham woke Garbo from his sleep. He apologized and explained why he was calling at such a late hour and Garbo asked him to wait on the line while he moved to his study in order to light a pipe and continue the conversation without waking his girlfriend. In his imagination Garbo wore a thin dressing gown and sank into a leather armchair in front of a dark wooden writing desk. He had listened to Avraham patiently and finally said, 'Wonderful idea. In a few more minutes the document will be sent. And I thank you for taking the initiative.'

That was the breakthrough, and Avraham was as proud of it as he had been of only a few investigative actions in his life.

Ilana strongly disapproved of the idea, as expected, and told him in a harsh voice, 'You did something that is *not done*, Avi.' She was still certain he was fabricating a missing-persons case and added things similar to what she had said during their previous conversation, and he waited for her to finish having a go at him and said, 'Maybe you're right, Ilana, but there's nothing that can be done now. The complaint has been submitted. And

I promise you we won't have to apologize. Would you prefer Sara to be arrested in Manila?'

He knew that she wouldn't have any choice but to authorize him to detain Sara for questioning at the airport, and even before he called her, he summoned Zaytuni and Ma'alul from their homes in order to prepare the operation.

At first he thought they'd need to instruct one of the security agents at the airport, but it turned out that Zaytuni had worked there while he was at college. He contacted the heads of security and obtained permission to impersonate a security agent and greet Sara when he arrived at the terminal. The security company's uniform suited him better than a police uniform, and Ma'alul snapped a picture of him on his mobile so that they'd have a souvenir.

The time was Thursday, 1 a.m., and not one of them went to sleep.

The official request from the External Relations Unit of the Philippines Police arrived by fax and email:

> Brigadier General Anselmo Garbo, chief of the Manila Police's Department of Criminal Investigations and Surveillance, demands that the Israeli police open an investigation without delay into the disappearance of Philippines citizen Jennifer Salazar.

Avraham added the official request to the file of the new investigation: *Salazar case.* In his office, when they reviewed the few materials that had been collected in the file, Ma'alul surprised him and said, 'Do you remember the weird neighbour from Ofer Sharabi's building? Avni? The telephone ruse reminds me of what we did to the parents then – you know, with his help – remember?' Avraham smiled and didn't answer. Would Sara have been caught had Avraham not read the report that Ilana produced about the mistakes he had made in that investigation?

Zaytuni had arrived at the airport at a quarter to five and grabbed a spot among the security personnel in Area E, across from the Korean Air counters. Avraham and Ma'alul waited at the station to be notified that Sara had left his home, then set out in a cab towards Ben-Gurion.

They travelled in Avraham's car and entered the terminal through a rear entrance a few minutes after Sara arrived.

The two of them sat tensely in the small interrogation room next to Charito, the Filipina woman who spoke in the name of Jennifer Salazar, when she received the phone call from Zaytuni, disguised as an agent, and heard her say to Sara, as they had asked her, 'Chaim, you won't forget to buy me what I asked for from the duty-free, right? Don't forget,' and Ma'alul signalled to Charito with a rolling hand motion to keep the conversation going. She was married to the brother of one of the police officers in the district, and in the past she had assisted the police with simultaneous translation and in deciphering documents. When she returned Avraham's phone to him, she asked in Hebrew, embarrassed, 'Okay? You think?' as if she had just turned in a performance in front of an audience on *Israel's Got Talent*, and Ma'alul said to Avraham, 'Maybe you and me and Zaytuni should go to the Philippines with their tickets?'

In his eyes the phone conversation was a sure sign that Sara was hiding something from them and a green light to continue the investigation, but Ilana listened to his detailed update without enthusiasm.

All the police officers at passport control were briefed and waited for Sara and his sons.

An adjacent interrogation room was put at Ma'alul's disposal in order to watch the children during the father's interrogation, but also, unofficially, so that he might try to draw them out and glean from them as much information as possible. He prepared drawing paper and marker pens, ostensibly so that they'd have something to play with while they waited.

Avraham drank black coffee and hastily smoked a cigarette in a smoking area for airport employees, next to a cleaning woman who leaned on a squeegee and let the ashes of her cigarette fall slowly into a bucket of water. The waiting continued, because Sara lingered in the departure hall after checking in his suitcase. At seven they finally saw him on the monitor, advancing towards one of the police work stations, and Avraham entered the interrogation room, to wait for him.

Like his office at the station, the room was narrow and naked, and windowless. At its centre was a grey table, on both sides of which were simple metal chairs upholstered with purple fabric. And a folding partition stood in the corner. On the table, at the start of the interrogation, there were only a recording device and the cardboard folder in which was printed the report Garbo had sent and the formal appeal to open the investigation and a sheet of paper that summarized in black Sharpie everything he knew.

Jennifer Salazar left Israel on 12 September and has not returned, he wrote at the top of the paper. Then:

She's forty-two years old and has resided in Israel continuously since 2005.

In his testimony from the previous interrogation, Sara said that she had travelled to Manila to take care of her sick father, but the local police officially confirmed that she hadn't entered the Philippines, and that her father had died quite a few years ago. And the main thing: a short while ago Sara had pretended that he was conversing with her on the telephone even though he wasn't speaking with her but rather with a stranger. For now, that was the only concrete sign that Sara had lied when asked where his wife was – not she who had lied to her husband about the place she'd travelled to, as Ilana thought.

The time was 7.09 a.m. on Friday, Yom Kippur Eve, when Sara opened the interrogation room door in the Department of Border Control at Ben-Gurion Airport. Avraham saw the handle turn and after that the expression on Sara's face when he recognized him, then turned around as the door was closing, but not so quickly that Avraham didn't manage to get a look at Sara's sons for a brief moment, for the first time.

His firstborn was tall and thin, almost adolescent from his appearance. The skin of his face was dark and his eyes were long and narrow. The younger son had long, straight brown hair, and his eyes were also foreign, but less so than his brother's.

This wasn't how Avraham had imagined them when he visualized them the day before – being led to the plane, with Avraham extending a hand to them but failing to reach them.

He sat on the chair facing the door and waited to meet Sara's eyes when the door opened.

Shock and fear were evident in them, and Avraham thought that they immediately gave him away.

He wasn't in the interrogation room when Ofer Sharabi's father had broken under the heavy pressure administered by Shrapstein and admitted to killing his son, but Avraham had no doubt that the same look had been there in his eyes. And Sara didn't evade him. He had fallen into the trap he had set for him and now he was in his hands, and Avraham had no intention of letting him go until he knew what he had done to his wife and what he had planned to do to his children, and, even more so, why. He didn't yet have an answer to this question, and without it he couldn't eliminate his doubt about what Sara had done and what his plans were.

He waited for Sara to understand that he had to sit down across from him, and with a very slow, very deliberate motion removed the photograph of Jennifer Salazar from the cardboard folder and placed it on the table without saying a word. He recalled that the last time they had sat across from one another, in his office at the station, he had felt a certain pity for Sara. He pictured the older father leading his son into the nursery among all the parents many years younger than he was. His son had come home from nursery bruised, and he had tried to speak about this with Chava Cohen, who had humiliated him in front of parents and children and refused to listen to him. Only a few days after this, Sara had become a prime suspect in the placing of the fake bomb and the assault on the teacher, and Avraham had looked at him differently when he trailed him into town and saw him enter the travel agency. He had to imagine him waiting for Chava Cohen in the middle of the night in south Tel Aviv and attacking her cruelly, and he had succeeded in visualizing him doing this, because Sara had had a motive. But he was mistaken – Sara wasn't the assailant, it was Uzan after all. And now he had to imagine Sara doing something else. To imagine if he was capable of harming his wife, and why, and, beyond that, if he had intended to harm his children. And perhaps precisely because he was sure of so little, Avraham felt the need to project confidence. At the start of the interrogation his questioning strategy was direct and aggressive. He battered Sara, hoping to shake him. He often fell silent, extending those moments in order to intensify Sara's fear and uncertainty. He asked his first question at 7.13. It was: 'Where is your wife?' And Sara didn't answer.

The two of them were quiet for some time before Avraham said, 'I have no doubt that you know where she is,' and again waited.

Sara sat across from him expressionless, without moving. His gaze wandered all over the table, though he avoided looking at the picture lying in front of him.

Avraham asked his second question at 7.16.

'Aren't you worried about your children? Are you going to let them wait a long time?' he said quietly, and Sara looked at him with amazement, as if he hadn't remembered that until a few minutes ago his children were with him.

That was one of the things that had confused Avraham that morning.

When the initial surprise had passed, Sara looked to him less tense than he had been during the interrogation at the station. In that first meeting he'd identified a stressed nervousness in his face, but now he seemed almost calm. He wore brown slacks secured with a belt and a thin, dark-green sweater under which the tattered collar of a white button-down shirt that had gone grey peeped through. He ignored most of the direct questions Avraham presented him with at the start of the interrogation regarding his wife, and only to the general questions that were asked about their life did he respond briefly and without fear. In Avraham's eyes the calm and silence were signs that he hadn't been mistaken. Sara didn't object even once to being detained for interrogation, not even when the questioning was extended and it was clear that he would miss his flight, and he didn't demand to know for what crime he was being questioned or where his children were.

This is the calm that descends on someone when he's finally been caught, he thought.

Sara no longer needed to escape.

He hunkered down into his silence as if it were a cave and waited for the storm to come, and Avraham wasn't able to extract him from there, not that day.

But what if Ilana was right and he was mistaken, even in the way he interpreted Sara's calm and his silence? Almost until the end of the first interrogation he couldn't entirely manage to eliminate the doubt she had stirred up in him. He recalled that when they had worked on one of their first cases together, an investigation into the abuse of senior citizens at a nursing home in Holon, Ilana had asked him, 'Do you know what the difference is between human beings and animals? Human beings talk. They can't not talk. Do you know what I mean? If you're patient and ask enough of the right questions, in the end everyone starts talking.'

Sara was one of the few people for whom silence was his natural state.

Avraham said to him, 'I don't know you all that well, Mr Sara, and it may be that you don't understand your situation at this moment. I'll explain it to you. We are searching for your wife and trying to understand why you lied with regard to her whereabouts.'

For a moment Sara lifted his gaze from the table, and Avraham used the opportunity to move the picture of his wife closer to him, then noticed how much she looked like her first-born, whom he'd seen through the open door. The faces were the same, with the thick, dark eyebrows over those dark eyes whose gaze was narrow and direct.

'I'm asking why you lied to the security agent and pretended that you were speaking to your wife even though you knew it wasn't her.'

Sara didn't respond, and Avraham continued battering him: 'That wasn't the first time you lied about her. You told me a few other false things about your wife. But let's start with the phone. Why did you pretend you were speaking to her?'

Sara didn't answer, and he repeated the question another time, in vain. Then he moved the picture still closer to Sara, up near his chest. 'Take a look at this picture, please, Mr Sara. This is a picture of your wife from many years ago. Do you know how I got it?' Sara didn't even shake his head. 'From the Philippines police. They demanded we investigate your wife's whereabouts. Do you know why? Because in our previous interrogation you said that your wife flew to Manila and because of that I couldn't call her in for questioning concerning the bomb next to the nursery, correct? Do you remember? You suggested I call her there. I'm looking at the summary of the interrogation, which you signed.'

The first words Sara said were, 'I remember,' and they were said so quietly they weren't captured by the recording device.

'Do you stand by what you said to me then?'

Again he didn't answer the question, and Avraham continued: 'Because that's not correct. We conducted an inquiry with the Philippines police, and your wife did not enter that country on the twelfth of September, or on any other date. So why did you lie? What were you trying to hide?'

If Ilana had been correct in her hypothesis and Sara hadn't lied, but rather didn't know that his wife had flown somewhere else, now would be the first time he'd hear of this and should then have responded differently. He didn't appear surprised.

'And you lied about another detail. You said she travelled there to take care of her father. Here is an official document that I received yesterday from the Philippines police. Look. Do you read English? Rizaldo Salazar, the father of Jennifer Salazar, who is your wife, died in 1985. You wife was how old then? Fifteen? You made up that she's taking care of a sick father. I don't know why you made it up, and why that of all stories, but you made it up.'

Avraham got up from his seat and stood behind Sara, who didn't turn around and fixed his gaze on the wall. He bent over and spoke close to his ear, 'You know where your wife is, don't you? I'm not mistaken, am I?'

A little after eight there was a knock at the door and Avraham left the interrogation room.

Zaytuni was waiting outside, wearing the uniform of the security company and with white latex gloves. He looked concerned when he said to Avraham, 'You should take a look at his suitcase,' and Avraham followed him into a small room, whose walls were lined with shelves of bags and suitcases. Sara's suitcase was open on a table in the corner. Avraham asked, 'Have you found something?' And Zaytuni took a paper bag out of it and said, 'Have a look.' That was the moment his confidence faltered, after which he contemplated releasing Sara so that he might still manage to catch his flight.

'I had no choice, I had to tear the wrapping,' Zaytuni said and extended to him a pair of white jeans and a thin, purple woman's blouse. He held them with the tips of his gloved fingers as if he were holding a rat by its tail. 'Presents for his wife. Take a look at the paper too.'

The letters were folded at the bottom of the paper bag, written on pages that had been torn out of a notebook. On one was a drawing of a plane in a blue sky, and next to it someone had written, in a child's hand, in red, *Dear Mum, This is the plane we're flying to you in after so long.* There wasn't a drawing in the second letter, on which was written in large blue block letters,

> *Dear Mum I missed you and I'm egsited that Dad's taking us to the Filipines. I want you to retirn home with us and stay with us like always. From you older son Ezer*

He burrowed into the suitcase with exposed hands and found at the bottom two more women's shirts and a nightgown inside an orange nylon bag. 'Other than this?' he asked, and Zaytuni said, 'Nothing. Children's clothes and a few toys and his clothes. And towels and toiletries.' Avraham looked at the letters for another moment, folded them up and placed them gently in the paper bag. Zaytuni followed him to the smoking area, even though he didn't smoke, and asked, 'So what will you do with him?'

He didn't know.

He asked Zaytuni if he had updated Ilana about what he had found in the suitcase, and the young detective shook his head. If Avraham were to call her, Ilana would instruct him to release Sara, and therefore he didn't call. He entered the room adjacent to the one where Sara was waiting, mainly to consult with Ma'alul, but perhaps more to look at the children, because he hoped that when he saw them his determination would return to him. The younger boy, whose hair was long, stood in front of the table with his back to the door and drew on a sheet of paper. Ma'alul leaned over him, hand resting on his shoulder. There was a marker pen in the boy's hand, too. The two of them turned around towards Avraham when he entered. Ezer, who sat on the chair facing the door, didn't lift his gaze from the paper, as if he hadn't noticed him.

They stood outside the open door, and Ma'alul whispered to him, 'What's new?'

Avraham said, 'Nothing for now. He's not talking, but I have no doubt he knows where she is.'

Afterwards he told Ma'alul about what they had found in the suitcase, and Ma'alul sighed. Now that they weren't looking at him, Ezer lifted his dark eyes and examined them through the opening of the door. 'So what's with them?' Avraham asked, and Ma'alul said, 'They're coming around. At first they didn't want to talk to me at all, but now they've already told me they're going to see Mum. That she's waiting for them at the airport. The little one talks more. The older one is more suspicious.'

'Did you ask them when she went away?'

'I don't think they remember. The little one said two days ago. But don't worry, Avi, I'll come back to it. Give me time. You think I could have another hour or two with them?' and Avraham was decisive again when he said, 'Yes. I'm not releasing him today under any circumstances.'

Nevertheless, when he returned to the room where Sara was waiting for him he spoke to him differently. Perhaps because of what had been found in the suitcase. Korean Air flight 958 to Seoul had received permission to take off and the plane taxied towards the runway. At least he had prevented them from getting on the plane.

He returned to his seat across from Sara and said to him, 'I saw your children just now,' and it seemed to him that something moved in his face. The following words he said quietly, almost softly, 'Do you know why I detained you for questioning? Do you want to know? Only because of them. If I hadn't done it, you would have been arrested the moment your plane landed in Manila. And your children would have remained there, alone and unattended. Do you understand?'

Sara raised his head and suddenly said thanks to him.

Apparently this was the right path, and Avraham continued on it.

'I understand that you've decided not to answer my questions, and that's your right, despite the fact that you're making a mistake,' he said. 'All in all, I'm just trying to understand where your wife is. I have no other issue with you. You said she's in the Philippines but she's not. And she's not in Israel, either. So let's assume for a moment that I got it wrong and that I believe you that you don't know where she is. Won't you help me find her, then? If you'd co-operate with me and tell me about her, it would be easier for me to believe you – and more than that, it would be easier to know where to look.'

Avraham didn't mean a single word of what he had said, but Sara didn't know that and asked, 'How are the children?' And Avraham answered, 'They're in the next room. They're waiting for you.'

Sara placed the palm of his hand on the table, next to the picture of his wife. 'Tell me what you want to know about her and I'll try to help you.'

A narrow crack opened up at the entrance to the cave where he was hiding, and Avraham dashed inside. 'How many years has she been in Israel?' he asked immediately, and Sara answered, 'Nine. Maybe ten.'

'And how did you meet her?'

'I met her at my mother's.'

'Does she work at your mother's place?'

'She worked at a neighbour's. Until they put him in a geriatric hospital and she was left without work.'

Avraham asked for his mother's phone number and address, and it seemed to him that Sara provided them unwillingly. He asked, 'And can you tell me who she's in contact with?' and Sara said, 'What do you mean, "who"? With no one.'

'She doesn't have friends in Israel? Acquaintances? She doesn't leave the house?'

'She leaves with the children. And goes to church sometimes.'

'Which church?'

'In Jaffa. In the old city.'

'And does she have family here other than you?'

'No. She was in contact with her sister. She lives in Germany.'

Sara didn't know where the sister in Germany resided or her phone number, or he knew and didn't want to say, but all the same, Avraham had succeeded in drawing him out of his silence. He asked him if he wanted something to eat or drink and Sara said no. He promised Sara that soon he'd be able to see the children. The conversation wasn't bringing him any closer to Jennifer Salazar – Sara still hadn't said anything about her that appeared important to him – but it seemed to him that it was bringing him closer to Sara's crime.

And, indeed, that was what happened.

He asked him, 'And she has no acquaintances from work? Friends?' and Sara said, 'She isn't working now. Before, she was taking care of the elderly, and afterwards she worked with me a little in the business.'

Avraham didn't remember what business he was talking about and Sara said, 'A catering business.'

'What does that mean? You sell food?'

'Yes. Sandwiches and warm meals.'

'Do you have a restaurant?'

'No, I sell at work locations in Holon. To companies. Now mainly in the industrial area. At factories, and at the Tax Authority and the Ministry of the Interior.'

He wrote the words *Ministry of the Interior* on his notepad, because he remembered that he had heard them already in the investigation, though he couldn't remember from whom he had heard them, or where, and he only remembered a few minutes later and knew that this was the breakthrough he'd been waiting for.

Sara no longer had anything to say to him and he didn't know what to ask.

'Do you want to tell me where you think your wife could be?' he asked, and didn't expect an answer, but Sara surprised him and said, 'If she's not there, then I don't know. She disappeared on us too. We wanted to go there to search for her.'

He wasn't speaking the truth now, either, but Avraham tensed because this was an answer he hadn't yet heard. He asked, 'What do you mean?' and Sara raised his voice when he said, 'She went away without saying a word to us. One day we came home and she wasn't there. She didn't even leave a letter saying that she was going, only called a few days later. We wanted to convince her to come back.'

'And she didn't say where she was calling from?'

'She said she had returned to the Philippines, but you say that this is incorrect. And afterwards we couldn't get in touch with her. She didn't answer her phone. Because of this I also didn't know what to do when security told me that she was on the phone. Maybe I no longer recognized her voice after so much time, you know? She didn't even say goodbye to the children. Disappeared on them one day without an explanation. I was sure she was there.'

The story lined up with Ilana's hypothesis and explained what was found in the suitcase, but Avraham didn't believe him for a second. 'Is this the first time she's disappeared on you like that or has it happened before?' he asked, and Sara looked him in the eye and answered, 'First time. She'd said she was going away a few times, that she didn't want to stay here any more, but she never left before. I don't know why she did it now of all times.'

'She didn't explain it to you? When you spoke to her on the phone?'

'She said she doesn't want to live with me. And doesn't want the children any more. I knew it was hard for her with us but I didn't believe that she'd ever really leave.'

The airport was empty when he left the interrogation room, after eleven.

He looked for Zaytuni and didn't find him, but when he tried his phone, he heard the ring behind him and saw the young detective dashing out of the room where they had earlier opened the suitcase. He asked him to call Sara's mother and check if she could take the children. He didn't know how old his mother was or what condition she was in, but he instructed Zaytuni to bring her to the airport in a patrol car, and to drive her home with the children, if necessary.

It was strange to see the airport like this; three hours earlier it had been buzzing with people. All but two passport control stations were closed. In one of them sat the policewoman who had escorted Sara to the interrogation room this morning. In three more hours Israeli airspace would be closed to traffic. The last plane that would depart before Yom Kippur was to take off for Warsaw at 12.55 a.m. and the last plane to land at the airport was to arrive from Brussels at 2.25.

He asked Zaytuni to try and get hold of the manager at the Ministry of the Interior in Holon, but this was hopeless on the eve of Yom Kippur. Then he knocked on the door of the room next to the interrogation room and opened it without waiting. Sara's younger son was sleeping in a corner, on the floor, covered with a blue sweatshirt. Ezer and Ma'alul were sitting next to each other at the table and were silent when he entered, and Ma'alul signalled to him that he'd join him in a moment. He appeared excited when he came out and whispered to Avraham, 'I think you're not off, Avi. Something happened there with the mother, and it's possible that his son saw it.'

He didn't need any more than this to decide that Sara would remain in custody until after Yom Kippur.

And only come evening did he grasp what was liable to have happened to the children had he freed him along with them.

Ilana would probably go through the roof, but Avraham already knew that he wouldn't ask her but would instead call Benny Saban, from whom he'd easily get authorization to detain Sara for twenty-four hours, take him to the holding cell at the station, and leave him there until after the fast.

'What do you mean, "saw"? The older one?' Avraham asked, and Ma'alul said, 'I went over the day she disappeared with him a few times. To see if he remembered how long she was gone and when she left. After the little one fell asleep he became less defensive and started telling me about how his father took his mother away at night and told him that she wouldn't be coming back. That is what he told me.'

He wasn't surprised, because it seemed to him that he understood everything when he recalled where he had heard the words 'Ministry of the Interior' before, but nevertheless he felt his heart beating fast. Sara was waiting for him in the next room and looked convinced that, having told Avraham the story of his wife's disappearance at length, he'd be released.

But Jennifer Salazar had never left Israel.

He asked Ma'alul, 'Do you think he really saw something?' and Ma'alul said, 'Could be. But he also says something odd. He keeps repeating that it wasn't Sara.'

Avraham didn't understand what he was saying.

'I don't know what he means either,' Ma'alul said. 'He says that it wasn't *this* dad of his who took her. That it was the previous father. Do you have any idea what he might mean? Is there some other father in the picture?'

Not that he knew of. According to the report that Garbo had sent him Jennifer Salazar had been married to another man before she married Sara, but she had divorced him after four years of marriage and the couple had had no children. And this had taken place many years earlier.

Was there something else he didn't know?

Only in the evening, after the start of Yom Kippur, did the complete picture become clear to him. The streets were dark and quiet, and faint lights shone in the windows, but the darkness lifted and the strange details came together, as he had expected they would. He then guessed not only how Sara's wife had disappeared but why he was determined to kill his children.

It was impossible to track down the chief of the Ministry of the Interior before the start of the holiday, but now there was no need. As he had done on every Yom Kippur since his childhood, Avraham went out to wander though the empty city and walked alone in the middle of the street. When he was a boy, before he learned to ride a bike and take longer trips with his friends, on Yom Kippur his father had taken him for walks through the city, which seemed to him then as giant as the whole world. They had walked westward from Kiryat Sharet to the other side of the city, almost to the edge of Bat Yam, and he remembered that on the way he would pepper his dad with questions about this strange day in which cars didn't drive in the streets and adults didn't eat or drink, and his father tried to explain it to him, but couldn't quite, perhaps because he himself didn't fast. When they returned home the three of them would sit down to eat a festive meal, and once the young Avraham had asked his father, 'If you eat on Yom Kippur, does that mean you'll die this year?' His father looked at him and didn't answer, but the question upset his mother and she said angrily to Avraham, 'Such nonsense you're speaking to your father,' and asked him to apologize.

If Marianka were here, they would walk endlessly in another direction entirely.

She continued not answering him, even when he called her for a long time without letting up.

A young man passed him with a *tallit* sack under his arm when he reached that building on Histadrut Street. In the apartment where Ofer Sharabi had been murdered a few months earlier, the windows were shuttered.

It wasn't for no reason that he'd walked there, but rather because the circle had closed.

Sara's children were protected, beyond his reach, and he was imprisoned in the holding cell at the station. Avraham could have entered his cell and continued interrogating him, but he preferred to wait. That evening he didn't walk to the other side of the city, but turned round and returned home.

14

Even days later, Chaim wasn't sure what had happened on the night that he admitted to the murder.

Had the police been honest with him? Had they lied?

Perhaps the order of the events had got mixed up and forgotten, but he did remember the small actions they had taken, and it seemed to him that all of them had a significance that he hadn't noticed that night. For instance, the chair that he was asked to sit on. Or the detective's violent outburst and his hand banging the door of the interrogation room. Were these part of a plan? He had no one to ask, but maybe it didn't matter any more. The only question that continued bothering him was whether or not the things the police had said about his son Ezer were true, and he got no answer to this, and perhaps he never would.

He understood that the Yom Kippur fast was over by the noise that reached him in the police station.

The phones outside the holding cell began to ring again, and people disturbed the silence with the sort of shouts he hadn't heard earlier. A radio was turned on, to the Voice of Israel, and through the door it was possible to hear the news, as well as the sound of cars being started in the car park that the lock-up's only window faced.

He understood that in a short while the interrogation would begin again.

His cellmate was lying on a cot and Chaim stood by the door in order to listen to the sounds up close and wait. A few minutes passed before the door opened and a policewoman instructed the cellmate to accompany her. Chaim asked the policewoman if he could have warm water and something to eat to break the fast and the policewoman said to him, 'Inspector Avraham is on his way for you. He'll make sure you get a snack.' The two inmates didn't say goodbye because they'd barely spoken during the hours they'd shared in the holding cell. The cellmate had been brought there during the night, while Chaim slept, and at first he suspected that they'd put him there in order to get him to talk. He was twenty years younger than Chaim, wore glasses, and looked intelligent and stylish. From the scraps of conversation with the police officers who brought him food and water, Chaim understood that the cellmate had been driving his car on Yom Kippur, hit a cyclist, and fled. Had he turned himself in to the police or had he tried to escape and been caught? He didn't dare ask. After the cellmate arrived, Chaim hadn't been able to get back to sleep, perhaps for fear that he'd get up in his sleep and say things he mustn't, and perhaps because his cellmate kept crying. But the cellmate didn't try to start a conversation with him, not even in the morning, and only once, when he was served a meal, did he politely ask Chaim if his eating next to him on Yom Kippur was bothering him, and Chaim said no.

A long time passed between the moment the cellmate was taken away and when Inspector Avraham opened the door, peered into the cell, and left.

Chaim was wrong about the detective, and he was convinced of this even before what would happen later.

The day before, at the airport, when he had told him about Jenny's trip, about the wife who had disappeared on him and the children without notice, it seemed to Chaim that Inspector Avraham had looked at him with understanding. That maybe he believed him when he said that he wasn't sure about the voice on the phone because he hadn't heard Jenny's for a long time, and that therefore he had kept the conversation going and didn't immediately tell the agent that the voice speaking to him wasn't hers. Deep inside, did he still hope that he could get away, even though he knew that the police were searching for Jenny? He felt that he had been caught even before he opened the door to the small room at the airport and saw Inspector Avraham inside, and then the hope arose in him that he was wrong and he told Avraham that Jenny had left them. The hope arose because Avraham's questions grew less aggressive and his face softened, and the panic Chaim had felt at the start of the interrogation had relaxed into an inner silence. Avraham was a bit shorter than he was and looked like a simple man. And Chaim wasn't as scared of him as he had been when Avraham questioned him a few days before about the suitcase that had been placed near the nursery. He had asked Chaim how he had met Jenny and where she worked and who she spent time with in Israel, and didn't yet accuse him of knowing where she was. But then the detective had left the room, and when he returned he had announced to Chaim that he had decided to detain him at the police station and continue the interrogation after the holiday, and the hope was gone. He asked what they were going to do with the children and was alarmed when Avraham informed him that his mother was on her way to the airport. He didn't see her when the detective brought Ezer and Shalom inside to say goodbye to him. He said to Ezer, 'Sleep at Grandma's, okay? We won't fly to Mum today because there's a problem with the plane. And I need to stay here a bit more in order to help the police,' and Shalom, who looked as if he had just woken up, asked him with tears in his eyes, 'But what do you need to help them with?' Ezer was tired as well, but tried hard not to cry like his brother.

In his cell at the station Chaim thought only about the two of them on Yom Kippur, and sometimes about his mother, too. About the fear that must certainly have gripped her. And hoped that the children believed what he had said to them about the reasons for postponing the trip.

Avraham returned to the holding cell with a large bottle of water and a prepared serving of couscous with vegetables in a plastic cup. He stood in a corner of the cell, his hands in his trouser pockets, and looked at Chaim, without saying a word, while he sat on his cot and ate. When his prisoner had finished eating, he instructed him to follow him. Avraham wore blue jeans and a black shirt, and Chaim hadn't yet identified in his eyes the crazed look that would appear in them later on. Avraham opened the interrogation room door and Chaim entered before him; he wanted to sit down in the chair close to the door, but the detective asked him to sit on the other side of the table, in the far chair, facing the door, and he sat down across from him. That couldn't have been a coincidence.

He turned on the recording device and asked, 'Would you like to see a lawyer?' and Chaim said no.

Avraham opened the folder sitting before him, glanced at his watch, and wrote something with a black pen on a sheet of paper.

The inspector's outburst had apparently been planned as well, since at the start of the interrogation Avraham was calm and asked his questions in a quiet, unaggressive manner. His face was wide and tired and he hadn't shaved. His gaze sought out Chaim's eyes throughout almost their entire conversation.

He asked Chaim if he insisted on continuing to claim that his wife had left Israel on the twelfth of September and Chaim didn't answer. Just as at the airport, in his questions Avraham didn't call her Jenny but rather Jennifer Salazar.

Avraham waited a moment before saying, 'Because I know that that isn't correct,' and asked, 'Do you want to know how I know?' Chaim tried to avoid his gaze. He didn't want to know. He tried to hear sounds from the other side of the door, maybe the radio that was on.

He had felt a dull pain in his stomach and chest since being arrested and brought to the police station, and the pain grew more intense when Avraham said, 'I'll tell you anyway, because I'm sure you're curious, even if you're embarrassed to ask. Do you know why it took me a while to get here this evening? I had a long talk with a man you know. Ilan Babachiyan. You know Ilan, at least *that* you won't deny, right, Mr Sara? He's your cousin, if I'm not mistaken. And you can imagine what he told me.'

His last hope of escape was gone, but he still didn't intend to speak.

The pain inside him grew still more intense, and he held fast to his silence and continued to lower his eyes, and only when Avraham read to him from the scribbled-on piece of paper that he held in one hand did he raise his eyes for a moment and look at him. 'Ilan Babachiyan acknowledged the following facts. You requested from him, by virtue of his work at the Population Management Authority at the Ministry of the Interior, to forge a false exit registration for Jennifer Salazar, purportedly because of problems with her visa. You explained to him that your wife's visa was running out, which according to him checked out, and that the documents you were asked to prepare in order to submit a request for citizenship weren't ready, and that it was necessary to create an exit registration for her so that she wouldn't become an illegal alien. Do you confirm these facts?'

The pain pierced his stomach and his chest but was still bearable – at least he hadn't yet burst.

The idea hadn't been his but rather his mother's: it had popped into her head two days after he'd killed Jenny. He had thought it was a mistake from the beginning. He'd planned to tell everyone that Jenny had just gone away, without forging any registrations. And he had been right. Had they not forged the exit registration, Avraham wouldn't have had proof that something was fishy, he thought then, before Avraham shocked him again.

It seemed to him that the pain didn't stem from anger. He wasn't angry with his mother, or with himself. He felt that something would burst in him when the pain exploded. He wouldn't blame anyone for his getting caught, not then and not later, it was just the bad luck that always dogged him. His mother had simply convinced him that they had to forge the exit registration, because if they didn't do this, one day the immigration police would come looking for Jenny, and that had seemed logical to him.

He maintained his silence, and Avraham said, 'You don't need to confirm the facts, Mr Sara. And I understand that it's hard for you to speak. It would be hard for me, too, if I were in your shoes. In any case, Ilan Babachiyan offered to help you in getting Jennifer Salazar's visa extended – without the missing documents, apparently – but he says that you refused and urged him to execute a false exit registration. That was the explanation you gave him. He vigorously insists that he didn't know your wife had disappeared, and we will examine this claim before deciding what to charge him with.' And suddenly he raised his glance from the piece of paper and looked at Chaim, and added in a less official voice, 'You hoped that everyone would accept that she had travelled to the Philippines and didn't return, correct? But if that's so, you need to explain something to me, because I want to understand how your mind works, if it works at all. Didn't you think Ilan would ask questions? Didn't you think that in a few weeks he'd ask if he should create an entry registration for your wife? Or that he might ask you where she was when he didn't see her?'

The detective's attempts to hurt him didn't hit home.

From outside the room he heard a man and a woman conversing, and the sounds of laughter. He had no intention of telling him that he thought they'd forget. That in the first days this was his only plan. That Ilan wouldn't think of it afterwards. After all, he rarely saw Jenny. Neither was he about to explain that in the beginning he even hoped that, little by little, the children would also just . . . forget. He had told himself that as time passed things would fade, the way things always do. He had been mistaken.

Why had no one forgotten this, of all things?

If he remembered the order of things correctly, a short time after these questions were posed, the interrogation room door suddenly opened and he saw, for a split second, his son Ezer standing in the opening with a policeman he didn't recognize. That had been the most horrible moment that night. And if he had been sitting in the chair closer to the door he wouldn't have noticed Ezer, even if he had managed to spin around when the door opened.

Ezer was wearing the festive clothes that Chaim had dressed him in before they had left for the airport: the blue trousers and the white shirt with the picture of the boat. Chaim immediately noticed that his hair was messy and that his eyes were red. The older policeman placed his large hand on Ezer's narrow shoulder, and therefore he could not run to Chaim and hug him, even if he had wanted to. They stood close together, and Ezer didn't flinch at the touch of the policeman's hand on his shoulder, even though he was extremely sensitive to strange contact, and this pained Chaim, because he felt that someone was already trying to take his son away from him. He wasn't able to say a word to Ezer because the older policeman shut the door, panic-stricken when he recognized Chaim, and Inspector Avraham tried to continue with the interrogation as if nothing had happened, merely saying to him, 'Sorry, that shouldn't have happened.'

Chaim asked, 'Why is Ezer here?' and Avraham didn't answer. Those were the first words he had spoken in the room, and this was the first time their glances met. He asked again, 'Why did you bring Ezer here?' and Avraham said, quietly, 'Mr Sara, in this room I ask the questions.'

From that moment on, Chaim saw nothing before his eyes other than his son, and his frozen expression, and the hand resting on his shoulder.

The pain in his stomach and chest exploded but the explosion didn't flood him with blood, as he had imagined, but with memories. From somewhere beyond his thoughts he heard that Avraham's questions were becoming more aggressive, even violent, and he recalled Ezer falling asleep on the sofa next to him the day before the trip, and how his son's head had fallen on his shoulder while he read to him from the children's book and made up the rest of the story. A blindfold of moments from recent days was tied over his eyes, and through it he saw Avraham, blurry and distant, and listened to the words of the detective as if they were coming from another room as he raised his voice again and again and said to him, 'I know that you murdered her. Tell me how it happened and where you buried her.'

This lasted for what felt like a few minutes, and afterwards a brief silence prevailed in the room.

And only after this did the policeman's temper flare, though that might have been faked, but he didn't know it then. He thought that Avraham lost his cool, and that through his blindfold he identified the crazed look burning in his eyes when the detective got up from his chair and approached him from behind, as he had done at the airport. This time he didn't whisper. He screamed into his ear, in a voice that grew louder and more frightening: 'She cheated on you, Mr Sara! Isn't that it? How many men did she sleep with before you discovered it? Did you find her in bed with someone that day? With a younger man? You can't get it up any more, can you? That's your problem, isn't it? That's why she went looking for younger men. And when you discovered it, she announced to you that she was taking the children and leaving you?' And suddenly he turned around and walked away from Chaim and struck the closed door forcefully with the flat of his hand as if he couldn't contain his fury.

Nothing of what he had said was correct.

And what crushed Chaim's wall of silence wasn't Avraham's outburst. Jenny never cheated on him, and if she had cheated on him, he wouldn't have touched her.

A minute or two passed before the door opened again and he saw the older policeman who before had held Ezer's shoulder. Only after the fact did he understand that the blow to the door might have been a signal of some sort. The man said to Avraham, 'You're needed out here for a moment,' and Avraham said, 'Not now,' and he came in and whispered something in his ear.

Chaim was left alone in the room.

The vulgar questions that Avraham had taunted him with about Jenny hovered in the air.

The pain inside him was different now. More horrible, actually. That was what the children would hear if he continued his silence.

You found her in bed with someone that day? And you can't get it up any more, right?

Avraham came back – Chaim didn't know exactly when because there was no clock in the room – and sat down on the table, in front of Chaim's chair. It seemed he had calmed down.

Suddenly he extended his hand and touched Chaim's chin with his fingertips, trying to lift his head. His voice was almost soft when he said to him, 'Chaim, don't you understand that nothing will save you now? You're lost,' and Chaim tried to prevent the words reaching him without covering his ears with his hands, and instead of asking Avraham not to touch him, different words came out of his mouth. He asked again, in a voice suffused with shame, 'Why did you bring Ezer here?' and Avraham said, 'Your son told us everything, Chaim. Do you hear me? He told us everything. And you knew the whole time that he saw.'

Chaim wanted to get up and lay him down on the table and beat the crap out of him, but his body was paralysed with shock and he could do no more than lift his eyes.

He asked, 'Who saw?' and Avraham answered, 'You know that Ezer saw you take her down in the suitcase. Don't pretend you didn't know. Because of that you felt it was urgent to go to the Philippines with them. It took me a while to understand why you wanted to take them to Manila, but in the end I understood.' He didn't touch Sara's chin with his fingertips again.

The inner pain had disappeared entirely, and from that moment on, Chaim thought about nothing other than what Ezer had seen that night.

And at first he didn't pay any attention to the things the detective was saying about the trip. Had Avraham lied to him? How could he have known then? He thought that maybe he'd lied, but Ezer had said some strange things about the suitcase that was found by the nursery. Chaim remembered that the boy had lain in his bed in the evening, on his back, in the frozen position that had frightened him, when he told Chaim for the first time that his first father knew who had put the suitcase there and that he was forbidden to reveal it to others. Ezer's words gave rise to a vague anxiety in Chaim, but he couldn't imagine how this might be connected to the suitcase. What troubled him, he thought, was the mention of the first father. And in the days that had followed, Ezer had barely spoken and was guarded and wary around him, and then he had told Chaim that his first father had helped Jenny escape at night with a suitcase and said to him that she wouldn't return. But afterwards he had stopped mentioning the first father, and Chaim also stretched the thread across the door to their room at night, and in the mornings it had become clear to him that Ezer hadn't got up in his sleep.

And on the night he had murdered Jenny he had made sure that the two of them didn't wake up.

'He can't have seen that,' he said to Avraham, without thinking, and the detective responded immediately, 'But that's exactly what happened, Mr Sara. Unfortunately for you, and for him. And you knew very well that he saw you. It won't help you to pretend otherwise, because he told us not only what he saw but that he told you, too.'

What if all this was true?

If he could have a clear answer to this question, it was possible he'd confess immediately.

Yet it seemed to him that everything he had done that night he had done without making a sound. He had opened the blinds in order to let a bit of light into the dark room and packed up Jenny's clothes in the small suitcase, and then he had taken the suitcase down to the car. And on the way he had checked to see if the boys were asleep. Had he made a noise and woken Ezer when he closed the door behind him? He remembered distinctly that the door hadn't creaked. Jenny was still on the floor in the bedroom, rolled up in a blanket that he'd found in the wardrobe.

But it seemed to him that he had peeped into the boys' room again when he returned, and that the two of them hadn't moved. When he left the second time, carrying Jenny in his arms, he'd locked the door with the key and hadn't paused there to hear if they had woken up because he was in a hurry to get to the car. Only when he started driving did he notice that it was getting late and he speeded up in order to get back before the children woke up, until he realized he didn't want to attract the attention of a traffic policeman and slowed down. He returned to Holon at a quarter to seven, and as it turned out Shalom was the one who was already awake. Not Ezer. He had turned on the television and sat in front of it on the floor in the living room and asked him, 'Dad, where's Mum?' And Chaim hadn't answer.

Avraham returned to his place behind the table, and waited silently. Chaim recalled that Ezer had woken up late that morning and that they hadn't got to school or nursery on time. Was this a sign that he, too, had woken up during the night? But Ezer didn't say a word that morning, and only a few days later, when the bomb was discovered next to Shalom's nursery and they were held up because of it, had he started talking about the first father and about what he had seen. Ezer had also asked him where Jenny was when he woke up that morning and discovered she wasn't there, and Chaim had told them for the first time that she had taken a trip. He hadn't had a plan then – he'd thought up the trip to Manila many days later.

Avraham said, 'So do you want to tell me how you killed your wife or should I be satisfied with what your son told us?' And Chaim suddenly understood what the detective was implying when he said that he knew Ezer had seen him and that he had been planning to take the children to Manila because of this. He didn't answer but instead asked, 'You think that I wanted to take Ezer so that he wouldn't speak to the police? Because he saw me with Jenny?' And Avraham said to him calmly, 'I don't *think*, Mr Sara. I know with certainty that you planned to kill the two of them there. And you'll pay for that as well.'

He should not have said those things, and Chaim screamed as much in a broken voice not his own.

Only a few days later, when the indictment against him was filed, did he understand that Avraham had indeed meant the things he had said. Chaim again screamed at him, 'Don't say that! I didn't plan to kill anyone,' but the detective had stared at him with that crazed look and said, 'Don't raise your voice to me, Mr Sara. You planned to kill your two children there and then return to say that they had decided to remain with their mother in the Philippines, correct? Maybe that could have worked for you. Why, your wife is already there, right? And who would have checked? Their mother went away, and what could be more natural than the children travelling to be with her, and then staying there with her. And you just took them to Manila, right? You were the courier. And when their bodies were found there, no one would have a way to identify them because in the Philippines your children don't officially exist. Isn't that exactly what you planned to do?'

Chaim saw the crazed look burning in his eyes, so why did he try to convince him?

Maybe he should have demanded then that the interrogation stop, or at least continue with a different detective, or in the presence of a lawyer. How could someone accuse him of wanting to kill his sons? He covered his face with his hands, then removed them, but still tried to defend himself when he said, 'Ezer and Shalom are all that I have. Do you think I'd give them up? I could never harm them,' and Avraham asked immediately, 'Then why take them to Manila? Explain that, please.'

But how could he explain it?

They were supposed to fly to Manila and not see her at the airport and be disappointed, then go to the house where she was supposedly staying and not find her there either. They would receive the farewell letter that Chaim had written in Jenny's name, either there or at the hotel, the letter that he had buried in the suitcase. They wouldn't have to know that she was dead, only that she didn't want them and that he was all they had left. In recent weeks he could picture, endless times, in his imagination their life once they returned to Israel, a life without pain. And that was the only thing he wanted, for him and for them. He didn't get to respond and tell the detective why he had planned to take the trip, or about the letter – because Avraham screamed, like someone who had lost control of himself: 'And don't tell me that you bought the children return tickets, because you also bought your wife a ticket. You repeated the same pattern. Where did you plan to bury them there? Or maybe you planned on throwing their corpses into the ocean? That's what you would have done with their corpses, right? You would have dumped them in the ocean,' and Chaim, maybe because of the horrible repetition of the word 'corpses', cut him off: 'Don't say that. Don't you understand that I killed her for them? To protect them?'

Avraham was smiling when he looked at him.

And Chaim understood very well that he had confessed, but that wasn't important.

'To protect them from whom?'

The smile didn't leave Avraham's face when Chaim said to him, 'From her.'

'From her? Did she beat them? Is that your story? So you had to kill her? Do you expect me to believe that?' and Chaim said, quietly, not to himself but not to Avraham either, because he didn't need to hear it, 'She didn't beat them, she just didn't love them.'

That was the moment when the interrogation ended, even if the detective didn't immediately understand that.

Chaim was already preparing himself for another conversation, in which he'd speak only to the children and explain the truth to them. This was the first time he'd ever uttered those words aloud: he'd told his mother something different. And immediately after they left his mouth he knew that he wouldn't have another chance to make them heard, not even to the children.

Avraham didn't listen to what he said at all. He said to him, 'Mr Sara, I don't believe a word of what you say. I want you to tell me now where your wife's body is,' and Chaim said suddenly, 'Bring Ezer here.'

Something had changed in the room, because he no longer had anything to hide. And it seemed to him that after the detective saw the farewell letter he had written in Jenny's name that he'd be convinced that Chaim hadn't planed to harm the children and that the goal of their trip was nothing like the detective imagined. 'Bring who?' Avraham asked, and Chaim was more decisive when he said it a second time: 'Bring my children if you want me to tell you where she is. I'm ready to tell you everything.'

At first Avraham refused to respond to the request but Chaim insisted and returned to his cave of silence.

His determination deepened, and it seemed to him that Avraham hesitated.

Finally the detective glanced at his watch and left the interrogation room, and Chaim remained alone.

In the time that passed he thought mainly about the things he'd say to the children.

He had planned for this to happen in Manila, but they'd never get there now.

If they'd had time, and if they were alone, perhaps he would have told them everything from the beginning. From the day they had come into the world.

Ezer was born in the autumn and Shalom in the summer, at the peak of the heat, and he remembered every moment at the hospital, the first touch, and how he had held Ezer in his hands for the first time. He had carried the baby when they had brought him home, and the baby's eyes were open and looked all around as if he could already see everything. Everyone said that he very much resembled Jenny and not him at all, but Chaim saw himself in him. Jenny didn't want to nurse him, and from the first day he himself fed Ezer with a bottle. And went to the baby at night when he cried. He would get him back to sleep in the rocking chair in the living room, in silence, without songs, as they told him his father had done for him. He continued thinking about what Ezer had seen that night, if in fact he had indeed seen anything, and recalled how he had carried Jenny rolled up in a blanket past the door. On the day they returned from their wedding in Cyprus she had asked him to carry her over the threshold and he had refused. And when he had wrapped her body in the blanket he had seen for the last time, under her pyjama top, the downy hair on her stomach that rose to her breasts. He remembered that he had repeatedly told himself on the day after the murder that this was what he had to do. That he had no choice. The children were suffering because of her; because of her, Ezer grew more and more distant. She encouraged Ezer to talk about his imaginary first father in order to hurt Chaim. He had gone to work that same day, as usual, but returned early to straighten the apartment up. Everything was silent when he entered, and the place was empty, exactly in the state he'd left it, and perhaps only then did he understand what he had done.

For some reason he grabbed a duster and went over the furniture in the living room and bedroom. Gave a once-over to the floor with warm water, without soap.

All of a sudden, seemingly out of nowhere, he thought about how he wouldn't dress his boys in the morning any more, that someone else would be doing this. Maybe the reason was that since he had remained alone with them he had, at precisely the time of night it was now, arranged the little shirts and little pants on the blue chair in their room, and afterwards gone to the kitchen and worked an hour or two in silence.

He also wouldn't be travelling any more through the dark morning streets, deserted except for the street cleaners.

Chaim wasn't sure that Avraham would bring the children until the sound of the door opening jolted him out of his thoughts and he saw the two of them before him. And suddenly he didn't know what to say.

15

The digger operator commenced work at five in the morning, and continued ever so slowly for some time in order not to compromise the integrity of the dead body. Jennifer Salazar was hidden in the yard under a cement path leading to the house of Sara's mother, which had been paved after she was buried. Upon first inspection, there were no marks found on her corpse that contradicted the account Sara had given during the night. There were no evident signs of violence or injury, and the general swelling of the buried body suggested that the murder had indeed occurred approximately three weeks earlier. In the brief report that Ma'alul composed at the scene in small, round letters and in his typically direct language, he wrote the following:

> *Salazar was buried in her clothes and wrapped from head to toe in a few layers of plastic sheeting in order to ward off the stench. And her possessions were found in the shed in the yard, as the suspect mentioned during his confession.*

Avraham was not a witness to the disinterment of the body, and afterwards he regretted this.

He had brought Sara before the judge on duty for his remand and then overseen the re-enactment of the murder, which took place immediately afterwards, so that Sara wouldn't change his version or have any second thoughts.

★

The building on Aharonovitch Street was dark and silent when they arrived there at three in the morning.

None of the neighbours woke up, or at least no one peered into the stairwell when they walked up and paused before the door on the second floor. Sara's left hand was cuffed to Zaytuni's right and with his other hand he pointed out the correct key and Avraham opened the door.

It was his first visit to the apartment, but nevertheless it was familiar.

He entered all the rooms and turned on the lights in them. The apartment was clean and organized, perhaps because of the planned trip, and a sweet smell of cleaning supplies rose from the floor. This time Avraham planned not to leave a single door closed.

Sara looked confused even before the video team got started, as if his thoughts had wandered somewhere else. Prior to this, at the station, after he had collapsed before his children in the interrogation room, he had actually calmed down, and delivered his detailed confession to Avraham in a quiet voice, while sipping the tea he had asked to be brought to him. But when they arrived at the apartment he again grew tense and quiet and looked upset, as if he hadn't understood that they'd return there when he had agreed to carry out the re-enactment. He stood next to Zaytuni in the narrow entranceway and followed Avraham with his gaze while he opened the doors to the bedrooms and the bathroom and went into the small kitchen, with the old cupboards and the table covered with red Formica and surrounded by four low chairs. Afterwards Avraham returned to the entryway and asked him to indicate which was the children's room, and with his free hand Sara pointed to the tiny room with the bunk beds on which sheets and blankets were folded.

According to his confession, the time of the re-enactment was close to the time of day when the murder had taken place.

Zaytuni removed the handcuffs and Avraham asked Sara to show him on which side of the bed his wife had lain and in what position – and he asked Zaytuni to lie in her place.

Jennifer Salazar lay on her back on the right side, close to the wardrobe, and her eyes were closed when Sara got up from the bed, he wrote in the report summary of the investigation. He stood behind Sara with a black microphone in his hand, the photographer standing next to them. Sara walked to the children's room to confirm that the two of them were sleeping and on the way back to the bedroom took the blue cushion from the sofa in the living room. Avraham hoped that he wouldn't close the bedroom door behind him, and he did indeed neglect to close it.

Zaytuni lay on the bed with eyes open as Sara placed the large cushion on the face of Jennifer Salazar and pushed it down forcefully with both hands. According to his confession, he couldn't see his wife wake up because her face was covered with the cushion, but she swung her hands towards him and tried to grab his hair and kicked the mattress a few times, and afterwards stopped. Sara left the cushion on her face for a few minutes before removing it. And throughout this entire time the bedroom door was open.

Avraham asked Sara to repeat the action and Zaytuni to kick at the bed, and he left the bedroom and waited next to the doorway to the children's room. Because of the angle he saw nothing, but he heard the sounds of feet striking the mattress quite well.

Two hours after this, at six in the morning, on the Sunday after Yom Kippur, Amos Uzan and Ilanit Hadad were each put inside a squad car and transported from the police station in Eilat to Holon. Sara had already been moved to a holding cell in the Abu Kabir main detention centre and Avraham returned to the station to wait.

Twenty minutes after the start of the trip the radios in both cars broadcast an announcement about an infiltration from the Egyptian border. All policemen in the southern district were asked to join the search, because some of the infiltrators were Bedouin who had smuggled in weapons from the Sinai. The police escorting Uzan and his girlfriend asked if they were to continue travelling to Holon, as planned, and received clear instructions over the radio, which both prisoners could hear. At a service station they stopped and Ilanit Hadad was moved to the car in which Uzan was being transported, and the other car joined the search. Actually, it stopped and waited two kilometres away for additional directions from Avraham. In the meantime he drank his first coffee since the evening and ate a dry cinnamon roll, and went to smoke a cigarette outside the station. A bus rolled past him in the dark along Fichman Street with its headlights on and three passengers inside. Was this really the end? Visions of the re-enactment and Sara's unclear confession wouldn't let go of him. He returned to his office and opened the investigation file in order to review his notes and suddenly noticed that the old picture of Jennifer Salazar that Garbo had sent him wasn't in the cardboard folder. He had no particular need of the picture, but he looked for it among the documents in the folder and on his desk, and couldn't find it. He dispatched Zaytuni to search again for the letter that Sara claimed he had written to his sons in the name of Jennifer Salazar and had buried in the suitcase that was moved from the airport to the station on Friday.

The police officer who remained at the service station went to the bathroom, but first he asked the two detainees to exit the vehicle and handcuffed them to an electricity pole next to the entrance to the convenience store. He instructed them not to speak to each other, and when he returned he put them back into the car. A quarter of an hour later he received a radio message that the infiltrators had been caught and that the second car was returning to the service station. The trip to Holon continued.

Amos Uzan smiled when Avraham entered the interrogation room where Sara had confessed a few hours earlier. He appeared relaxed when Avraham sat down across from him and said, 'I promised we'd see each other again. Do you remember?'

He wasn't supposed to interrogate him then; in fact, he had returned to the station for a meeting with Benny Saban, in white trousers and the ridiculous peach-coloured shirt that Marianka had bought him and which he hadn't worn since then. Uzan laughed. 'Right, you promised. So take a good look, so you won't miss me, because I'm not staying for long this time, either,' and added, 'Can I have a cold drink?' But the smile was wiped off his face when Avraham turned on the recording device and played him the short conversation he and his girlfriend had had next to that random electricity pole they had been handcuffed to at the service station. 'Motherfucker,' he said and added, 'That's not admissible, so you might as well slather it in Vaseline and shove it up your arse.' On the recording Uzan could be heard asking his girlfriend to be quiet during the interrogation and threatened that if she did speak, he'd dump everything on her and say that she had asked him to attack Chava Cohen. Ilanit Hadad didn't say a word during their brief conversation, only cried, and Uzan said, 'Give it a rest. Just watch that mouth of yours and everything will be fine.'

Now it was Avraham's turn to smile, but he didn't.

In many senses he was indebted to Uzan, he thought.

If Uzan had broken during the first interrogation and admitted that he was involved in placing the bomb next to the nursery, Chaim Sara would be in Manila now with his two sons, if they were still alive, and no one would have thought of searching for their mother's body. He just said to Uzan, 'We'll see about that in court. Now tell me, please, why you attacked Chava Cohen. Just because your girlfriend was fired from her job, or were there additional reasons?'

Uzan looked at him and asked, 'Who's Chava Cohen?'

There was no point in persisting.

In the adjacent interrogation room Zaytuni played the same recording for Ilanit Hadad and easily convinced her to talk. And she told him everything: how Uzan had thought up the plan to blackmail Chava Cohen, and how the teacher hadn't given in to his demands despite the threats and fired her from her job, and how she had placed the suitcase with the fake bomb that Uzan had assembled next to the nursery, and arranged, at his request, the meeting with Chava Cohen by the beach in south Tel Aviv. She hadn't suspected that he planned to assault the teacher, and as far as she knew maybe he hadn't planned to do that at all, but the meeting turned into a violent argument and she wasn't able to stop Uzan when he lifted a rock and struck Chava in the chest and head.

Avraham rose from his seat and left, and Uzan called out behind him, 'Did you give up? Just like that? Don't I even get a kiss goodbye on the cheek?'

In the entrance to the station Ilanit Hadad's parents sat waiting, and at first he didn't recognize them. But her mother ran up to him, weeping bitterly, and he remembered as she grabbed both his hands and said to him, 'Let my girl go, I'm begging you. He kidnapped her, I swear, he took my girl and made her his puppet. None of this was her fault.'

The father stood next to her and didn't say a word, just as he had during the questioning in their apartment.

And only then did Avraham grasp what had happened since the day before.

Policemen stopped in the hallways of the station in order to shake his hand and his mobile rang much more than usual, until he turned it off. Even Shrapstein knocked on the door of his office, peeked inside and let slip, 'Way to go.' At noon Benny Saban's secretary invited him up to his office and Saban received him at the entrance to the room with an awkward pat on the shoulder. He said to him, 'You did great work, Avi. If you get a call from the commissioner, pretend you're surprised and don't let him know I told you he was going to call. And get ready for the star treatment from me,' and Avraham thanked him with an embarrassed smile.

The two investigations that had started together, without him knowing at first, concluded on the same day.

One opened with a suitcase holding a fake bomb placed near a nursery on Lavon Street in Holon, which had led only himself to a second suitcase, in which were packed the clothes and toys of two little boys who were en route to be murdered in Manila, and to a third suitcase that was hidden in a shed and into which were hastily stuffed a dead woman's personal possessions.

Had he eaten in the cafeteria the flow of praise would have continued, but he ordered a tray and shut himself up in his office. He tried to transcribe the full confession that Sara had given at night in order to attach it to the investigation summary report but he couldn't do it. He ate slowly and felt the exhaustion spreading through every part of his body. The stewed beef he chewed had a strange taste, and he left most of it on the tray. There were moments from the tape of the interrogation that he watched again and again, but in the meantime he hadn't written a word.

He wanted to go home, to sleep, but he still had a long day ahead of him. He searched again for the photograph of Jennifer Salazar in the cardboard folder and among the papers scattered on the desk but he didn't find it, and he debated whether or not to call the jail and ask the guards to search for it among Sara's possessions. But there was something else he was missing, other than the picture, as if there was a false bottom in one of the suitcases that he hadn't discovered, or a secret compartment hidden inside it. He went to the evidence room, where Sara's suitcase was being kept, and tossed it onto the table, rummaged through the children's clothes, and even checked the toiletries bag. The letter that Sara claimed he wrote to his children in Jenny's name wasn't there. Had he lied about that as well? But if he hadn't lied, how had the letter disappeared?

The telephone in his office rang and Anselmo Garbo was on the line.

The Philippines detective sounded excited when he said to him in his sharp voice, 'Inspector Avraham? Is that you? Can you hear me?'

He forgot that he had promised to keep Garbo apprised of developments.

'I have good news. We have located Jennifer Salazar's sister in Berlin.'

Avraham waited a moment before saying quietly, 'We already found her,' but Garbo misunderstood his response and asked, 'The sister?' And Avraham said in a louder voice, 'No, no. I mean Jennifer Salazar. The missing person. We found her corpse this morning. She's dead.' He apologized for not contacting him earlier, because he had been busy with the investigation. The connection was bad, or Garbo was phoning from a place with poor reception, because he didn't hear his voice for a few seconds.

'How did she die?'

'She was murdered. Her husband murdered her.'

Garbo asked him to wait on the line and his voice disappeared again. The time in Manila was 7 p.m., and he was calling Israel in the middle of a dinner with the minister of police and other senior officers, so he went out to the smoking vestibule at the Hotel Makati Shangri-La in order to continue the conversation without interruptions.

'Can you hear me better, Inspector Avraham? You said she was murdered by her husband?' he asked, and Avraham confirmed this. Jennifer Salazar was asphyxiated, in her sleep, in the bedroom of the apartment where she had resided for eight years, since she had married Sara.

'So why did he plan to enter the Philippines?'

'In order to murder the two children there. One of the children was a witness to the mother's murder, and he discovered this. He denied that this was his plan, but we think that he planned to murder them, then return to Israel without them. To say they stayed with her.'

Again there was silence. From the other end of the line the sounds of a match lighting and the rustle of tobacco burning in a pipe could be heard. Garbo blew his nose a few times. Was he crying? Avraham said, 'I can send you the summary of the case in another day or two, if you want, in English,' and Garbo suddenly asked, 'Did you identify the body with certainty? Did you see it?'

For some reason he said that he had seen it himself.

'What will you do with it?'

He hadn't thought about this before. The body had been moved to the Institute for Forensic Medicine, but he had no idea what would be done with it after that. Was the Philippines detective offering to transport it to Manila for interment?

Garbo said, 'I will nevertheless give you the sister's details. Her name is Grace Ilmaz and she resides in Berlin. Perhaps she can help you with the children. And besides this, I succeeded in speaking with Jennifer's first husband. Andreda. They divorced in 1994, after four years of marriage, because he travelled to work in Qatar, but they kept in touch by telephone and post for some years because they still loved each other. So he said. Her most recent visit to Manila, in 2005, was the last time they met; she learned then that he had married again and had had children, and since then they didn't speak any more. He did not know that she had married in Israel and had two children.' Avraham didn't understand why he was telling him all this now, when the investigation was over. Before they got off the phone, Garbo said to him in an official tone, 'Inspector Avraham, I would like to thank you in the name of the Philippines police for your efforts. In the Philippines we say, "Wherever there is life, there is still hope." But I believe that even when life comes to an end, we must continue to hope. Do you not think this way?'

They promised each other that they would keep in contact in the coming days.

Avraham decided to put off transcribing the tape of the interrogation until the evening and went off by himself to Ilana's office at the Tel Aviv district headquarters. The car windows were closed, and the traffic in the streets on the Sunday after Yom Kippur was sparse, and for a moment he drove in complete silence. He opened the window and a dry wind came inside.

Ilana was wearing her rectangular glasses and had her uniform on when he arrived at her office. She rose slowly from her chair in order to close the door behind him instead of asking him to close it. 'How are you?' she asked him, and he said, 'Tired, mainly.'

She said further, 'You need to celebrate, no?' And he answered, 'This is how I look when I celebrate.'

Ilana laughed.

That day offered more than a few sights and sounds that would stay with him afterwards, but he would never forget his conversation with Ilana. They sat across from each other and she removed her glasses, and he didn't notice the spots around her eyes. She glanced at him with her painful look and said immediately, 'I owe you an apology,' and he asked, 'For what?' even though he well knew.

'For doubting your gut.'

He had imagined this moment differently.

He had been waiting for her to apologize, but when it happened he didn't feel happy. Three days earlier he had sat in her office and she had insisted that he was fabricating another missing-persons case and another father who planned to harm his children, and for a moment she had succeeded in shaking his confidence. And now he had returned to her office, victorious. She looked tense to him, and he thought that this was because it was hard for her to acknowledge her defeat and his victory, and later on he would be ashamed to have thought this.

He tried to avoid her stinging gaze and told her that it didn't matter, and Ilana said, 'It actually does matter, Avi. And I'm glad you went with your instincts against what I asked you to do. You conducted this investigation alone, and at times behind my back. I know I should be angry with you, but this means that you've grown as a detective. And mainly it means that you've got past the trauma of the Sharabi investigation.'

After their conversation, Avraham didn't understand why he felt that these words had crushed something inside him. It was then that he remembered Sara's meeting with his children in the interrogation room at night.

He had reviewed the meeting over and over again in his office while he ate lunch. And knew the words by heart, though he still hadn't written them down.

The children had stood in the entrance to the interrogation room but didn't dare enter until Avraham gestured his permission. And then the younger son ran towards Sara. The older one remained in the entrance to the room, next to Ma'alul, and didn't move.

He didn't know what Sara wanted to say to them and warned him that if he said anything that might hurt the children or affect the investigation, Avraham would remove them from the room immediately. Sara breathed heavily and stroked the hair of his younger son, who burrowed in between his knees. But when he spoke, he spoke to the older son, the one far from him, as if he were the only one in the room. Sara said to him, 'Ezer, they're going to tell you all sorts of things. Don't believe them. Believe me only. You know I had no choice, right? Shalom doesn't understand because he's still small. And from now on you'll have to protect Shalom. You'll be like a father and a mother for him now, okay? Like I was . . .' and then he crouched on his knees in front of his smaller son and a strange sound emerged from his mouth, deep and unintelligible, and Ma'alul called out, 'Enough, Avi, that's enough,' and Avraham pulled the boy's hand and removed the two of them from the room.

Ilana felt that something was a little out of balance with him and asked, 'Avi, are you okay?' and he answered her without thinking, 'Something's not sitting right, Ilana. Something's missing.' He hadn't planned to talk to her about this, but he was so used to this sort of exchange with her over the years, here in this room, and before that in her old office on the second floor of the Ayalon district station.

'Do you mean with the case?' she asked, and he nodded.

'You have the suspect's full confession and a video of the re-enactment and a body, no?'

She asked if it was the testimony that Sara's mother had given that was bothering him and he said no. In the morning hours, when the digger operator was disinterring the body, Ma'alul had questioned the mother in her home and she had testified that her son killed his wife in his sleep. Or at least that was what he had told her when he brought the body to her house after the murder. Sara had been a sleepwalker since he was a child, she said, getting up at night and doing things without knowing it, in his sleep. But that wasn't what was bothering him, because they didn't believe her story. And Sara had explicitly confessed to premeditated murder and made no attempt to imply that he killed his wife accidentally. And the new testimony from the son about the 'first father' wasn't the problem, either. The child repeated that he had seen his first father take his mother down from the apartment with a suitcase, but he insisted that the first father wasn't Sara and that Sara was asleep in bed the whole time. After Sara's detailed confession they had no need of his testimony, and, anyway, it was clear to everyone that the child was having difficulty dealing with what he'd seen and therefore was transferring the responsibility for the murder to an imaginary father and clearing his real father of blame. According to the report he submitted, Ma'alul asked the child, 'Do you know where your father took your mother?' and the child said, 'Yes, to her country.' And when he asked him why his father had taken her there, the child said, 'Because she missed it. She wanted to live in her country with our first father and have new children.'

Ilana didn't understand.

'So tell me what's not sitting right,' she said.

What bothered him wasn't only the photograph of Jennifer Salazar that had disappeared from the investigation file, or the letter that hadn't been found in the suitcase.

'I just can't understand him,' he said.

'Who?'

'I don't understand Sara. Why did he do what he did?'

'Didn't he explain it to you?'

He had tried to explain. But the more he explained the less Avraham felt he understood. The confession Sara gave was detailed, but something in it remained unclear, and Avraham had a sense that the more details they added to it the blurrier the picture of the murder actually became. 'He said that he did it in order to protect the children. Because she didn't love them.'

According to the tape from the interrogation, that first, spontaneous confession was spoken at 10.38 p.m. Avraham repeatedly questioned him about his intentions to murder the children in Manila, and Sara vehemently denied this and suddenly erupted and screamed, 'Don't you understand that I killed her for them? To protect them?' Avraham was shocked when he observed that he was smiling in the video upon hearing Sara's confession. He smiled because this was the confession he had been trying to prise out of him, because his investigation plan had proved itself, because this was the moment when it finally became clear he wasn't mistaken; but perhaps he smiled because something scared him as well.

And then Sara had fallen silent once more.

Ilana asked, 'So tell me, what's not clear?' and Avraham said, 'I don't know. That explanation sounds reasonable to you?'

'Why not?'

'So why did he plan to murder them afterwards? And why is he denying it now, after he already confessed to murder? And why does she have pictures of the children in her wallet?'

Ilana didn't understand who he meant.

'Jennifer Salazar. That was what we found in her wallet, which he hid in the shed.' From the case file he removed Ma'alul's notes from the scene where the body was found. Sara's mother had shown Ma'alul where her son had hidden the suitcase, and in it he found a lot of clothes, two pairs of tennis shoes, and some inexpensive jewellery, bracelets and plain necklaces. At the bottom of the tool drawer in the shed Ma'alul found the wallet and the passport and the mobile. *In the wallet there were neither credit cards nor cash*, Ma'alul had noted.

> *In it were receipts and business cards and an elliptical wooden coin, perhaps a foreign amulet, and a dog-eared photograph of a young man, apparently a picture of the murdered woman's father, and two passport photos of the children.*

Ilana looked at him puzzled.

'Avi, I don't understand what you're trying to do.'

'I'm trying to understand why he did what he did' – and as he spoke, the following questions formed in his mind. 'Do you know that he explained to me that he loved her? He even sometimes misses her, but he had no choice because she'd hated the children ever since they were born and didn't want them. Does that sound like an explanation to you?'

'That is not what you want to do, Avi. You're trying to cast doubt on the findings in your case.'

'Not true, Ilana. I know that we caught the right man. And that we caught him in time. I'm just trying to understand him. He could have confessed to killing her in his sleep, let's say, but he chose to confess to premeditated murder and wanted to explain to his children that that was what he had done. And now he's trying to convince me that he planned to take them to the Philippines in order to stage some kind of farewell. And I don't understand her, either. I don't get what kind of person she was. If what he says about her is correct, why did she marry him at all? Or have kids with him?'

If he hadn't lost the old picture that Garbo had sent him he would have placed it on the desk and asked her to look at the wide, young face that so resembled that of her son Ezer. Ilana spoke to him like she always did, as if nothing had happened between them before this and as if nothing was about to happen afterwards. 'But that's not your job, Avi. Your job is to understand *what* happened, not *why*. To prove what happened with the help of evidence. And that's exactly what you did. Sara murdered his wife. And planned to kill the children because one of them was a witness to the murder of the mother. There can be a thousand reasons for the words that come out of his mouth in an interrogation after the fact, and you know it. It could be that he says he murdered her for the sake of the children because he's trying to convince you that he didn't plan to harm them, right? He's ready to confess to the murder of his wife in order to evade blame for his intention to harm the children, that's my best guess.'

He hadn't thought about this, but it seemed to him that Sara wasn't so sophisticated. Was he mistaken?

Even when he had questioned him the first time, about the suitcase that was placed next to the nursery, he had been disturbed by the gap between his short, clipped answers and the complete and organized story he had told about the argument with the teacher. And last night as well, Sara had been mainly silent, and it had seemed like he'd never open his mouth, until after the meeting with his children he suddenly told the story about his wife, in a quiet voice, as if he were reading it from a script. And continued to deny, vehemently, that he had planned to harm his children. But his explanation for the trip to Manila was absurd and unconvincing: he'd said he wanted to take his children there in order to say farewell to their mother, in order for them to understand that she didn't love them; and he insisted that a letter would be found in the suitcase proving what he intended to do on the trip, but the fictitious letter hadn't been found.

Avraham was quiet, and Ilana asked, 'Do you understand what the child meant when he spoke about the first father?'

Avraham wondered what she was getting at. 'I think so.'

'Yes? What?'

'That he saw Sara with his wife's body. But it was unbearable for him to admit this.'

'And are you sure of this?'

He had no doubt.

'Okay. And do you understand why you're doing everything that you're doing?'

'I think so.'

'Really? You understand why you chose to be a police detective? Or why it's so hard for you to get over Ofer Sharabi? Or why you and I haven't been getting on lately?'

Avraham closed his eyes, and when he opened them he still didn't notice anything.

'We don't get on?' he asked.

They didn't talk about Sara any more because the time was short and Ilana asked him to present the findings from the other case.

'There you do understand what happened and why?' she asked, and he smiled and said that he did.

'Ilanit Hadad told Uzan, when she worked at the nursery, that Chava Cohen was abusing children. Everything started from there. Uzan thought he could make money out of this. She took a few pictures with her mobile, per Uzan's instructions, and tried to blackmail the teacher, but Chava Cohen refused to be blackmailed and fired her, and Uzan lost it and decided to take a harder line with the extortion. That's why she didn't tell us. She knew all along who had placed the suitcase next to the nursery and who had called her, just as I thought from the first moment. But she was sure that she could deal with them by herself and didn't want to risk us learning about the abuse. She took a recorder to the meeting, apparently in order to record them saying that they'd placed the suitcase, and Uzan discovered the device and attacked her. I don't know if he was trying to kill her.'

'And I understand that Hadad confessed, correct? So that case is in fact closed,' Ilana said, and he answered, 'Not yet. There is one more thing. I want you to authorize me to open an investigation of Chava Cohen regarding the abuse of children at the nursery. Ilanit Hadad will send us the photos she took and there will be at least a few parents who will have something to say.'

He thought about Sara's younger son and things Sara had told him about the day he had murdered his wife. These two cases were connected in so many ways he hadn't foreseen.

Ilana asked, 'We're not going to wait until she gets out of hospital?' and Avraham shook his head.

'We're not going to wait.'

And it was then, when the meeting was about to end, that Ilana got up from her chair and opened the window facing out onto Salame Street and placed the ashtray on the desk and asked him how he hadn't smoked until now and if he wanted coffee. He lit a cigarette and Ilana said, 'I've wanted to tell you something else, for a while now, though maybe you already know.'

Until the moment she told him, he was sure that she was about to say that she was separating from her husband. That strange email address from which she'd sent him the report about the previous investigation; and the family picture that had disappeared from the desk. And because of her hypothesis about Jennifer Salazar, that she had probably lied to Sara and fled Israel with a lover, before the truth was discovered. Until the last moment he was sure she planned to tell him she was getting divorced.

'This is my final week with the police. You know, my final week *for now*.'

He set his cigarette down in the ashtray. He didn't have to ask, because things became clear immediately.

'Cancer. It's unclear if it's terminal or not, but the treatments will last a few weeks. Maybe more.'

He didn't know what to say.

'Are you sure?' he asked, and Ilana laughed.

'*I* think it's a mistake and the nurses at the hospital switched the test results. But the doctors seem sure.'

Was he supposed to get up and hug her? That was what he wanted to do, but he couldn't. He examined her face and neck, and she noticed his gaze and said, 'You can't see it, Avi, it's inside. Very deep down.'

'Can I help with something?'

'You can give me a cigarette. It's not lung cancer. And, actually, that's the reason I went back to smoking with you.'

He brought the lighter up to her pale face and saw spots on the back of her hand, but he couldn't remember if they had always been there. He wanted to ask her so many questions: Are you in pain, Ilana? When did it all start? And why didn't you tell me anything until now?

Are you scared?

They had met for the first time more than ten years earlier and a short time after that began working together.

And now he asked himself just one question: How can I continue?

They were silent, and Ilana wanted to make it easier for him and said, 'I don't know who they'll nominate to replace me. They haven't asked me yet, but I intend to recommend you. I'm hoping that this office will be yours. Temporarily, of course. That you'll watch over it for me until I'm able to return. And now, since you've got over the previous investigation and solved this case, maybe there's a chance that'll happen.'

He couldn't look her in the eyes. Was it so she wouldn't see what he wanted to tell her, that she had actually been right before?

That he hadn't got over it.

That he had indeed fabricated another missing-persons case in order to make right what he'd mishandled in the previous investigation.

That since his return to Israel he had sat for long hours facing the sea that had swallowed Ofer Sharabi's body.

That he still desperately wanted to save him.

That, to be honest, he was still searching for that suitcase.

Ilana hugged him at the door, and only then did he feel how thin she had become. Her body was so fragile, it seemed to disappear in his arms.

He didn't go home, despite his exhaustion, because he sensed he wouldn't be able to bear the grief in solitude. He returned to the station, which was almost empty in the late evening, and made himself a cup of coffee. Across his desk lay a bouquet of flowers.

He didn't think about the investigation any more that day, only about Ilana, and perhaps for this reason he found the strength to watch the interrogation video again and finally transcribe Sara's confession. Looking for a pen in one of the drawers, he found the lost photograph of Jennifer Salazar, which he didn't recall putting there, but he no longer had any interest in it and turned it over quickly and filed it away in the investigation folder. He wrote and erased for a long time.

Question: You said earlier that you had planned to murder her for a long time, so why did you do it on that particular night?

Answer: Because the day before, my boy returned bruised from nursery.

Question: Which boy?

Answer: Shalom. The younger one.

Question: Okay, continue.

Answer: On Tuesday he returned from nursery with serious bruises on his forehead.

Question: Right. You've already said that. And what happened then?

Answer: I asked how he got the bruises and she said she didn't know and that it didn't interest her. I said to her, why didn't you speak with the teacher, ask her how it happened? Maybe some kid hit him, and she said, You speak with her, they're your kids, I'm not interested in how they get their bruises. She would talk about them like that all the time.

Question: Then what?

Answer: The children were standing there and heard her, both of them. She didn't say it quietly. Ezer heard too.

Question: When was this?

Answer: When I returned from work. In the afternoon.

Question: So why didn't you kill her that same day? How did you answer her?

Answer: I didn't answer. What could I have said?

Question: And you murdered her because of this?

Answer: Yes.

Question: Did you suspect her of beating Shalom?

Answer: No. She wouldn't dare touch them.

Question: So, then, I don't understand what you're saying. Did she threaten to take the children from you?

Answer: She wouldn't have taken them because she didn't want them with her. One time she said she'd take them just so I'd suffer like she suffers in life. She knew how attached I am to them, and because of this she would insult me around them.

Question: When was this?

Answer: That was a long time ago.

Question: And why didn't you do anything then?

Answer: I hadn't thought about it yet.

(. . .)

Question: But on the day the child returned from nursery with bruises you did think about it?

Answer: (nods) She refused to speak to the teacher, and so because of this I went to the nursery myself the next morning, and then there was the fight with the teacher. She didn't listen, either.

Question: That was on Wednesday morning?

Answer: Yes.

Question: And what happened later that day?

Answer: Nothing happened. When I returned home from work we had dinner, and afterwards Jenny put them to bed and went to sleep early and I finished working in the kitchen, and then I prepared the blanket.

Question: Was there another incident between you that same evening?

Answer: What do you mean, 'incident'?

Question: She didn't feel that you were planning to do something?

Answer: Why would she feel that?

Question: Did you beat her in the past?

Answer: I never in my life touched her.

Question: And was there anything different she did that evening? Describe for me exactly what she did.

Answer: There was nothing different. She watched TV in the living room and then went to bed.

Question: Did you sleep with her that night?

Answer: (no response)

Question: Did you have sex that night?

Answer: No. I worked and she fell asleep.

Question: And did you already know how you would kill her?

Answer: Yes.

(. . .)

Answer: I set an alarm clock for four a.m. but I didn't fall asleep.

Question: Why didn't you do it as soon as she fell asleep?

Answer: Because she sleeps deeper in the middle of the night, and so do the boys. And then it would be easier to remove her without anyone seeing.

Question: So the murder was carried out at four?

Answer: Slightly before. And I checked that the children were fast asleep.

Question: And then? How did you carry out the murder?

Answer: I suffocated her with the big cushion.

Question: Which cushion is that?

Answer: From the living room.

Question: And is it still there?

Answer: Yes. A blue cushion.

Question: Show me how you did it. Did you put it on her face?

Answer: Yes. I put it on her face and pushed with both hands. (Extends his hands forward.)

Question: And she didn't struggle?

Answer: No. Well, she tried grabbing with her hands, and kicked the bed with her legs, but after a while she stopped. I stayed there with the cushion on her face for a long time.

Question: Have you washed the cushion since then?

Answer: No.

16

Avraham saw the children whom he so badly wanted to save once more, at a mass in St Peter's Church a week after the body had been discovered.

It was a grey Sunday morning in the middle of October, and even though winter was still far off, strong winds blew outside, battering the tops of the palm trees. Avraham searched for Sara's sons but didn't spot them. Dozens of Filipina women were already crowded into the church pews, some of them with children. And that was the only reason he had come. Two days earlier, Garbo had sent him a fax with an announcement about the mass in memory of Jennifer Salazar and that the murdered woman's sister would be arriving from Berlin to take part, as well as a representative from the Philippines embassy in Israel, and it seemed to Avraham that Garbo expected him to be present as well. He told no one from the station that he planned to go to the ceremony. He sat down in one of the rear pews and waited.

The American priest who rose to the pulpit looked like a hippie who had come home from Vietnam in the sixties and become religious. His mane of hair was white and his beard long. He started by saying that he was dedicating his sermon to Jennifer Salazar, a beloved member of the community who was murdered, but he didn't mention her again in his sermon, whose subject was miracles. He tried to impress upon the believers that even if they had never seen a miracle in their own lives, that didn't mean they didn't take place all the time, and that if they continued to hold their faith dear to them, one day they'd be granted the vision, with their own eyes, of a miraculous revelation.

Each of Avraham's coughs echoed inside the space of the church like thunder.

Orange lights flickered around him in the dark space, and colourful figures gazed down on him from the stained-glass windows.

He was certain that someone would speak in her memory, but it didn't happen.

Had anyone among those sitting in the church even known Jennifer Salazar? Had the priest seen her when she sometimes came alone to the church on Sundays, as Sara told him she had in one of the interrogations? From time to time the congregation stood up from their seats, according to some hidden signal, and Avraham got up with them in order not to stick out, but when they knelt in the wooden pews, he stayed seated. A tall Filipina woman passed among them with a padded straw basket and they put notes and coins into it, but Avraham avoided her gaze and did not reach for his wallet. He didn't believe in any God, yet still it occurred to him that he might well pay dearly for his visit to the church.

He noticed the children only after the service. The priest approached the first pew and shook the hands of the worshippers, and that was when Avraham recognized the older son, wearing a smart shirt, and the younger boy, and a woman next to them with long black hair.

A chill passed through him.

From where he was sitting she very much resembled the young woman in the old picture.

The priest paused before the children and placed his hands on the head of the smaller boy, as a blessing, and afterwards bent down in order to whisper something to him, perhaps words of condolence, and Avraham recalled that a few days earlier he'd thought he should adopt the children and raise them himself, but that was an idiotic thought that had come to him only because of a novel he'd read years ago. He introduced himself, in English, to the sister, who up close resembled the murdered woman less, her face more narrow and delicate, and told her that there were items belonging to her sister in the police's possession that she could take.

She thanked him and asked what items, and Avraham said, 'Mainly clothing and jewellery that were found in a suitcase. And a few documents and pictures that we found at their home. And there are letters that you wrote to her that you will probably want back,' and she looked at him with surprise and said, 'I never wrote Jennifer letters. We haven't been in touch since I went to Germany.'

He presented her with the picture of the man that had been found in her sister's wallet, but she didn't want it because, despite Ma'alul's assumption, it wasn't a picture of their father, but rather a picture of Jennifer Salazar's first husband, Julius Andreda, 'The man who broke her heart,' her sister said.

Ezer stood next to them during this conversation and didn't let go of his younger brother's hand, as if Sara's final injunction in the interrogation room continued to echo in his ears.

Avraham walked the narrow alleyways of Jaffa's old city, down to the old port, and sat next to a fisherman who with his net caught small, dead fish that floated open-eyed in the shallow water near the boat docks.

Perhaps because he saw the children alive, a sense of satisfaction rose in him, even though he still felt that the case wasn't completely settled, as he had admitted to Ilana; and one night when he again couldn't fall asleep he would go to Lavon Street and with a small flashlight scan the courtyard where the suitcase with the fake bomb had been hidden, as if he might find something there so many days later.

The wind picked up, and the waves that crashed against the docks soaked his shoes and the hems of his trousers, and he went back to the station.

The newspapers' interest in the Salazar case was brief and superficial.

Information about the murder and the plan to dispose of the children in Manila appeared in the back pages of most of the daily papers, and in one of them Avraham was mentioned by name. On the same day he was interviewed by telephone for a radio programme on the Voice of Israel, but two minutes after the broadcast began, it was cut short for a report on the elimination of a senior member of Hamas in Gaza, and he didn't even get a chance to say the murdered woman's name on the air. He sat by the phone in his office and waited, because the programme's producer promised that they'd get back to him, but that didn't happen.

And life continued.

Sara's lawyer offered to sign a plea bargain according to which Sara would confess to the murder of his wife while the prosecution would shelve the baseless accusation regarding the plan to kill the children, and even suggested that the police were responsible for the disappearance of the letter that Sara had hidden in the suitcase, which would have proved his explanation for the trip. Avraham vehemently opposed the deal and no one was about to disagree with the opinion of the detective who had solved the case: his investigation proved that the plan for the trip was born in Sara's mind after his son had hinted about what he had seen on the night of the murder, and the fact that he had ordered return tickets for his wife and children confirmed that his pattern was identical. And they decided not to prosecute Sara's mother, due to her age.

The next case that was placed in his hands dealt with the assault of a bus driver, who had been beaten with an iron rod by two passengers, and there was an additional case, exceptional and wrapped in mystery. It began with some writing that had sprung up on walls all over the city, in black spray paint, *Soon you will understand why*, and continued with three break-ins of senior citizens' apartments in the course of a single night. Nothing was stolen from the senior citizens' apartments, but in the three bedrooms were placed rusty metal cases in each of which was a folded page of an old newspaper.

In one apartment, on De Shalit Street, it was a page from *Yediot Ahronot* from Thursday, 5 May 1949. The central item on the crumbling paper told about a plane crash in Italy, on Mount Superga, south of the Po River, in which all the players on the celebrated Turin soccer team perished. Underneath it, circled with black marker, was an item about a murder in the city of Holon: *The body of a widower was found in the sands in the Moledet neighbourhood.*

In the second apartment the newspaper clipping was from 4 November 1979. There was a central item in it as well, this time about a massacre in North Carolina: Ku Klux Klan operatives opened fire on activists marching for human rights who were joined by representatives from labour organizations and Communist movements, and five were killed. Next to it was a smaller item about an eighteen-year-old woman, a resident of

Holon, who was abducted from her home. In the third incident, which was reported a few days later, a section of the 18 November 1962, *Davar* newspaper was found, in which was an item about the murder of a disabled shoemaker in a suburb of Tel Aviv.

> *Moshe Stolero, age 35, hunchback and limping, locked up his shop for household goods, books and newspapers, and prepared to go up to his parents' apartment on the third floor of the same building. He had with him the day's revenue in the amount of three hundred lira and began the climb home. When he entered the stairwell and extended his hand to turn on the lights, a volley of three shots was fired in his direction. He was struck in the chest, shoulder, and head. The unidentified shooter fled the scene.*

On each of the three newspaper clippings an anonymous person had written in black marker: *Soon you will understand why.*

For the first time since joining the force Avraham visited the police's archive basement and met the archive's director, a strange man in his seventies who was known as Dr Bartoshek, even though that wasn't his name. Despite his age, Bartoshek was restless, fuelled by some kind of inner fire, and as he moved with dizzying speed in his wheelchair among the shelves of old files he treated Avraham to a short lecture on the history of police work in Israel.

'Did you know that thirty years ago when a policeman needed to report a criminal incident, he had to run to a public telephone and call the station with a phone token?' he asked, and his eyes sparkled. 'And that's if he had a phone token on him, of course! But in those days every policeman had in his shirt pocket a small bag of tokens. Can you imagine?'

Together Avraham and Dr Bartoshek discovered that the three old crimes had a common denominator: none had been solved. And none of the three senior citizens had a clue as to why the newspapers were placed in their apartments.

The case stirred Avraham's curiosity, but he struggled to be drawn into it. He had a feeling that there was something contrived about it and that it wouldn't lead to a crime carried out by a real person, as if he had read about it in one of the detective novels he loved and wasn't actually investigating it himself. For long hours he stared at the old news items about the disasters and the dead and the crimes that had no apparent meaning or explanation. And to make matters worse, he couldn't speak about the case with Ilana. Ostensibly his work continued as usual, but there was no 'as usual' without Ilana. Not a day passed without him wanting to talk to her, but she had asked not be visited in hospital or to be called during therapy. In his imagination he saw her sitting up in a hospital bed, her head bald, wearing a green robe. Her feet bare and her skin hard and rough. From time to time things were whispered about her replacement in the corridors of the station, but in the meantime no one had been nominated to replace her; nor had it been hinted to Avraham that he might get the job. And until the last moment he hoped that she'd surprise him and come to the decoration and promotion ceremony, which took place on a Wednesday afternoon, in the courtyard where the Rosh Hashanah toast had taken place back in early September.

The station's courtyard again filled up with policemen and -women in uniform, and the wooden tables were covered with tablecloths and plastic plates with small sandwiches and bottles of pop. Avraham searched for Ilana among those who came and saw his parents, who stood at the entrance to the courtyard, embarrassed. His mother was well dressed and wore makeup, as she used to wear makeup during his childhood when she would go to hear a concert in Tel Aviv, and he saw his father for the first time in a while wearing jeans and the black beret that he had begun wearing after he'd retired. They sat next to him in the first row during Saban's speech, which the district commander presented in a lazy manner, repeating entire paragraphs from the speech he'd given at Rosh Hashanah, about his vision for a safe district free of violence, and at the end he added that, thanks to the diligence and courage of police officers such as Avraham, this vision was becoming a reality.

When Avraham spoke there was complete silence in the audience – anyway, that was what his father told him afterwards.

His mother complained that his words of thanks were too brief, and that he hadn't talked about himself enough.

He thanked Sergeant Lior Zaytuni and Sergeant Major Eliyahu Ma'alul, without whose contributions the case would not have been solved, and especially Commander Ilana Lis who, all the officers of the district were praying, would soon return. Like the priest at St Peter's Church, and like Saban in his speech, he didn't mention Jennifer Salazar, even though in the first draft he had written the night before at home there had been a few sentences devoted to her memory.

Two days later, a Friday morning, Police Superintendent Avraham Avraham flew to Brussels.

He kept the trip secret, and told his parents that he was going for three days of professional development in Nazareth.

He landed in Brussels in the early evening and took a train from the airport to South Brussels Station, and continued from there by cab to the Hôtel Espagne, where he'd stayed during his first trip to the city.

Room 307, where he'd slept then, was occupied, so he settled down in a pricier, more spacious room, on the seventh floor, with a beautiful balcony facing north and looking out onto the residential neighbourhoods leading into the city.

He left his small suitcase in the room and, just like during the first visit, immediately went out to avenue Brugmann, but this time he knew the way and walked quickly parallel to the tram tracks until the turn at rue de la Victoire. Darkness had fallen and the streets had emptied when he arrived at Alfred Bouvier Square, out of breath. From a distance he noticed the window of the room that had been his room for three months, in the summer, with the light off, but he nevertheless went closer and stood under the grey, industrial-looking building, which Marianka said was the ugliest building in Europe but in his eyes was more beautiful than any palace.

Her name was still inscribed on the mailbox.

And no lights were on in the rest of the rooms in the second-floor apartment.

Avraham stood next to the doorway to the building until he realized that Marianka would see him if she suddenly arrived, and he retreated to the abandoned garden in the middle of the square. He smoked a cigarette under the protection of the darkness and the bare trees. A neighbour whose face was familiar to him walked through the garden with his dog, and the dog barked at Avraham as if it remembered him. From time to time he looked up at the dark window. But the cold grew sharper and deepened, piercing his thin jacket like a knife, and at ten thirty he decided to go back to the hotel. On his way there, he was overcome by hunger and stopped at Le Prétexte, and the waitress smiled at him and asked how he was doing, and he managed to answer her with the few French phrases he had learned over the summer. He ate pasta with seafood in a bland cream sauce and watched the chess game two loud old men were engaged in at the table across from him.

He was still quite familiar with Marianka's schedule, and the next day, at seven in the morning, he again hid in the garden across from her building.

His heart pounded powerfully when he saw the door open on the other side of the parked cars and his Marianka exit the building in a dark tracksuit and running shoes. She looked around and didn't notice him, warmed her hands with her breath, then started on her established run, in the direction of rue de Lausanne, and disappeared. Following the plan he had conceived in advance, he waited in a café through whose window he would be able see her upon her return.

But he didn't see her return.

And when he went back to the square, at nine fifteen, the window of her room was open.

The windowsill was decorated with the small cyclamen plant he'd bought for her a few weeks before he'd gone went away.

And each and every one of her movements, when she came out again, before ten, was completely familiar to him.

The quick, springy gait. The leather bag hanging from her shoulder.

Even when they walked together, he remembered, he always lagged slightly behind her.

He raised the collar of his jacket and wound the blue scarf around his mouth and nose and followed her at a safe distance so that she wouldn't spot him. As he had expected, she stopped in the small Polish store, in which he had bought her, every morning before she woke up, dark rye bread, and afterwards she walked quickly down rue de la Victoire, towards the market. While she waited at the crossing for the light to change there was a moment when she turned around suddenly and might have caught sight of him, but he managed to hide behind a recycling bin. She passed by the stands of fresh meat and stopped to buy fruit and vegetables, and he too paused in front of the stands and looked at the cheeses like any other customer. The market filled and it grew difficult to keep Marianka in his line of sight without getting too close to her, and then she suddenly disappeared. He increased his pace and turned into streets he didn't know, because he thought she might have turned down one. He didn't have a map and didn't know the neighbourhood he had wandered into, and even though it seemed to him that each turn would lead him back to the market, he was actually walking further and further away.

Rain began to fall, and he walked without an umbrella down a street that went on and on in who-knows-what direction. Suddenly he felt a tap on his shoulder and turned around.

Marianka was as wet as he was.

She asked him, 'What are you doing here?' and he said, 'I came for a visit.'

'And you didn't say anything?'

'I didn't know if you'd want to meet.'

He hadn't expected to see her from such a short distance, and up close her face surprised him. She asked him, 'Were you following me?' and he answered, 'I wanted to see you,' and in truth that was all he wanted.

'And you weren't going to let me know that you're here? You didn't think I'd see you when you've been walking behind me since this morning?'

Really, his only plan had been to look at her from a distance.

Afterwards they walked down the street in silence. She in front of him and he a bit behind, as usual.

Marianka asked him if he remembered where the shower was and how to turn on the tap, and under the stream of hot water he heard her open the bathroom door and lay dry clothes on the stool. The white vest was his. It had been forgotten in the tumble drier. She went into the bathroom after him, and he waited in the kitchen. On the dining table were two mugs of boiling-hot tea and a bowl of sugar. His wet trousers were drying on the radiator, which gave off a pleasant warmth. And the photo of the two of them, from the summer, in Bruges, was still on the refrigerator. Marianka sat down across from him with her hair short, wet and dark, and said to him, 'I know that I have to explain to you what happened, but tell me first how you are,' and he said, 'Fine.'

'Are you sure?'

'Yes. Why not?

'How did the bomb case end?'

When they had last spoken it had still been an investigation into a fake bomb inside a suitcase that had been placed next to a nursery. And Chaim Sara had been merely a witness then. She didn't know that Chava Cohen had been assaulted, or that it had turned out that the witness had murdered his wife and planned to murder his two children. He told her everything: about the suspicions stirred in him, and Ilana Lis's opposition to detaining Sara for questioning, and the ticking of the clock and the urgent communications with Anselmo Garbo and the arrest at the airport and the boy's ambiguous testimony, and Sara's confession and the re-creation of the crime in his apartment. Did he explain everything at length because it was easier than to talk about himself? Perhaps he hoped that, like the time before, Marianka would say something that would open his eyes and clarify for him what he didn't understand.

But this time she said nothing.

And when he told her that, thanks to his uncovering the murder and saving the children, he had been decorated for his service and promoted to police superintendent, Marianka got up from her chair, said to him, 'Wait a sec,' and disappeared into the bedroom. She returned with a small package wrapped in gold paper, which he began to remove gently, so as not to tear it.

'What is it?' he asked, and she said, 'A present. For you. Open it.'

He opened the wooden case and was surprised.

'A pipe?'

'I passed the shop one day and saw it in the window and thought about you and your detectives. You don't like it?'

He really didn't know anything about how to smoke a pipe.

But he was happy because she had thought of him one day.

And he heard the rustle of the tobacco burning in Garbo's pipe during the conversation in which he had informed him that Jennifer Salazar had been found.

Could he smoke a pipe, like Garbo?

He pictured himself on the steps of the station, blowing sweet smoke rings into the grey Holon sky.

He said, 'I like it very much. I'm just not sure how to use it,' and Marianka said, 'I'll teach you. It's one of the smells I most like. My father smoked a pipe – it's the smell I remember from home. I suppose I should have also bought some tobacco.'

Something between them had opened up, and Marianka smiled for the first time when Avraham put the pipe into his mouth and bit it with his teeth. He wasn't about to question her any more, and only then did she offer, 'I didn't come because I was afraid,' and Avraham asked, 'Of what?'

'Of leaving this apartment, and of my work with the police, and of travelling to you without knowing what would happen to us. Losing my whole life again – like what happened to me when we left Slovenia and came here. But mainly afraid of discovering in a few months, or years, that it had been a mistake. To give up everything I have and go far from my family to live in a strange country, then discover that I had stopped loving you. Or that you had stopped loving me. That you had cheated on me with your secretary because you were tired of me. Isn't that what always happens? I love you now, and maybe you love me, and our summer together was the most wonderful time I can remember, but everything comes to an end. And I can't allow myself to lose everything again like that.'

Avraham smiled, because all he'd heard were the words 'I love you now.'

He said quietly, 'That won't happen to us.'

'How can you know?'

He removed the pipe from his mouth and exhaled an imaginary cloud of smoke into the kitchen.

'It's elementary, my dear. I simply know.'

'But don't detectives always get it wrong, according to your theory?' she whispered, and he said, 'Not this time. And besides, I don't have a secretary,' but Marianka didn't laugh.

She said, 'Avi, I need to tell you something, to make things easier for myself. This is the real reason I couldn't speak with you any more. I didn't want to lie.'

Had he known, even before she told him, and hidden it from himself?

'I had an affair with another man. Brief. It lasted a few days and was over. I couldn't have talked to you as if nothing had happened and hidden it from you, and I couldn't tell you, either. I think I did it in order to prove to myself that I couldn't come to you. That we didn't have a chance. And I succeeded. Are you listening to me, Avi? Are you still here?'

He set the pipe down on the table.

'Who was it?' he asked, and she whispered, 'It's not important.'

It was important, but he didn't insist on knowing his name.

'Where did you meet?'

'At a family event. But let it go, Avi, please. It doesn't matter.'

'A family event?'

'Yes. He's a very distant relative. He lives in Slovenia and was here for a visit.'

He wanted her to say more, and also he didn't want her to say any more.

He recalled the questions that he had asked Sara about his wife in the interrogation room at the station, on the night he had confessed to murder. Marianka lay on the bed in the bedroom, the bed that had been his bed for three months in the summer, and a man he didn't know and whose face he couldn't picture slowly opened the buttons of her blouse, from her collar to the button at her navel, and touched her pale shoulder. It was during the time that he had been preparing the apartment for her arrival. That he ran after suitcases, and down hospital hallways, always thinking he wanted to go home and call her.

'Did he sleep with you here?' he asked, and she said, 'Yes.'

'How many times?'

'I don't remember. And I'm sorry that it hurts you so much.'

'You don't remember if he slept here one night? Or a week? Or a month?' His voice nearly broke, and Marianka said, 'Don't interrogate me, Avi. Please. I'm trying to explain to you that it was just an excuse. It won't help if you know.'

He hadn't looked at her until then, and when he looked he saw despair in her gaze. A pain he recognized, even though he'd never seen it in her eyes before. His wet trousers were still drying on the radiator, but he needed to get up and leave. And suddenly he couldn't understand why he had come at all. What had he expected would happen if he stood under her window, or followed her in the street? Would he have returned to Holon without speaking to her if she hadn't noticed him? And why didn't he get out of there immediately?

Someone knocked on the door and didn't stop, and Marianka peered through the peephole but didn't open the door. He said to her, 'You can open it,' and she said, 'I don't want to. It's the neighbour.' The rain beat against the window, and from outside the rattle of workers dismantling equipment in the street could be heard. Finally evening fell and the kitchen grew dark. They barely spoke until his phone rang, a bit after seven. And afterwards he thought that this was the reason he stayed, as if he had known that this call would come and he wanted to answer it next to her.

Marianka looked at him while he spoke, and she understood that something had happened.

He got up from his chair and walked away, then returned to the kitchen and asked her for a pen and paper. His hand shook while he wrote.

Her eyes didn't leave him, and when he hung up, she asked, 'Who was that?'

He said, 'Eliyahu Ma'alul. He called from the station.'

Ma'alul's voice had shaken when they spoke. He had said to him, 'Avi, I'm here with Chaim Sara's lawyer at the station.'

'Had something happened?' Marianka asked, and he nodded.

She didn't recognize the name Chaim Sara, because before now he hadn't mentioned the murderer by name.

'His letter was found. The letter he wrote to the children in his wife's name.'

He hadn't told her about the letter that Sara insisted he had written and hidden in the suitcase, which was supposed to prove that he hadn't intended to harm his sons in Manila but instead was going simply to stage a sort of farewell to their mother, and which had disappeared with no explanation.

'So how did they find it?' she asked, and he answered, 'His son returned it. The older son. His name is Ezer. He says that he stole it from the suitcase the night before the trip and kept it with him until now. This morning he mentioned it to the grandmother, or the lawyer, and the lawyer contacted Ma'alul and presented the letter to him. We still need to verify that it's Sara's handwriting and try to confirm when it was written, but Ma'alul believes the child.'

'And what does this mean?'

'I don't know yet. But maybe that he didn't plan to kill them there, like I thought. That he was almost charged with the attempted murder of the children because of me, and that this is what the children had heard since he was arrested.'

Marianka looked at the foreign letters he had jotted down and asked, 'And that's the letter?' He nodded and stared at the words in front of him.

'Can you read it to me?'

'What for?'

'I want to know what's written in it.'

He would have preferred not to. If Sara's version of events was correct, he had been planning to read this letter aloud to his sons in Manila, and here was Avraham reading it to Marianka in Brussels, trying to translate the contents of the letter but at the same time trying to resist the meaning of the words, or to forget them, as if he was afraid they'd stick to him somehow.

Shalom and Ezer, he finally read,

> *I know that you came from very far away to look for me with Daddy and that you want to see me and bring me back home, but I can't meet you here. I decided to leave you and our home because I didn't want to be your mummy from the beginning. I know that it will be hard for you without me in the beginning and that it will be hard for you to forget too, but you have a father who will protect you and take good care of you. He loves you very very much and he'll be a good and strong father for you and in the end you will grow up and forget me and start new lives with him. Please help him, because in the beginning it won't be easy for him alone. And maybe one day, when you grow up and are adults, we'll be able to meet. Mummy*

Marianka hid her eyes from him. And Avraham said, 'Do you understand that the child might have saved him?' And suddenly he also understood that he hadn't asked Ma'alul if Ezer had read the letter and if he thought that his mother had written it or knew that his father had written it in her name. But, really, which was more terrible? He didn't want to know.

Marianka brought her head close to him and rested it on his shoulder for the first time. He said to her, 'Every time it seems to me that the ending will be different, you know? At the start of every investigation. That everything that had happened can be erased or fixed. But nothing is erased, it only piles up from case to case. I was sure that this time I'd done it, but I didn't manage to save anyone this time either. Not her, and not them, and not even myself,' and Marianka came closer to him and said, 'Avi, I don't think it's possible to save children from their parents,' and then added, 'but maybe you'll succeed one day.'

He listened to her and closed his eyes.

The next day, when he was at the train station, on his way to the airport, he saw a teenage boy and girl kissing.

They were wearing heavy backpacks, and Avraham stared at them for a little too long, until they noticed him, and he thought that when people hold each other in their arms they don't ever see the other person. And apparently he and Marianka had also said the things that they had said that night, without seeing each other, like blind people, or like people talking to themselves. He had said to her hair, 'I want us to get married, Marianka,' and she had whispered to his neck, 'After everything I told you?'

'Especially after everything you told me,' he answered, and even though he didn't understand what he meant, he knew that it was the right answer.

He asked, 'Do you agree?' and she said only, 'Yes, I think so.'

On the table before them were two empty mugs and an uncovered bowl of sugar and two teaspoons, and wrapping paper that had been torn hastily, and a wooden case, and also a pipe – which Avraham packed in his suitcase and took back with him to Holon.